Kingdom of Solace

By Rachel Himelright

A novel of the

Rumors of War series

This is a work of fiction. Names, characters, organizations, places, events, and incidents are either products of the author's imagination, or are used fictitiously. Any resemblance to actual persons, living or dead, or actual events is purely coincidental.

FIRST EDITION

Cover design by En Kite

Marketing and Distribution by Independent Literature Brewing Company, Winchester, Virginia

For more information, please visit
www.bookbrewers.com

Printed in the United States of America

ISBN: 978-1-7360070-5-1

Breath I'm given, fingers to type
People to surround me
People who confound me
People who've unbound me
Mind to push the words to page
Inspiration to see them fall the right way
Place to write
Food for fuel
Air that's fit
Music notes for muse
How do I contain the transcendent with words?
Holy, Holy, Holy say the Seraphs best
This is for Him.

Prologue

Darkness provided just the cover he was hoping for. He crept into the deserted town square, furtively looking around, thankful for the clouds that covered the nearly full moon. Waiting on the cold stone bench, each second seemed to take an hour to pass. Finally, he saw someone approaching. The slim shape gave away the femininity of the figure. She silently moved closer and seated herself next to him. She took his hand but didn't speak. The look in her eyes spoke in a language her voice couldn't articulate.

"Thank you for coming, we needed to talk away from your house." He said in a hushed voice.

"What else could I do?" Her eyes shimmered with unshed tears.

"Don't cry!" He folded her into his arms and sighed deeply, his aggravation evident. "We can make this work." He whispered gently, right next to her ear.

She looked up expectantly. "We have to talk to the elders. There has to be a way you can stay. Someone else..." her words caught in her throat, not able to make their escape.

"Shh, hush now." He pushed her hood back from her face, revealing her finely etched features to the weak light of the clothed moon. "The elders can't change this decision. We must make ours, and quickly. Your father will not wait long to have you betrothed to another man now that I have to go. He can't be on our side, Alia. We have to go." His face was a banner of determination.

"Leave?" she pushed back out of his arms and stood. "Go where? What do you mean?"

"Listen, Alia, I know it sounds insane." He stood and took her hand. "I have to leave tonight if I hope to ever make my own choices again. I couldn't just disappear without giving you the chance to come along. We will find a place to settle far away from here and start a new life. If you choose to stay, I understand." He reached up and stroked her cheek, pushing her golden hair aside. "We can never come home, but this is our only chance to stay together."

Alia paused for only a second, thinking of the path that her life would take if she didn't follow Kai. She looked at the man waiting expectantly beside her. Emotions flooded her heart, and she grew angry at the unfairness of the situation for all of them. "I couldn't stand to be another man's wife. It would make my life a lie to care for his children and care for him, if it were you I wished to see every day. Even if you were far away, as you would be, my heart would leave this place. I have no choice but to go with you. When do we leave?"

"We have to leave now. The guards will be expecting me in the morning. If only it would stop raining." He gave the cloudy sky an anguished look, his mind still seeing failed crops. He looked back at the girl by his side, loving the determination and the willingness he saw there. "I'm sorry this happened, Alia." He lay his hand on her shoulder. "I have horses waiting at the edge of town. We should have plenty of food to make it there, and I took a few of my mother's things for you to wear."

Alia looked around the town she called home. She had witnessed many people leaving town for various reasons and had even had occasion to leave a few times herself when her father had allowed his family to accompany him to other towns for gatherings. This time she wouldn't be able to come home. "We'd better go, then." Her statement was a dismissal of her fears, as though she had put all the bad things that had happened from her mind and embraced the good with open arms.

Kai took her words to heart, grabbed her wrist, and whirled toward the wooded area at the edge of town. The cloud cover grew thicker as the forlorn couple ran to their waiting horses. Each footstep seemed to Kai to pound as loudly as a slamming door. He thought that surely his heart would beat out of his chest, driven by the adrenaline that burst unchecked into his veins. After what seemed like an eternity of dodging imaginary adversaries in the shadows and hiding alongside stone walls from invisible foes, the pair arrived unmolested at the two horses that stood patiently waiting. Kai boosted Alia into the saddle and then climbed aboard his own horse. At the encouragement of the two riders, the horses broke into a fierce gallop away from the warmth and comfort of familiar stables. Rain started seeping from the clouds one drop at time, its path downward like a commentary on the actions of the two torn souls. Within minutes, torrents of rain fell like tiny erasers, wiping clean the slate of the couple's disappearance.

Morning dawned in the town like a bad dream, and to the families of Alia and Kai, it soon became apparent what had been the fate of the two lost youngsters. No number of tears shed, or anger expressed, would reveal to the families the location of their loved ones, so silence became the precedent in the usually smiling village. Alia's father, Harald paced the barn where he had last seen Kai. He had taken it upon himself to give the close family friend the news that he knew would be devastating. Kai was promised as tribute from the village to cover the shortfall of crops that the town had never before failed to be able to produce. Each village had a certain quota to make every year. Their village had always produced plenty and had enough left over to make sure that everyone within the boundaries had plenty. How could he and his wife have known this would happen? How could they have made the mistake of letting the two youngsters become close? They had assumed, as had many this barren year, that the grain would always stand tall enough and the fruit trees would always bear un-blighted and generous fruit. There had been no thought that any of their young men would have to become soldiers to make up for a deficit. Kai had been a natural choice for tribute. He was tall, strong and impressive. Harald dropped his head in grief. Since the building of the chapels, young people in this village had been married as expected at regular intervals, and perhaps the laws meant to protect the people from all manner of hardships had been relaxed too much. Even he, a village elder, had allowed way too much interaction between the young people. He should have known better! They had lost the fear that permeated other towns in the kingdom, and so they had planned the marriage of their children without thinking of the consequences of a lean year. He suddenly stopped pacing and thought through the portion of the law that he had studied for years and was required to enforce without question. The law was clear. Anyone caught assisting a soldier who had deserted his post was subject to several punishments, some more severe than others.

He realized he had to find the young people before Arne knew he was missing a tribute. He loved Kai like a son, but he wouldn't allow his daughter to be subjected to these kinds of consequences without trying his best to bring her back before her treachery was known. He felt the scandal of what he was about to do creep up like a poison, and he choked back the bile that rose in his throat. He'd always erred on the right side, standing in judgement over the various infractions that had happened while he was on the council. He'd never taken a bribe or been tempted to bend the rules for a friend. Now he hoped beyond hope that an entire village of people who wouldn't even look him in the eye because of their fear would look into his heart and understand the desperation that drove him. He ran into his bedroom, finding his wife strewn across the bed sobbing her eyes out. "It is necessary," he had once told her, "to keep a tight rein on wayward youngsters and not to allow unlawful love to flourish into something we cannot control. It is for the good of everyone that we listen to those who are wiser than us." Why hadn't he listened to his own words of wisdom? Now he shook her shoulder roughly, forgetting tenderness in his haste. "Runa, get up! We have to go after them!"

His wife turned, startled, and glared at him. "What could be gained from running after the pair of them? She is willing to turn her back on us and everything to be with Kai." He could see decades of resentment giving way to hatred in her face. Its usual calm resoluteness had surrendered to flint-like disdain.

"We can bring her back. We can find the pair of them and leave him to flee on his own. He had no right to drag her into this horrible decision.

I'm sure if we find them, we can open her eyes to the reality of this decision and bring her home. The law says..."

"What good is such a ridiculous law!" She nearly shouted and he closed the distance between them and quickly caught her arm with one hand and covered her mouth with the other.

"Do not blaspheme the law, Runa. It is our obligation to remember. It is our obligation to obey. It is our obligation to serve." His eyes burned like embers as he slowly lowered his hand from her face, the warning in them clear. He continued in a whisper. "Runa, you can't abandon the law now. You have to help me get Alia back. We need to go after her."

She looked confused. "This feels like bondage," her voice now low enough to appease him. "Kai doesn't deserve this." Still, she turned and began gathering supplies for travel. "If we can't find them today?"

"May the gods help us." He turned and strode from the room. "May the gods help them."

Within the hour, a new set of hoof prints wound its way out of the village, its course different than the first. There was love in the reasoning of both sets, and a driving force that would not be denied.

Chapter 1

"I will not marry the girl!" The boy said it with finality, the decision made and firmly planted in his conscience. He stood feet apart, arms folded across his chest; his brow arched in a defiant grimace. The stance caused his father to chuckle under his breath. His boy was certainly becoming a man. His father walked around him, pondering his next words carefully.

"So be it, if you wish to bring her dishonor among her own." He said it with a taste of the unknown, a flavor he knew his boy could not resist, and he turned to walk out of the dimly lit barn where he had found Evin when he'd missed dinner.

"Wait." It was the word he knew he would hear. He turned back to face his son and found the boy's arms now hanging loosely by his side.

He arched his brow in a questioning glance. "Yes?" The question invited all queries from the young man without offering any condemnation.

"Why would I dishonor her by leaving her free to choose? I don't know her at all, but I heard that this girl doesn't even want to marry. Worse, I heard that her heart is set against it. Why do I have to be the one to cause her pain? I don't want to be responsible for her hurt!"

The older man seated himself on a nearby bale of hay and invited his son to sit next to him. "My boy," he said, "there is so much you do not yet understand. The law has made it clear what is right and good, and for years we have lived peacefully by living within it. Before the law, the people worshipped their own desires, and the needs of the community were left in the dust. This marriage will help you and Inkeri leave aside the selfish parts of a union with another and cling to the beautiful parts that will make for a stronger unit in the end. You and your wife will study the law together and you will discern for yourselves the wisdom of following the ways of the elders."

"Why should it matter what the elders say if our hearts aren't in it?"

"It matters. The heart will turn you astray. For years, you have been taught how to be a good husband. You have been taught the ways of our people. You are fortunate that you have not been chosen to serve our country in other necessary ways. You are fortunate that the rains that have plagued some of the outlying villages haven't touched our city and have left you free to move forward. The time has come for you to honor the position that you have been given and that position is best fulfilled with a wife by your side. Tomorrow, you must either marry the girl that has been chosen for you or dishonor her and the law by rejecting her. She may not be chosen again, and if she is, it will be at least a year. People will question whether you would be a good elder. Is that what you want?"

"Why must she be chosen at all? Why can't she choose?"

"Did you choose? It is not for the young and foolish to know best. Only time will show you what is right. For years I have poured my soul into yours, to help make you a productive member of a larger whole. I have grown to love your mother. Indeed, we were among the first to follow the choosing as prescribed in the law, and if I had ignored the teaching, I wouldn't have her as my wife. Rest assured, your mom and I helped to choose this girl for you, and we have carefully considered your desires. You will love her. Now you must choose to do what is right or live with the consequences. It is our obligation to remember. It is our obligation to obey. It is our obligation to serve. That is the way of things."

Evin thought back to the ritual his village had just finished the night before. They had built fires and repeated well-known chants to ask for the blessing of fertility and health, many donning flower crowns and dancing. It was thought to be lucky to join in betrothal right after this festival. It had been like many ceremonies he'd seen in his life, but aside from planting and harvest ones, he'd never imagined one of them might have some weight in his life. He had never felt connected to the rituals, even last night. He thought with his own handfasting in the mix, he should have at least felt ready at the end of it. "I don't like it! My life is bound by strict rules I don't have any control over. If I choose to marry this girl, as you wish, then my life will drag on in this place and I will grow old with nothing but softness to show for the years on my face. I feel in my bones I wasn't meant for this existence!" The boy hung his head and sighed. His sorrow was evident. "I just want an adventure!"

"There's nothing wrong with adventure, Evin, but you must remember it has many faces. If you can find the adventure in this life, you can be fulfilled in it. If you keep pressing against it, you will only find disaster. Remember you have a journey ahead of you. You and your wife have to travel to one of the sacred chapel sites and spend your first season together learning the laws and learning how to govern your home well. It is said to be a nice time. If you want to hear more about what it's like, I'm sure you could talk to Inkeri's parents tomorrow at the wedding. I remember when they went away. I had just come from the war, and I was wounded, so the council gave us leave to remain here, so we didn't get to participate in what was then a very new ritual. Your brothers both have nothing but glowing things to say. You've heard their tales. The shaman there will help you learn all the laws and understand them better than you do now. You do have a choice where to go, you know. You are free to choose a sacred site that you think will offer a different landscape than the ones closer to here. All of the chapels are renowned for their teachings, and I trust that you will choose well where you will step into the future together."

He rose to go, followed only by the gaze of his young son. Evin stared at the wall long after his father left, his hazel eyes searching for meaning in the lines of wood. His thoughts traveled a world of possibilities, and his heart longed for the freedom to make his own choice. His mom had spoken to him of a different, more powerful god, but he had never heard anyone else speak of this deity. His mother had been adamant that the only real future lay in the hands of this god she served quietly. She warned Evin never to speak of him aloud because worship of him had become dangerous. These sacred places and their shaman were supposed to help him understand his responsibilities, but would that understanding be rooted in truth? It seemed that everyone thought so. Even his brother, Othniel, whose wife had died of a fever less than a year after they were betrothed expressed that he was glad they had spent that time together in that way. Now Othniel was pledging his life to be a soldier for Diederick because he was so sure about the altruism of the rulers that kept order and peace. Evin was bothered by his own perception of reality. Nagging questions hung on, and he couldn't push them aside so easily. Why had his parent's generation married much later in their lives than the current one? Why were so many people happy to just blindly follow every law these men handed down? What of the god his mom spoke of in stories told quietly at night? Everything seemed to lack the fire and heart that he could feel beating in his own chest. Was he alone? He finally rose to follow his father into the house, his slight frame stiff from sitting in the same place for so long. He had let time get away from him. When he entered the cool air of the early spring night, he gazed at the twinkling stars in all their glory, and into his mind rushed all the fanciful stories his mother had told him years before. The tales spoke of miracles of old and of men who had risked everything to serve an unknown god. "If you are there, please hear me!" he yelled into the silent sky. "I need to know the way I am to travel, and I want you to show me the path!"

His voice echoed off the empty barn, and he stood still and waited until the silence grew oppressive around him. He made his way quietly and dejectedly toward the small wooden structure that would be his home for this last night, unaware of the form of his mother as she slipped away from the front window.

Chapter 2

Evin's mother Sanna stepped through the door to find him staring out the window. "My little boy is now a man. In a few hours, you will find yourself in charge of a household of your own."

"The reminder is a bitter thing. There is no joy for me in a ceremony like this," he stated flatly.

"Ah, my son, you can choose bitterness or joy. Don't let a bad thing come out of a joyful situation. The girl that has been chosen for you is going to be an amazing asset in your life." She closed the door to the room carefully. "I have something to share with you, Evin. I see in you a heart that mirrors my own, the heart of a seeker, looking beyond yourself for something more." She paused, gathering herself to pour out years of knowledge to her son. The tension in the room was tangible, and even someone as young as Evin could sense her inner struggle. "What I will tell you could change things a great deal, Evin. Do you want to hear it?"

The question caught him off guard. He laughed, a nervous sound, and scooted to the edge of his bed. "I have always loved your stories, Mom. They've taught me a lot. Go ahead."

"What I tell you must not reach your father's ears. He doesn't have the seeker's spirit to handle its telling. Do you swear this to me?"

Bewildered, Evin blinked and then replied. "Of course. I won't share it." His mother began to nervously pace the room. "Calm down, Mom. I'm ready to hear whatever it is you have to say." He smiled warmly and she settled on the edge of the bed like a frightened bird.

She fidgeted with the edge of the quilt. "Understand, Evin, that for years, I have hidden in my heart what I'm about to tell you, because if I said it in the wrong place, it could have meant my death. It has given me the strength to raise three boys to men without worrying that one of them would be the one to be able to hear it. It took a lot of faith to watch my youngest grow up in the footsteps of the others, when I knew he was the one. I saw you through the window last night as you begged god for his help, and it was the answer to years of questions in my mind. One of my boys knows the stories are more than that, much more. When I was a child on the outer islands of our country, my father shared with me the same stories that I have passed on to you. My mom and brothers had died unexpectedly when a plague swept through when I was a baby, so I was all the help left to my dad. We would spend hours working alongside one another, and he would tell me every story he knew about El Olam. For many years we lived in peace in that fishing village, our way of life so uncomplicated. I was ten when the tide changed, and I will never forget it. My father came to me in the middle of the night, bade me get up and get dressed and meet him out in the front of the house. I was scared to death, but I did what he said. When I made it outside, he was standing there with a freshly saddled horse. It was so long ago, and so dark."

His mom got a faraway look in her eyes, as the pain of the memories crossed her face. He dropped his eyes to his fingers in his lap, suddenly feeling like an intruder. Her voice continued, quieter. "I can still remember the look on my dad's face in the torchlight. It was a scary thing. His eyes were filled with terror, and he told me I must flee the islands and never return until there was peace. He said he'd taught me all I needed in my life in his stories, and that I should treasure them. He handed me a crudely drawn map and some meager provisions and told me to take the family fishing boat to the mainland. From there I was to journey to a place I'd only seen once in my life, a small chapel in the north of the mainland, being careful to avoid danger along the way. It was a two-day journey from my home, but by some miracle, I made it. I still don't remember much of it. When I left, my father told me to ride like my life depended on it and not to look back. I didn't look back, but I could hear the hoof-beats of what sounded like hundreds of horses arriving at my home. I traveled in a daze, and upon my arrival, my father's old friend welcomed me. The chapel was a refuge untouched by the wars that raged around it, and there I was able to hear again many of the stories that my father had told me. They told of the god my father had trusted, and I too grew to love him. After two years, things settled into an uneasy peace, but when I emerged into the world again, there were few of the things I remembered. My home and my father were gone, but his legacy remained in my heart. I was finally taken to live with my aunt in this village, and I was soon after pledged to marry your father. I was warned that I could never speak aloud again of that god, El Olam, so I didn't. Though my choices in life were seemingly gone, I thought often of him, and I knew he was watching, so I made the decision to make the best of my life.

Evin moved closer to the edge of the bed. "You made this journey by yourself?" He looked incredulous.

"Once I got away from the house, there were other people leaving the island to go to the mainland, so not entirely alone. I was with other families I knew." She continued speaking "Ten years into our marriage, the fighting spread to this side of the mountains, and I knew that your father would go to fight in the war on the side of the people that had killed my father. I knew his absence was a chance to teach my boys the truth I had learned. They only halfway listened to my stories because they were distracted by the war that raged outside. I was pregnant with you, and the time was near for you to be born. One night, as the fighting moved into our village, I cried out to god and asked him to keep us safe. The night was a wild, stormy one, black as ink, and I had just put your brothers to bed." She stood and walked to the window. "Someone started banging on the door, and I was terrified. Without your father here, we only had his status as an elder's son to protect us. I felt a peace come over me, and I knew that I should open the door. When I did, there stood the man who had kept me safe at the chapel as a ten-year-old girl. His every move was frantic, like he was in a state of panic. He was badly wounded, and it didn't seem to me there was any way he would survive the night. I made him as comfortable as possible and tended his wounds. He indicated the chapels had this time been the direct target of all the warring, and that he had barely escaped the leveling of the one closest to our village. Our rulers had become aware that if they were ever to have complete control of the people, they had to rid the country of those who stood against them. He told me that although all seemed to be lost, we still had friends on the other side of the mountains. Those people may still have this truth we've all but lost. He said they were still powerful enough to help free us from the oppression these lords sought to crush us underneath. Everyone who tried to flee that winter was killed, either by the weather, or by the enemy, and he feared greatly for our friends on the other side, but he seemed to think they were our only hope. Since then, the lords have continued to meet with our brothers on the other side of the mountain, which leads me to believe they must have conquered on that side as well. Some people still talk about the lawless lands over the mountains. I don't know if they have wiped out the worship of El Olam over there yet, but I fear there may be no one left to help us. He said I would need to be wise about when to send for help, about who to send for help." Her voice trailed for a minute, and Evin raised his eyes to find her staring into his eyes, her own eyes filled with a bevy of emotions ranging from confusion to fear, and he felt those same emotions rising in him. She repeated, "he said I would know the right time, and that god would provide the right person. Until then, those of us who were left here would only be able to contact one another in secret. He begged me to remember his words when the time came, and I swore to him I would. He gave me a small piece of cloth with a map carefully drawn on it, and a small leather pouch with a small colorless stone fragment. He said the fragment had been with him since I had come to him the first time, where it had been hidden in the things my father had sent with me to give to him. I had always thought those things were only items my father had sent to pay for my care, but apparently that stone meant something more. He said that the map would take us to a place where we can find help, and that the stone is the key. I'm unsure what that part means exactly, but I know the stone is one part of a seal that was broken into three. I have seen all of them in my days."

She turned from the window to face him. "Then he left, retreating into that terrible storm, and that was the last time I saw him. Hours after he'd left, my birth pains started, and you were born as the sun pushed the storms away and flooded through the windows. I was not alone, because I had awakened your oldest brother and sent him next door to ask our neighbors to send the midwives. They handed you to me and busied themselves with caring for the boys and cleaning up. I put you on the bed and kissed your tiny brow and counted your fingers and toes like every new mom does, and when I took your hand in mine and uncurled your fist, a second fragment of the stone tumbled out. You were born holding a shard of the stone." She moved across the room and raised his chin to look into his face. "I swear to you, I do not understand it, but I knew I had to hide it away with the other one and never speak of it until the right time. You are doubtless the man he spoke of that night, Evin, and now is the time." She looked suddenly terrified and raised her hand to her mouth to stop herself from trying to take her words back.

For a long minute, the young man stared into the soft eyes of the woman who had loved him unconditionally. "I think I like your other stories better." He sighed a deep sigh and fell backwards on the bed with a thud. Confusion clouded his features, and he folded his arms and used them to cover his eyes. He felt like he'd been punched in the gut. He let his fingers rub absently against his palms, looking for evidence his mother was telling the truth. What motivation would she have to lie? What was she asking him to do?

"Will you accept the gift of my secret and the responsibility it brings? The reason I tell you now is because you and your bride will be given leave to travel to whichever chapel you choose to pursue your training for a season. This is the only chance you're going to have to travel without arousing suspicion. You're to be a farmer, so you'll be expected to settle and live here without wanderlust. These fragments indicate there is more for you to do before that happens. You have to take them together and find out what it means that they are the key. After the war, many of the chapels were replaced with holy sites and staffed with shamans who know nothing of god. We still call them chapels, but there is no worship of El Olam there anymore. The worship of the true god has been replaced with the ancient ways. The new shamans train our young people and our soldiers in the ancient ways in an attempt to stomp out any remaining worship of the true god. I have watched as our people go and return as happy citizens, willing to give far more than they receive without question. I don't know what this training is like, Evin, because it started after the war. Because we were already married, your father was granted reprieve from going while he recovered from some relatively minor wounds he acquired in the fighting, but something is wrong about the people who return from its tutelage. Be aware of this. You must go to Fjall chapel. It is furthest away from here, but closest to the location on the map. It is still some distance, but it's as close as we can get you without anyone knowing something is wrong. Remember the things I told you, Evin. Remember the faithfulness of El Olam. In every story I know of him, he always proved to be steadfast, and I promise you can trust him."

Evin rolled over on the bed and pounded the pillow into a shapeless mass and proceeded to bury his face in it. For a minute, he lay still, breathing heavily, calming newly stripped nerves. Then he rolled to the side and sat up, looking like a tousled sleepy boy. "Today, you're asking me to be joined to a girl I've never met, and tomorrow, to leave the only life I have ever known, forcing that girl to do the same. Now in addition to that, you ask that I drag her all the way across this land to a place I've only heard of today in a story about your girlhood, so that I can solve a puzzle about a key that will free people, who don't even seem to be unhappy, to worship a god they don't even want to know?"

His mother looked appropriately chastised by these questions. "Evin, I don't want this for you either, but when god makes something this clear, we can only choose to obey or not. I would never presume to push you to this drastic measure if I could see any other way. Time and circumstances have pushed us to this point and to this solution." Her eyes were pleading. "You have to go. Things are getting worse for people in many of the villages around. Our turn is bound to come." Tears welled up in her eyes, but she took a deep trembling breath and buried them. She pulled a cloth and a pouch from the folds of her dress and handed them to her son. He unfolded the cloth on the bed and poured the contents of the pouch into his hand. Two minuscule pieces of light stone tumbled into his palm, and he held them lightly as if they might burn him. Instead, they felt warm and welcoming, like they were inexplicably always his. It was like a confirmation that his mother hadn't lost her mind.

"Where's the third stone?"

His mom took a breath and stepped back. "It is safe with someone who knows its purpose." Her gaze dropped and she looked embarrassed for a fleeting second before she regained her composure. "This map will tell you where to go, but god will lead you. Let his peace protect you as it has me. Let it go with you, my son, to your handfasting, and to your life beyond." She bent to kiss her son on the forehead, then left him staring at the pieces and fled from his room. For the second time in Evin's short life, he prayed.

Chapter 3

Inkeri lay on her bed, massaging her forehead, willing her headache to go away. "If I could have slept a little more," she complained. She rolled to her side and sat up, sadly gazing around the house in which she'd grown up. Everything took on a different look when you were seeing it for the last time in its setting. She paced the room, looking at the curtains and the furniture pieces that held her things. She knew that while she was away, a home would be built for her and her husband, and that many of these things would be there to welcome her when she returned. Her mom had promised her the washstand and basin she loved, and she let her fingers trail the delicate glass of the basin as she washed her face, lingering over the ritual she loved. She hoped her husband would choose one of the bigger and more comfortable chapels. She had heard that some of the outlying ones were almost comparable to a night in the woods, which had always had a certain appeal, but not for an entire season. She finished and moved to the dress hanging carefully on the back of the door. She smoothed the beautiful material and looked at the carefully embroidered flowers that circled the hem. "I guess I need to make a good impression; I do have to spend the rest of my life with this man," she mumbled to herself. Her thoughts were drawn away by the sound of her mother's voice calling her to breakfast. "I'm on my way!" she called out. She would wait to put on the dress until she had finished eating. She laid it across the bed and started out the bedroom door to head down to the kitchen. At her bedroom door, she stopped, unable to continue no matter how much she pushed forward. She looked in puzzlement at the door as if it had somehow developed the power to stop her forward progress. She once again tried to take a step, but still couldn't move beyond the doorpost.

Out of the darkness of the hallway, a voice spoke. "Hold still and listen."

Inkeri didn't know the voice, and was terrified by it, but her fierce spirit refused to allow the fear to cross her face. Instead, steady defiance settled on her face. "Let me go!" she growled.

"I'm not holding you."

Inkeri surveyed the situation and found this to be the truth. "What do you want?" The question was fearful. She peered into the darkness and still saw nothing. "Where are you?" A young man stepped forward, dressed in the strange clothes of some foreign warrior and carrying the full equipment for battle. He looked as if he'd stepped off the battlefield victorious, but not untouched. He wore a breastplate with a circular symbol on it. Inkeri tried to scream but couldn't find her voice to do so. She stumbled back into her room and stood dumbfounded, mouth agape.

"I am a messenger from El Olam, a humble servant of the almighty. I have brought news, Inkeri." His use of her name was the most unsettling thing to happen yet. "You need to know the man you will marry today is no ordinary man. He seeks truth that will set people free. Do not think him foolish or come against him, but instead serve with him and fight alongside him. He will find the truth of the healer."

Inkeri's headache had suddenly grown worse. "I don't understand," she stammered. "Today I'm going to marry a boy from the village. An elder's son. From all accounts he is a sober person, one who follows the laws in the strictest manner."

"He is the man El Olam has chosen to bring a message." The warrior turned away, and he began to fade back into the darkness. Before he was gone, he whispered "You will speak of this to no one."

Inkeri stood looking at the spot where the warrior had stood. She was so intent on staring at the place, that she failed to hear her mother's footsteps. "Inkeri? Inkeri, what's the matter with you? Your food... Inkeri? Are you even listening to me?"

She turned her gaze to her mother. Surely the warrior didn't mean she couldn't tell her mother. "Mom," she said, "I just..." Inkeri's voice caught in her throat, and she began to cough. The fit lasted a full minute with barely a breath between coughs.

Her mother grabbed her shoulders and held her at arm's length, staring at her. "Has the stress of the day made you ill?" At last, the cough subsided, and Inkeri looked at her mother and tried to speak, but nothing would come out. She clutched at her throat and tried again but could say nothing.

"I think you need to rest, child." Inkeri shook her head defiantly as her mother busied herself cleaning off the bed and turning back the covers. "Climb in now, don't argue." She found herself shuttled into bed against her mild protestations. She hated getting up anyway. Maybe she did need to rest. After all, she was seeing things. After her mother left the room, she tried to speak but couldn't issue forth the smallest sound. She lay for a long time trying, even though she knew she couldn't. The warrior had said she could speak of this to no one, and he obviously meant to enforce it. As she lay still, her thoughts had time to wander to the things he had said and for the first time, and she began to eagerly anticipate laying her eyes on this great man she was to marry. She must have heard the wrong things spoken of him in the marketplace. After a bit, she could tell the time was drawing near for her to leave the house. She climbed out of bed for the second time that day and retrieved her dress from the back of the door where her mom had replaced it. She dressed carefully, making sure that everything was in place, and braiding her hair into shimmering ceremonial ribbons that were meant to show her father's status in the village. He was not an elder, but an important liaison between the people of this village and Lord Diederick. As a result, fine clothing and the choicest goods found their way into his coffer with every job well done. She left the room, heading down the stairs, pausing as she neared the kitchen. Voices echoed up the stairwell toward her.

"She isn't as strong as I apparently thought, Torsten. Maybe she needs another year. She just might not be ready for this yet."

"Nonsense, Birgit, she is a strong girl. She's just a little overwhelmed, I'm sure." Her father's voice was a balm to her soul. He was always taking up for her. The thought of the warrior's words took sudden hold on her heart, and she found herself fighting back tears. She must say goodbye to the family she held so dear and pursue some course about which she knew nothing. The road before was clear. She could cry on her mother's shoulder and slip quietly back to bed unsure if she would ever speak again, or she could step out on her own and trust a god she'd never heard of to catch her.

Her parent's voices carried on discussing her fate and her impending marriage, and into the midst of their turmoil stepped a woman who minutes before had been a frightened girl. She stepped between her parents' chairs and mustered her full height. With her chin held high, she found her voice again. "Isn't it time for us to leave for my handfasting?"

Chapter 4

Evin shielded his eyes from the bright sun that threatened to blind him and searched the gathering crowd for his family. His mind wandered again to his mother's secret. Upon finding help, what was he to do? According to his mother, he had been chosen for some greater purpose, but was this spindly boy the man to do such a dangerous thing? The weight of the pouch he'd secured to a cord and strung carefully around his neck reminded him this craziness was real. Inside, the map and the fragments rested safely.

"Evin, did you hear me?" The voice brought him back to the present.

"What, I'm sorry?" He grimaced and looked at the oldest elder in the village, unsure what else to say.

The elder smiled with understanding, "I asked if you are ready to begin the ceremony and receive your bride?"

Evin looked at the man for a second as if seeing him for the first time. He spoke as if in a daze. "Yes, I'm ready." The words signified much more than the man knew. Layers of buried meaning rushed to the surface and threatened to smother him. Was he? He doubted he ever could be. He gathered himself as if he was being asked to jump into an abyss and had decided to do it with all the grace he could muster.

When the sun reached its apex, a ram's horn was blown, and the group of people gathered around the stone circle of the ceremonial ring. The service began with an admonition to Evin to grow his family, to teach them well, and to carefully maintain the plot of land he would be given by the elders so that he could happily take part in helping to fulfill the offering his village was required to provide to the overseers. He was reminded that this portion would grow as the number of families in the village grew, so he and the other boys that would marry this year would feel the weight of that responsibility in the coming season. Evin knew his father and brothers would work his land this season and provide the time for him to travel, and for the first time, he realized the burden his choice to travel so far would put on them. The elder continued to speak while Evin listened to the different voices that were playing in his head. He was acutely aware that everything was about to change. He stared through the man, looking into his own soul for strength and purpose, but he only found a painfully blank slate. He was not ready to let go of the years of simple life that he had led. Despite his search for adventure, he felt lost now that it was staring him in the face. The elder finished droning on and turned to the right side of the circle. "Evin son of Erik, behold your bride!"

Evin turned in time to see a young woman striding confidently across the space between them. There was a fire burning in her eyes and purpose in her gait. Highlights played like fireflies across the ribbons in her auburn hair as she moved, causing her hair to shine like distant fire on a hillside. Her blue eyes reflected the color of an iceberg he'd once seen as a young boy, and the spark in them only served to make her even more beautiful. For a moment, he felt unable to breathe as he watched her close the space too quickly. A finely woven blue dress embroidered with delicate pink roses brushed the ground and a silver cloak fastened with a silver brooch sparkled at her throat and spoke of her family's obviously high standing. She looked at him with no smile of acceptance, and he began to feel as if he was being sized up like an animal to be sold at auction. She drew near in what seemed like seconds, and the chaplain began to speak again. Her appearance made the weight he felt even heavier, but despite feeling like the wind had been knocked out of him for the second time today, he couldn't help but grin when he saw her.

"Do you accept this man to be your husband, Inkeri?"

"I accept gratefully the gift that the counsel has given of a husband to care for me and work alongside me to build a home and family to ensure the growth and health of our village." She quoted the oft said words with conviction that was often missing in this ceremony. Inkeri reached to take the hand of her husband as was expected, turning his hand over and placing a necklace in his open palm. Then she stared at the chaplain with resolve. Evin couldn't take his eyes off her. He looked at her as he slipped the cord around his neck, careful to make sure it rested above the pouch. She seemed so incredibly strong, and he felt in his bones that his mother was right about this girl. There was more to her than he could imagine in this moment. Though Evin had seen many of these same rituals, he was not prepared for the emotions that went along with all of it when he was the one whose life was being dramatically altered. Their hands were bound together with ribbons of various colors, and they looked into one another's eyes and took turns vowing eternal faith and lasting fidelity.

"Till death divide us,

In good faith,
Two bodies, one heart."

He and this girl had everything any couple in this world could hope to start out with, and he was suddenly filled with an overwhelming desire to live that life he'd always been promised instead of the one he was now staring down. The sudden and complete shift in his thinking was not lost on him as he looked into her eyes. He remembered not even a day before standing in the barn refusing to marry her. Now they grasped hands across the space between them and made promises to each other and to the assembled village. Before he was ready, their hands were freed, and the customary dancing, over-filled wine goblets, and plates of rich food were soon entertaining the entire village. This seemed to Evin to drag on forever. He looked up more than once from conversation to find his new bride at the other side of the square engrossed in a conversation of her own. He managed to get away from the crowd by backing into a small alley and finding a crate to sit on with a good vantage point. Evin had always liked to watch people more than talk to them, and he knew there was a great deal to learn from watching people interact. He spotted Inkeri in the crowd and watched in awe as she talked to the people that flooded around her. She handled the crowd with matchless grace, smiling at all the right times, or bowing her head just so. He was stricken suddenly with the fact that he was not worthy of such a prize. As he watched, he knew that having her on his side would make everything so much easier to handle. His face set in a frown as it occurred to him that she had not offered him so much as a smile at this point. Maybe she didn't think he was worthy of her either. His first act as her husband was going to have to be to drag her away from everyone she loved under false pretenses. He knew what a fool he looked like to all of them.

"You found a place to think alone. That could be good or bad." The voice startled Evin. In his reverie, he had neither seen nor heard any approach. He nearly jerked his head off his spine, turning it to face the sound. Upon examination, it proved to come from a middle-aged man, maybe twenty years Evin's senior. His clothes were dusty, like those of a traveler, and he had a well-trimmed beard and piercing eyes.

"How could it be bad," Evin asked "and how would you know?"

"I know more than you give me credit for, young man." The man laughed, a booming sound that seemed to originate from his belly. "Being alone makes people sad."

"You sound like an authority on the subject." Evin jumped down from his perch on the crate and held out his hand to the man. "My name is Evin."

"Evin, yes I know. Evin son of Erik." A ghost of sadness flitted across the man's features for a moment, but it was quickly replaced with a grin.

"How do you...?"

"Your parents hired me as your guide," the man interrupted. "Your father thinks you might need help finding the place you've chosen for you and your bride, seeing as it's far away."

"My father is mistaken." Evin sighed "I can figure out the way, or I wouldn't have headed there. We won't need your services." Evin turned to walk away, back toward the crowd.

"Oh, so you don't think so?" The man laughed heartily again. "My company isn't that bad, lad. Your parents and I have known each other for years. You'll get used to having me around." He started to follow Evin.

"I said I don't need your help!" Evin raised his voice a little bit and turned to face the taller man. "Look, I need to do this on my own. My dad's just not ready to let go yet, that's all. Let's just pretend you missed me in the crowd, and I left without meeting you. Now you're off the hook, ok?"

Evin once again turned to walk away, this time sure he'd be allowed to go without harassment. A now serious voice proved him wrong. "So, you're going to navigate a poorly mapped wilderness with your blushing bride, knowing the kinds of things that lurk out there? Do you want to die for a reason, young man?"

Evin stopped short of his next stride. "My name is Evin, if you didn't get that. My mother encouraged me to go to the chapel at Fjall, which is only next to the poorly mapped wilderness, so that is where I am going to go. I know the way." He stood still, waiting for the guide's next words.

"How can you know the way? There is rarely travel to that chapel from this village, and I have been many times, but you've only stepped foot from this village a few times. Your parents asked me to take you there. They are concerned for you both, Evin. You may be strong, but you are still young, nonetheless. Let me guide you there, if only to help your parents feel safer. You are the youngest of the brothers and your father's heart lacks the courage it once did. He wants to ensure you're safe while you're away. If you don't want me along, pick a closer chapel. In Fjall, there is nothing. By the time you get there, much of the time you should be enjoying together will be gone. You will be allowed to stay longer because your brother and father are willing to farm for you, but your father thinks your choice of Fjall is silly. I don't even know if there is a good shaman there." He sized Evin up carefully.

The map that Evin's mother had given him burned in his mind. He would have to go beyond Fjall. He knew better than to mention it to this man. His mother had been very clear on that point, but he was also wise enough to know that his insistence on going alone would seem even more foolish, and his lack of protection would cause more talk than it was worth. "All right. You're right. I should have seen it from the beginning. You're welcome to go along, granted that you leave upon our arrival in Fjall and return home. I want to have the time alone at the holy site to learn all the things I'm supposed to. I'm sure you understand." His voice lacked any kind of sincerity, but both chose to ignore that.

"What about your way home? Your father hired me for the whole trip, and I want to be able to give him what he paid for, you know?"

"You can teach me to defend my campsite effectively. That can be the second half of your pay."

"You're quite the bargainer, young man. Just like your mother. Strong willed as an ox. It's a deal, but let's see how the journey goes and then you can decide if you want my company for the trip back or not, all right?"

"I don't want your company for the trip there." Evin turned once again and strode back into the thick of the crowd, leaving his new guide standing shaking his head.

"That boy's just like his father." He muttered under his breath as he ambled into the crowd after Evin.

~~~

Evin had spent his day listening to so many congratulations and saying so many hellos that he was exhausted with all the talking to people. After meeting his guide for the journey, he had tried unsuccessfully all day to lose him for a few minutes. He didn't even know the man's name yet, but he had already decided he didn't like him. He was always annoyingly present. The few minutes he'd actually spent in the company of Inkeri had been spent answering questions, mostly about why they had chosen such a faraway chapel for their training in the laws. As the end of the day drew near, Evin finally found himself alone. He figured the guide
~~~

had decided he could trust him not to run and had gone to get some rest for tomorrow. Evin felt the leather pouch to make sure the cloth map and stone fragments were secure and looked around to find his mother. He had a few things to discuss with her and his father before he left. He knew the customs of his people concerning marriage, but his request to travel so far was unusual, and he knew it had only been granted because of his father's status as a war hero and elder. Suddenly Evin felt like he needed to know more about what was expected of him at the chapel. He wanted his mother's reassurance that he was doing the right thing. Careful study of the map that morning had confirmed that Fjall chapel was the closest to the location of this help that he was supposed to be looking for. Were he to spend his time there, he felt confident he would find it, but he didn't even know how Inkeri felt about such a long journey. He looked toward the setting sun, and quickly made his way to the last place where he'd seen his parents. He only needed a moment with them before he took his bride to the Hall of Elders. There they would be blessed and sent on their way by the assembly. They would spend the night there and begin their journey in the morning with provisions provided to them by the council using animals belonging to their families. Evin found his father in the rapidly thinning crowd and called his name. "Dad, wait, I need to ask you something." He quickly made his way across the square and to his father's side. "There is so much I'm unsure about. I need your words of wisdom."

His father grinned, a look that quickly faded into remorse. "It seems I have given quite enough advice, Evin. In the barn, I didn't mean that you must find an adventure in your trip, only that you must make the most of your stay at whichever chapel you chose. I didn't mean for you to choose one as far away as Fjall." Erik frowned as if to make a point.

"The choice was mine, and I think I made it well. Also, you hired a guide for us. We'll be fine."

His father's face brightened discernibly. "Then you met Roald? I'm glad. He's a good man, Evin, and he knows his way around a tight spot. He will take care of you and Inkeri. Still, Fjall is a long way and a fierce journey. What would make you choose such a place?"

"That would be my fault." Sanna stepped up at his father's elbow. "I'm afraid I told our boy too many stories of the ruins near there and now he has it in his head to go there and explore them. He thinks it will give more time for Inkeri and him to get to know one another."

"Well, they'll have the rest of their lives to do that. You must talk the boy out of it. He's too hardheaded for me."

She chuckled. "He has chosen, my love, and preparations have been made for his journey. I think we should bid him farewell and offer him our support. Besides, I see his wife all alone at the other end of the square." She turned toward Evin. "Can I walk with you to meet Inkeri?"

"Of course, mom." Evin placed his hand on his father's shoulder. "Don't worry, dad. We will remember to take care of ourselves for you. The law keeps this place peaceful. We won't encounter trouble."

The words seemed to soothe the older man. "Please go swiftly, my boy, and return to us in one piece." He turned toward his home and walked off without looking back.

"Let's go, Evin, before Inkeri thinks you've forgotten her. His mother reached for his arm to guide him. "We'll talk on the way."

Evin watched his father go. "But I have so many questions."

"Now is not the time for questions, Evin. It is time for you to be with Inkeri. She needs you to be strong for her. Tomorrow when you leave, she will have to go with you, a stranger, far away from any life she has ever known. Don't expect her to sit in the background and take commands. She will have questions too, and she has the right to have answers to them."

"Are you telling me I should tell her?" Evin stopped and twisted out of her grasp, giving her a hard stare. She took his arm once more and continued to tug him toward Inkeri.

"I'm telling you that you should use discretion, but don't ever lie to her. She must be able to trust you if she is to be any help to you at all. Fjall is a long way from here, and the two of you will need each other. You will be far away from us, but instead of being in some cozy chapel, you will be in the wilderness. You have to choose your friends carefully and guard against your enemies."

"Enemies. Makes you sound a little bit crazy. What about this guy that dad hired? I had to say he could go, but he has no idea a map exists. What am I supposed to do about him?"

She paused for a minute, choosing her words carefully. "He's a great friend of ours, and a good man. He knows more of this situation than you think, but don't speak to him openly. You can trust him if you have questions. You are going to Fjall, Evin, and very few people know why. People will consider you a fool, but if you seek out El Olam, your heart will not be foolish, even though your actions will appear to be. You have to be prepared for that. As your knowledge of god grows, you will look more and more foolish, but he will protect you. He will help you, Evin. Don't be afraid."

"I'm not afraid, Mom, only full of questions. I don't even know this god, and you ask me to trust him?" Evin looked at Inkeri as they drew closer to her. "You're asking me to drag her into this, not knowing what each day will bring? You have always been a wise woman, so I have chosen to trust you. I will make the journey you have asked me to make. I only hope it is not in vain."

"It will not be in vain, Evin. If yours is the only heart that is changed, then your journey will have been worthwhile. You go now and take care of this precious girl. I will see you when you return, but I will be looking at a new man, not the boy who leaves."

The pair stopped in front of Inkeri, and Evin's mom once more turned to him. "It was wonderful today to see you wed, and I hope one day to see your children." The traditional blessing sounded sweet. Then she turned to Inkeri. "I have admonished my son to be attentive to you. If he is not, just let me hear of it." Her eyes sparkled with a kind of mischief Evin supposed only women could understand, and Inkeri smiled broadly.

"I will see that he is careful to obey his mother. I won't let him get away with anything else."

Sanna took Inkeri's hand in hers. "Good. Now I wish you two the happiness that I have come to know." This part of the blessing sounded more rehearsed than genuine. "Goodbye both of you, and may the gods bless you on your journey." She squeezed Inkeri's hand and released it, then grabbed Evin and hugged him fiercely. She released him and walked away quickly, leaving her very uncertain son standing beside his silent wife-to-be.

He looked at her nervously. "Well, I'm not really sure what to say. They didn't give me any words to memorize." He smiled shyly. "This day has been a whirlwind, and I still haven't had a chance to say more than a couple of words to you. Now that I have the chance, I'm speechless."

The night began to creep up on them, its dark fingers seeking the last of the natural light and vanquishing it. Inkeri watched as the lamps were lit around the square to ward off the impending night. "I think I have so much to say I don't know where to start. For days, I have thought I didn't want to be your wife, but today, my life has changed. Whether good or bad, I must look back on my past as only a starting point for whatever is to come. Since you are to be the author of my future, I have no choice but to trust you." She reached out her hand with decision and clasped Evin's fingers tightly. "Take me to the Hall of Elders, Evin. I grow weary of this square."

Evin was filled with appreciation of the strength of the girl who held his hand. All day, he had seen it, and now he saw the resolve that was its backbone. He gently led Inkeri toward the biggest building in the square, aware of the warmth of her fingers resting trustfully in his hand. "If I am to be the author of your future, may the one who authors mine teach me how."

Inkeri glanced at him with puzzlement but chose silence as they plodded along. The thoughts in her mind had claimed her attention all day, and though Evin looked still more a boy than a man, she remembered the messenger's words. Evin might look like a mere boy, but she was acutely aware there was more to him than even he imagined.

Chapter 5

Inkeri stared out across the wide plain in front of her. The sun peeked over the horizon, making the plants stand out in bold relief like giant eyelashes. The sight was beautiful. "Inkeri, I think we're ready to go." Evin's voice was as enthusiastic as his face. His eyes were lit up like a little kid's, and his smile was the sincerest she'd ever seen. "Have you ever seen such a perfect day for traveling?" He kept going as though he didn't expect an answer, so she offered none. Instead, she watched him tie the final bundles to the cart provided by the elders. Just five minutes ago, she'd met Roald for the first time. She watched him talking to another group of travelers, then he stopped and approached Evin. They talked intently for a few minutes, and then seemed to agree about something. Evin finished adjusting the straps on the donkeys and walked to where she stood. "Roald said these other people want to travel with us as far as Vatna. We'll be going that way to replenish supplies anyway, so I don't see any trouble with it. I thought you might like the female company." He smiled, obviously uncertain whether he had made a decision she would be pleased with.

"That's good. How long will that be?"

"It should take us a couple of weeks to reach the town if the weather stays fair, and we rest the animals often enough. Roald thinks the weather will stay good."

Inkeri looked at the group of travelers curiously. There were three of them, two female and one male. The women chatted comfortably with one another, while the man busied himself with fixing some bundles at his feet. From their interactions, she gathered they must be family. The younger girl's belly swelled with a fairly advanced pregnancy, and she sparkled with young health, her long blond hair catching the sunlight beautifully. They looked like they had traveled a long way already. Evin turned away, handed Roald the donkey's reins, and mounted his horse. The rest of the group did the same and began to slowly move away. Inkeri turned once more to look at the sleepy town she was leaving behind. The buildings were bathed in the first light of morning, each one just starting to yield its inhabitants to the business of another day. Although goodbyes had been said yesterday, she felt like she was leaving without a word. She reached out toward the buildings in an unconscious wave, as if she could carry with her each of the things that had formed her life up to this point. From this high spot the entire village was visible, each structure outlined against the green fields behind it. Inkeri's eyes lifted in the direction of her home, and a tear rolled down her cheek as her hand dropped to her side. "Goodbye, for now." She whispered the words and turned to join the group as they rode away.

She stayed in the back wiping tears from her eyes in awkward privacy. When the last of the tears had washed its way down her face, she looked up, studying the back of her promised husband curiously. Today he wore the simple clothes of a farmer, not those he had worn yesterday. Then he had worn rich textiles woven with color and accented with gold thread. He didn't even seem mindful that he was one of the only men in the village decked out in all that finery. His father was an elder. There had never been any hardship or uncertainty, and she had expected his bearing to resonate with that. She had been pleased to discover that instead of a being a spoiled brat, he seemed to be considerate and good natured. Furthermore, she'd heard how lanky he was from the girls who had met him along the years. Their village was large, so not everyone knew everyone else, and people who were pledged to be married were kept apart, so she'd relied on these accounts to give her some idea of what to expect. She had been a little stunned to discover that lanky didn't describe him so much as young. He looked as if he'd just made the cut for actually old enough to marry. His frame was still the thin and unsure build of a boy, but with the promise of wide shoulders and strong muscles that would not only rival those of his older brothers, but in all likelihood surpass them. She had watched the three of them together yesterday, and he didn't look like either of them, who favored their father instead of their mother, who Evin looked more like.

She knew that pairings for marriage were made for people as close in age as possible, and rarely was the girl older, but she felt in their case this must be the situation by at least the better part of a year. She watched him chat with Roald as they made their way along. He had hair that could not quite be called brown or blonde, but somewhere solidly between the two and eyes that matched almost exactly. These things he did share with his brothers, Othniel and Gunnar. Fair was the best word that she could imagine describing him. His looks, his manners, his disposition. All those things were very fair. This man was the reason she must leave her family for so long and trade the comfort of the past for a big unknown, yet she could not bring herself to feel anger towards him. Something told her that his choice of destination was beyond his control. She only wished he would yield some part of the burden he carried to someone else. He had proven this morning already that he took the planning and execution of this trip very seriously. She wondered if he was the kind that would ever ask for help. He seemed to carry a great deal around on his shoulders, yet he was so unsure of himself. She remembered his goofy grin at their wedding ceremony when she'd walked across the ring to meet him. Inkeri smiled to herself despite her sadness. She knew from the few hours they'd spent together so far that he had as much heart as he had stubbornness. Although he must not be used to caring for anyone but himself, she felt like it was a lesson he would learn easily. She also felt like she could trust him to give her space and time, so she decided to keep her distance, and watch and learn as much as she could about this enigma that was to be her husband. She spurred her horse to move beside the pregnant girl and settled into stride close enough to carry on a conversation. "We haven't met yet. I'm Inkeri."

The girl smiled sweetly and genuinely. "I'm Alia. These are my parents, Harald and Runa."

She smiled and nodded in their direction. "Congratulations on the coming little one. It must be a hard time to travel."

A cloud of confusion and then sadness crossed Alia's face. "Oh, yeah, the baby will come in a few moons. I didn't have a choice but to travel now. My husband died unexpectedly while we were on our wedding journey." She seemed to be thinking way too hard about this.

Her father stirred uncomfortably in the saddle to the left of her. "Alia is really just in shock, I'm afraid. As soon as her mother and I got word of the tragic situation we came to the chapel to get her.

I can see why her husband chose for them to travel here. It's a beautiful place in which you live." He forced a smile and swept his arm out to indicate the pastoral scene that surrounded them, changing the subject.

Inkeri caught the look in his eyes, and assuming he didn't want to continue to discuss a painful topic, she followed his prompt. "Yes, we are most blessed. Our village grows by the year, and Evin and I are only a small portion of the young people that will marry this year alone."

"The land looks very fertile and healthy." Harald sounded a little bitter about it, but Inkeri let it slide without comment. Runa looked up at this point, and the depth of sadness that covered her face at her husband's comment seemed to sum up the mood that had settled over the four of them.

"Yes," she intoned, unsure what else to say to that. She fished around in her brain for another topic, discarding the previous two. "Is there anything I can do to help ease the burden of traveling? Evin said you have a couple of weeks before you leave us. Will you be home then, or changing direction?"

"We will be leaving your party to change direction, but we only have a couple of days left to travel once that happens." Harald looked relieved to have settled on a neutral topic. For the next hour, the four of them discussed the similarities and the differences in the parts of the country they hailed from, and told stories of weather, farming, and fishing. She felt drawn to the forlorn family, and compassion for Alia rose in her as she watched her chat too excitedly about the things she loved about her hometown.

Soon, it became obvious to Inkeri that traveling on the horse was not a good fit for the very pregnant widow. She moved beside Evin and touched his arm to get his attention. He smiled warmly at her and listened attentively as she described the situation. "I'm thinking we could move some of the bundles off the cart on to her horse and reconfigure the others to make a more comfortable spot for her to ride while the road is smooth." He didn't even pause to think about it, but immediately flew into action to stop the whole party and spend the precious time moving the already situated cargo. They worked together to make the switch possible and carefully helped Alia into the cart. Evin's compassion wasn't lost on Inkeri. He could have insisted that these strangers make accommodations for themselves so that they didn't waste a perfectly good travel day, but instead, without complaint, he inconvenienced himself for them. He was oblivious to the fact that this was unusual, doing it all without gaining anything. Inkeri watched the men as everyone remounted their horses and caught sight of the admiration on Roald's face as he sized up the young man he was guiding. She felt the storm inside her calm a little to find herself in the company of decent men. If they would care this way for a stranger, she could realistically hope that that they would care for her. The rest of the day passed without any problems, and the party paused as the sun began to lower in the sky so that they could be sure of the daylight to set up a good camp.

A day's journey from home, Inkeri and Evin relied on the knowledge and patience of the other travelers as they sorted through the provisions and figured out the best way to set up camp. Roald and Evin worked comfortably alongside one another, laughing and falling peaceably into appropriate roles, the younger learning the few things he didn't already know about the task from the older. Similarly, Runa and the two younger ladies busied themselves with making sure they had a ready source of water for the night and preparing a fire on which to cook some of the provisions they had at hand. Camp was a bustle of activity, for a time. When they finished, two tents faced each other across the central fire circle, which crackled happily. Nighttime sounds settled in, and the group finally rested around the fire. They told stories of other campfires and of other journeys, all happy. Roald regaled them with stories, being easily the most traveled in the group. His jocular personality put everyone else at ease, and by the time the party was ready for bed, the mood was decidedly pleasant. It was decided one of the tents would house the ladies, and the men would reside together in the other one.

Inkeri tidied up a few things around the camp and moved toward the tent where the other ladies already waited. A gentle touch on her arm stopped her and she squinted to see her husband's face outlined by the campfire like some kind of otherworldly creature. She couldn't help but think back to the warrior in her hallway the day before.

Evin smiled sincerely, looking too burdened for his short years. "I just wanted to say goodnight. Thank you for being so kind to our companions today. My mom always taught me that a good way to know the character of a person is to watch how compassionate they are to the people around them." His face always had an easy smile, even when his eyes looked as though the fate of the world might somehow rest on him. It looked so comforting and welcoming.

"Of course." She let her eyes fall away from his face. He would be easy to like too much. Right now, she remembered her resolve to maintain her emotional distance from this young man, no matter what their marital status said about them. Thankfully, the actual beginning of their lives together as husband and wife wouldn't be expected to begin until they had been blessed by the shaman at the holy site. "Goodnight, Evin." She turned away and moved into the tent. The ease that had accompanied her evening was rattled by that little conversation with him. She was dying to know what he knew. She wasn't sure whether to muster some sort of anger at being a pawn in some greater story. She wasn't sure whether her marriage was contrived for some other plan. None of this was anything like she'd imagined this part of her life would look. She nestled into the blankets and let her mind whirl with all the thoughts she pushed out during the day. She was at best a supporting role in something she didn't understand, and she had chosen to walk into this with her eyes wide open. She suddenly missed her family, her room, and her comfort. Now that she was alone, she could no longer maintain the perfectly chiseled stone wall that she let the others see. She cried like a flood gate had been released, turning into the pillow to drown out the sounds of her sobbing. Yes, these were nice people, but they were not her people. The more she thought of it the heavier her heart seemed, and she felt lost in the tide of her own tears. Suddenly a hand was rubbing her back, and she raised her head from the depths of her pillow and found herself only barely able to make out the face of a very concerned looking Alia. "I'm okay," she maintained, attempting to hold on to her carefully crafted dignity.

Alia moved back into her spot. "I had to go out of the tent. This baby makes me get up every night now. You didn't even notice me, so I was worried about you." She was quiet for a minute. "Do you not want to marry him?" Alia spoke with compassion.

"Not that, I think." Inkeri tried to articulate part of what was bothering her without saying too much. "I didn't really want to marry at all." That didn't quite hit the nail on the head, but it was close enough to ring true.

Again, a moment of quiet. Alia was a thinker, it seemed. "I wanted nothing more than to marry Kai."

"Kai? Your husband?" Inkeri almost choked on the words as her body still struggled with breathing. "I'm so sorry."

"It's weird. I can't remember what happened to him. That makes it worse, I think. I just remember him, and loving him, and being ready to marry him, and now here I am and everyone's telling me about some accident we had that robbed me of him and of my most recent memories of him. I'm not able to be sad that he's gone. I'm just sad that I can't remember why he's gone."

Inkeri was aware of the sudden perspective shift that was taking place in her mind. How dare she sit here and sob like a little baby about having to marry a guy that seems like the nicest guy in the universe while this poor girl couldn't even remember losing the love of her life and the father of her child? "The baby will remind you." She didn't know where this certainty came from, but she had a sense that when Alia saw her child, she would never be able to forget the path that brought the baby to her.

Alia reached out and took her hand. "Thank you." Her voice was quiet and unsure. "Everyone else says it's just better to forget him."

Inkeri squeezed Alia's hand reassuringly. "I'm pretty sure you won't be able to do that. We'd better get some rest for tomorrow. Sorry I woke you."

Alia scoffed. "I'm pretty sure it won't be the last time I'm up."

Inkeri's last thought was to wonder if this is what it must be like to have a sister.

Chapter 6

The following days passed in much the same way, with no hiccups in the travel plans or the weather, and the path for the cart continued to be smooth enough to allow Alia to spend time in relative comfort there. The group became closer, growing comfortable with each other and developing close friendships. Inkeri and Alia grew especially close. Inkeri always listened to the things Alia could remember that others didn't have a taste for, and Alia was a good safe place for Inkeri to express her emotions about her marriage without having them destroy her again. They always worked together to gather sticks for kindling and water for bathing and cooking, where they would have time out of easy earshot of the others to discuss these more delicate matters. A week passed quickly and with no problems, and the second seemed as if it would go much the same way. Even Harald and Runa relaxed and grew more friendly every day. It seemed something had made them both suspicious and afraid, but as the days passed those emotions seemed to settle.

Evin and Roald spent much of the time together, and Evin eagerly learned many of the things the guide had to teach him. What had started as a business agreement eased naturally into a friendship, and Evin became happier every day that he hadn't managed to scare the man off with his gruff attitude that first day. With Roald's guidance, he learned to watch out for his whole team like they were family. The annoying feeling that Roald was ever present on his wedding day was replaced with an appreciation that the man was mindful of the situation and aware of any problems long before they became a threat. He was glad to have some of the responsibility for that transferred to his shoulders, and he was thrilled to learn to wield his short sword with ease. The style of fighting came naturally to him, and since the days of most boys were spent learning how to squabble effectively, he already had a fantastic foundation for this knowledge. Roald had years of experience that made him an excellent resource, but Evin's natural ability made him a worthy rival long before Roald had anticipated him becoming so. As week two aged, everyone remembered that soon they would part ways. Evin watched Inkeri as she grew closer to Alia, and he felt conflicted and sad. The girls' relationship meant he didn't have to feel guilty for asking Inkeri to go so far from home. He didn't have to feel guilty for hiding the truth from her. He didn't have to feel guilty for taking her away from her family. That was all about to end.

He became quieter and spent more time alone worrying about what was to come next for them. They'd still hardly spoken, and she avoided long conversations with him, which he understood, but he was also smart enough to realize that when she lost Alia, it was going to be bad for her. Would he be able to comfort her? Would she want him to? He could try all day to pretend she didn't exist and let her work through things herself, but that didn't seem wise or kind. Every time they rested, and he watched her and Alia talk and laugh, he was stricken more by her beauty and her natural grace. She belonged where she'd been born. Her fair skin had darkened like theirs all had in the bright sunshine, and she seemed to grow more beautiful each day. He almost wished his mom had chosen an ugly girl. It would be less distracting. He smiled to himself at that thought and realized right away how glad he was it wasn't true. Again, wishing he could brush the stray hair out of her face, he felt the waves of guilt come back, and he stood and marched off, feeling sick. It was getting so bad he couldn't even look at her without wishing he could take her home. He just had to find that other stupid shard, and whatever help he could. He was a seeker, nothing else. He would find information, hand it over to his mom, and then he would take her home. They would settle together and make a wonderful life. They would have children and laugh about the time they took a wild trip all the way to the opposite coast of their land. He found himself alone in the forest, the sounds of the resting party having long died out behind him. He sat on a log and pulled the pouch from around his neck for the first time on the journey. He carefully dumped the two shards and the map into his hand and gazed at them again. What could these mean? He held them up and watched as the light bent through them in miraculous ways. They reminded him of the glass beads he had played with in his mom's sewing stuff when she wasn't looking. Held up to the light in certain ways, they bent and reflected all that was one way and made it another way altogether. He marveled at one of them being in his hand when he was born, and he found himself tempted to doubt the story. What if the midwife had put it there as some sort of superstitious nonsense? As he looked, though, he riddled over the fact that they fit together perfectly, leaving space for a third piece. Where would she have gotten the right piece? He placed them carefully back in the pouch and looked reflectively at the map. For the first time since his wedding day, he studied the landmarks and the route, refreshing his memory. He noted that the town where they would part ways from Alia's family had a small holy site. They would soon stop there to replenish provisions and say goodbye. He would ask his wife to say goodbye again. He looked at the little chapel on the map longingly. What if they stopped there and did their training? Would it matter? He started thinking about it, and the more he mused, the more it made sense. He seized upon the opportunity to not be the bad guy and replaced the map in the waiting pouch and stringed it once more around his neck, tucking it into his shirt. He retraced his steps, and after a bit found the group waiting eagerly to continue the journey. He looked sheepish. "Sorry. I was just taking a few minutes to think." The others nodded pleasantly.

Roald sat up from the patch of grass he'd been sunning on and smiled lazily. "Good thing we're not in a hurry," he joked.

Evin kicked a stick at him as he walked by. "Give it a rest, Roald. It wasn't that long." He smiled and kept going past him to his waiting horse.

The good-natured group kept going, falling into the much-practiced rhythm of travel and stopping that they had all come to understand was necessary for Alia's comfort. By nightfall, they had made it within one day of the south bound road that the others would take.

Tents were erected with care in a plain on comfortable flat ground. Mountains loomed in the distance, and the group knew that soon the comfort they'd been experiencing would be a memory. Evin did his chores without thought and went through all the motions while he waited for everyone to meander off to bed. Roald was always the last in the tent, so Evin waited patiently for him to finish working so he could talk to him. The fire in the camp settled into a slow cadence and evening wandered into night. When he saw that Roald was slowing down, he called him over to a spot just out of the hearing of the camp, but still within view. A fallen log made an easy bench where Evin had been waiting.

"Kind of hard to take it all in, huh?" Roald sounded extremely wise, and Evin had no reason to doubt he was.

"I can't believe I'm on my way to being married, Roald, and there is so much I have to consider now. I'm not sure I'm doing the best thing."

"You mean with your marriage? You don't really have a choice, do you?"

"No, not with that, Roald. I think I'm very lucky where that's concerned and to be honest, that's what worries me."

Roald sat for a second with a puzzled look on his face. "I'm not sure that I follow you, Evin. You have a bride that pleases you, and that's the problem? Do you mind trying to be a little clearer? What are you wrestling with?"

Evin sighed deeply and stared at the ground. He clenched and unclenched his fists, then abruptly looked up into the older man's eyes. He decided to trust what his mom had said about Roald knowing more than he let on. "Roald, you have no idea what you're asking me. I can't tell you what's going on, but every day the shame gets worse knowing that I'm dragging such a wonderful girl so far away from her home and family. For now, I will just say that my reasons are not our marriage, like I have made it seem, and I feel a crushing weight of guilt for the cruelty I'm showing Inkeri."

"She seems to be doing fine, Evin. I wouldn't be concerned." Roald rubbed his forehead absentmindedly, trying to easily dismiss Evin's concerns and failing miserably.

"I can't help but thinking it's unfair to drag her so far. I'm considering stopping at the chapel in the next town for our training. We can move on later when she's had time to adjust to the idea of the distance." He looked into the older man's eyes. "I think you know I have a reason to go farther later, but I think that could wait. No one at home needs to know we didn't make the whole journey at the beginning. We have a long time before we're expected back."

Roald looked alarmed as he stared straight ahead and considered Evin's words. He twiddled his thumbs for a second, and then seemed to come to a serious decision. "You don't have a long time, Evin. If you stay here, you'll be dead long before that time is gone." His words were quiet, but full of raw emotion.

This had a terrific impact on Evin. His eyes narrowed and he looked at Roald suspiciously. "What do you mean?"

"Evin." Roald said his name in a strange, desperate-sounding way. "I wanted to tell you all this in a little while longer, not so soon. I'm no more ready to say it than you are to hear it. If you'd just gone on a little further away from here." He held his head in his hands dejectedly. "Why do you have to care so much about everyone else. What about you? Don't you want to see the mountains and taste the adventure? Just put one foot in front of the other and get there." His words seemed more for himself than for Evin, but they caused Evin to jump up, suddenly looking like a frightened deer. Roald raised his head and studied him.

"What are you hiding from me, Roald."

Roald smiled sardonically and turned his head away, looking off into the woods. What was he not hiding from Evin? What did he have to let him in on now to keep them moving in the right direction? "You're in extreme danger, Evin. There are those who would do anything to see you dead. My lifestyle has afforded me lots of jobs, and one of those is to work closely with Lord Diederik as a guide and to help him find and rid him of certain undesirable people in his circle. I was one of the guides," he emphasized the word to imply its real meaning, "that he called in less than a month ago to counsel him about a problem he was having. He had a dream in which a young man killed him. Mind you, he's crazy and we were all half listening to everything he was saying. He's always imagining enemies for himself." He paused and Evin furrowed his brow in confusion. "He described the boy that killed him, Evin. It was you. Down to the birthmark on your forearm that he saw when you reached out to slit his throat. You killed him in his dreams and now he has an unquenchable fire to see you dead. I pretended to listen to the rest of his ranting, and then he put a gigantic price on your head and sent eleven of us out searching for you. I raced as quickly as possible to tell your mother. We had to get you out of there, but we had to have a good reason to upend your whole life." Evin looked like he might be sick. Roald continued, "You were just old enough to marry, Evin. Inkeri provided a good means to move you. Remember, you're the one born with the third shard in his hand."

Evin stumbled backward into the log. His voice failed him, each sound coming with great effort. "Roald?" he tripped over the log and fell heavily back onto it. "My mom, did she tell you that?" His words trailed off, the pieces of the puzzle trying to fit together in his mind.

"Your mother said she told you about the shard. She didn't want me to scare you with the story. I've known your whole life. I'm sorry I couldn't stick to her wishes." His words rushed together, and his hands motioned wildly in his haste to quell Evin's angst. "It's so important you learn to rely on El Olam, and no one else, but Inkeri can become an ally. It wasn't expected you would start to feel so strongly for the girl. Your mother helped choose her because she could see that she was your opposite. She just thought you'd probably ignore her. I'm sorry it turned out to be a different way. She is nothing in the plan to send you for help, but we couldn't risk the questions of others if you were to leave without a reason. I mean, one of your brothers is going to be this man's soldier. It would have definitely come to his attention. As strong headed as you are, we couldn't risk telling you too soon, and it was bad enough you had to explain your decision to make this trip to Fjall."

"If she didn't want me to love her quickly, why did she pick the most beautiful girl in the whole village?" Evin sounded lost. Tears began to roll down his cheeks and he held his head in his hands and groaned deeply. His body shook with sobs, making him the picture of abject sorrow. "Why didn't she just tell me?" The sobs grew in intensity, threatening to bring Evin all the way to the ground. "Now that I think I might be able to love her, I find out she's an unwilling pawn in a plan to save my life. Roald, I can't do that to her." Evin wiped his eyes and forced his crumpled body into a sitting position. "I will not continue to lie to her this way. From what you say, we are living on borrowed time. She has to go home before that time runs out."

Roald looked panicked and walked briskly over to Evin. "Think about what you're saying, Evin!" You don't know the full reaches of this yet, nor can you until you've had the chance to see and hear and experience something outside of what you have already. Trust me, you will see the urgency of the situation for yourself soon. You don't even understand what we're up against. You've lived a cushy life on a fertile strip of farmland in a sleepy village without a care in the world." His words were like a slap in the face. "The prophecy about the shards. What did your mom tell you, exactly?"

Evin looked astounded. "She said the shard meant I was the one they were waiting on to go for help. I need to find information about who we can trust. I'm going to give it to her."

"There is much more Evin. The man indicated in the prophecy, you, will be the one to lead the army that will free the people. You were raised for a purpose none of us fully understand yet. Please don't be hasty in your dealings here. Inkeri's life may be in your hands, but more than that, the lives of many people depend on the decisions you will make. I have been careful to uphold the most innocent of appearances for this trip. Now what will you do?"

"Who else knows of all this care put into my upbringing?" Evin was obviously distressed, broken dreams giving way to relentless and crushing expectations to which no one could rise.

"Only your mother and I. There is a growing group of people who are longing for freedom, and they are waiting for a leader to coalesce their efforts into an unmistakable force, but they don't know of you, only that there is one prophesied."

Evin stood up and squared his shoulders. "A growing group?" He looked incredulous. "You mean this is an uprising? This is insane, Roald. Have you met me? First, some madman dreams that I'm going to kill him, and he's never even seen me, but that's concerning enough to ruin my whole life, even though I could never hurt a fly, much less kill another man!" He would have been yelling if he wasn't trying to be quiet. Instead, his words came out like a hiss. "You expect me to take on armies that must have amassed thousands of foot soldiers by this point, including my own brother!" He stared toward the tent where his new wife lay asleep. "What about Inkeri? What was it you said? She's nothing in your plan. Guess what, Roald, she's already everything in mine. I've already imagined my life with her and planned our future. What of her?" He looked truly anguished.

Roald stood in the growing shadows cast by the dying fire, glaring at the expressions on

Evin's face. "How am I supposed to answer all your questions, Evin? I told your mother a long time ago that your youth needed to be managed differently, but now there is no choice. It must be right now. No time for lengthy explanations or any kind of training. She hoped you wouldn't care for marriage at this age, and that the scent of adventure would be what would drive you to discover the truth."

"So, you hoped I'd be an impertinent, thoughtless jerk. Some leader for your little uprising."

Roald ignored his outburst and continued, "Your mother thought someday you'd make a good team. What if Inkeri were on our side, Evin. Would that change things?"

Evin stared incredulously at Roald. "I'm not even sure if I'm on your side, Roald. You want me to tell her what I'm not even sure of? What if she decides she doesn't want to be on our side? Do we keep her against her will to keep up appearances?"

"Will you keep her in the dark forever?"

"Why not, it seemed to suit you and my mother to keep me in the dark my whole life!" Evin's growing bitterness was apparent.

Roald sighed. "Evin, that isn't fair. As a boy, you couldn't be trusted to keep the truth hidden from your family. It's only the sudden urgency that causes us to tell you now. Your mom is very concerned for you. She doesn't want you to be hurt, but your life isn't in her control."

Evin looked at Roald suspiciously. "What if you're both just manipulating me? You talk about knowing everything about me for my whole life, but I don't remember ever seeing you for any part of that. Sounds like you and my mom know each other well. What about my dad? Why doesn't he know any of this? What if there's really nothing different about me. No shard, no dreams, just some lunatic vision and someone young enough to bend to your will. It is time you make me understand exactly why

I should stay with you and not go to another chapel with my bride." Evin's face glowed with new resolve. "You can go on some special journey, and I will live my life!"

"Evin, you aren't reasoning before you talk. Don't be afraid to think for yourself. You aren't a sheep that follows the whims of a few power-hungry men. You will realize that a life without freedom isn't really a life at all. There is something sinister going on here, and we must stand our ground. You're supposed to be the man, and the time is now. You have to go with me so I can show you some things along the way. If you desert us now, Evin, we may be at the end. You will certainly be at your end the first time Diederik lays eyes on you. It won't be long before everyone in this region that matches your description will be rounded up and taken in, and when he sees you, he's going to kill you right away. There are only a few people left who are willing to stand up against this, and there will be great forces moving to crush us as soon as we get organized. I can tell you stories of cruelty that will convince you that these people are evil, but it might be better if you hear those from the people who have lived them. Please understand, Evin. God has chosen you for reasons only he knows. You can't expect me to have every answer. I'm just following his lead." Roald stood trembling all over and pointed his finger at his own chest. "I will either live free or die trying, Evin." He pointed his finger in Evin's face. "You will have to decide which." He seemed to Evin like a man possessed. He lowered his hands to his side and stood glowering.

"Sounds like I don't have much of a choice then, Roald. I guess if I tried to leave, you'd probably kill me anyway, so I'm stuck here with you and your insanity. Besides, where would I go if you're right that I'm in danger in my own village? Unless I see something that changes my mind, this trip will be exactly what it is supposed to be. I'm going to stick to my wedding journey. I will not buy into some lunatic man's idea that people are suffering and longing for freedom, unless I see proof. Why should I start another war in a country full of people who don't even think they have a problem? Maybe you've misled my mom to see something that isn't even true to push your own agenda. I'm going to lie down now and get some rest, but first, I have to know if the people who are traveling with us are in on this whole thing?" Evin started pacing the small clearing.

"No," Roald said, "They're just part of the ruse, Evin. It's a common thing for a wedding party to share the rigors of the journey, and it would have seemed strange if I had insisted they travel alone. They will only be with us for a little longer, and then they will go their own way. What they do should have no consequences for our path."

"There are consequences for Inkeri, Roald. People aren't just playthings for your overactive imagination. I'm glad they're not with you, though. I was worried you were surrounding me. At least I know one thing. The vows I made to Inkeri were real to me even if they were a lie to you and my mother, and for now I'm going to focus on Inkeri. I won't change my plans for the trip, but I won't let myself believe anything until I see it. Now, I'm going to bed. I hope a good night's sleep will make this all disappear."

Chapter 7

Sleep wouldn't come. It wasn't long before Roald entered the tent behind Evin, and it seemed he was asleep within minutes. For some reason, this made Evin exceedingly angry with him. How could he upend Evin's whole life and then lay his head down and drift off to sleep in minutes? Anger coursed through Evin as he thought of everything he'd learned. The worst part was just not being trusted with the truth from the beginning. He was old enough to marry a stranger, learn to defend a campsite, and learn everything about being a husband. Evidently, he was not old enough to make decisions for himself about whether to get caught up in this whole suspicious tale his mom and Roald seemed to know everything about. He wrestled around, oblivious to the other men sleeping away in the tent. His mind went in circles, refusing to let him rest. He couldn't discern the truth in this situation. His emotions were in his way. He wanted to destroy something, but instead he was stuck in a tent with two snoring old men. Tomorrow, he'd have to pretend everything was normal, and he wasn't even sure how to begin to do that. He was so angry, he felt dangerous, and he was going to wake up in the morning to a group of smiling people who had no idea what was happening in his head. Could he muster the strength he needed to pretend everything was okay? He thought of Inkeri. She was everything any man alive could wish for in a companion, it seemed. He hadn't seen any flaws in her character, although he was smart enough to know they existed. His mom must have thought he was still eight. She chose the most beautiful girl near his age in their entire village, one with no discernible flaws, forced him to marry her, and then expected him to ignore her and run off to play war? He flipped over again in the blankets and tried not to let a bitter laugh escape audibly. She had to know better than that. He thought of what Roald said about telling Inkeri, but he couldn't even begin to imagine how that conversation would go. "So, by the way, Inkeri, I wasn't supposed to get married for at least another year, maybe two, but some important guy decided I need to die. In order to keep me safe, my mom and this insane guide guy I don't remember ever meeting decided to choose you to provide the perfect cover for my escape. Oh, and by the way, now we're going to traipse all the way across the whole damn country and start a war, so I don't know if I'll ever be able to take you home."

He flipped again in his angst. He felt like he'd never actually known anyone in his whole life. There was no way the people who had nurtured him all these years were the same people who could make these insane decisions. He thought of his mom. He thought she was the perfect mom. He couldn't deny that he'd thought in the previous few days of seeing her tell his children the same stories he'd heard as a child. Now he knew those stories had been used to make him think a certain way. Were they even true? What in the world was he being asked to dedicate his life to? What about the people that were apparently so tired of living under oppression? He remembered just days before questioning all these laws himself as he stood in the barn with his father. There was no doubt that the system they lived under was difficult, but the people he'd met seemed happy to continue to live that way. What were his mom and Roald seeing that made them think differently? Even in the furnace of his anger, his curiosity burned bright. He couldn't imagine that his gentle, loving mother would put him in this unstable situation unless she was truly convinced in her mind that it was the absolute only way to accomplish something truly necessary. Was he going to trust that was true, or was he going to go out kicking and screaming? She'd mentioned the peace of god that had carried her through some astonishingly difficult times, and he didn't doubt that might be true for her, but where was this peace for him when he needed it? Somehow the last thing he wanted to do right now was call out to this god that was supposed to provide him this peace she'd claimed he could find. He felt wronged and used, and he felt like most of that was the fault of people who he had been convinced would always have his best interest at heart. He had been betrayed, and he wasn't sure he wanted to feel peaceful about that. It seemed much smarter right now to stay on his toes and look out for himself instead of giving in to complacency. He gave up laying down for the moment and sat up. He thought of the confused look on his father's face when he'd declared he was going to go to Fjall. How did Evin even know about this faraway chapel? It was clear from his dad's consternation that he knew nothing of all of this. The same was true of his brothers, who'd both picked on him on his wedding day for making such an illogical choice. The choices he made now would determine if he would be their enemy. Would they see his side of things and come over to help him, or would he forever be alienating most of his family? Would anyone ever tell them the truth? He let his chin settle on his fist while he contemplated. There were supposed to be people to help him on the other side of the mountains, but all the stories he'd ever heard about that region indicated it was sparsely peopled with lawless meanderers. His mom even said that she couldn't be sure any of them remained. This whole thing was a maddening mess of proportions he was sure he couldn't even imagine yet. He thought of sending Inkeri back home alone now that they were safely away, or maybe of sending her to stay with Alia for a short time while he sorted out what he was supposed to do. He was sure she would rather be with her anyway than out here wandering around in the wilderness with him. He let a little groan escape his lips and threw himself back down into his spot. Fresh anger rushed back in, and it was all he could do to keep from beating his pillow to a pulp. Finally, just as his mind was beginning to give up on the idea of sleep, he lay still long enough to drift into a restless repose.

Roald lay awake listening to Evin thrash around for a long time. He was grieved by the incredible sadness he'd been forced to unleash on him. He and Sanna had talked for over an hour about how to tell Evin all the things he'd have to learn on this journey, and she had insisted that Evin be kept in the dark for as long as possible. "Let him hold on to that playful boyishness for a little longer, Roald." She'd been very convincing, and he knew that she'd be unhappy to discover that he'd only been able to do that for two weeks. He'd really enjoyed getting to know Evin more in that time, but now he felt like he might have given their relationship a death blow. He listened to the young man's angst play itself out in a wrestling match with his blankets. He lay completely still, afraid that if Evin knew he was awake he might decide he had more choice words to say to him. God, he thought, help the boy understand better. Roald wasn't sure himself what was going on. All this maddening stuff happening around this lanky farm boy didn't make sense to anyone. How could he be expected to explain any of that to him? It was madness. He was fully aware that Evin was on the edge of throwing it all out of the window because he wasn't sure he could believe anything Roald was saying. Also, though, there was no way that he could be expected to do anything about that. That was on god's shoulders. If he wanted to show Evin something that would change his mind, he could, so Roald decided to leave that up to him. Could they survive if Evin turned tail and ran right now? How would Evin help their cause survive? That had yet to be fully realized. What would he do to make any kind of difference? He had laughed at the idea of killing another human being, but Roald had never encountered a war that didn't involve bloodshed. He'd participated in plenty of it himself, even making a livelihood out of being willing to take care of unsavory business for other people. What was he doing, encouraging this boy in that direction? He hated himself for it sometimes, until he remembered the signs that pointed to Evin. Undeniable, solid proof that god had a plan for the young man. He heard Evin sit up and sneaked a glance in his direction. He watched him through half-closed eyelids as he rested his chin on his fists, obviously done with trying to rest. Roald closed his eyes and prayed that god would show Evin what his purpose was for him. Roald settled into his pillow. He hoped god would answer him before there were no relationships left for anyone to salvage.

Chapter 8

The weather the next day started as bright as all the ones before, but as the day continued, fluffy clouds began to gather on the edges of the horizon to the west. A heaviness had settled over the whole group because they all knew they had to part ways very soon, so no one noticed that Evin's mood was much darker than usual. They reached a good stopping place outside Vatna, where the road split to the south. They had decided some days ago to spend the half a day gathering new supplies from the village before they had to go their separate ways. This was by far the most beautiful place they had been. The mountains rose to the west of them, variegated with shades of green. A small lake sat between them and the village, which could be seen in the distance across the water. The buildings incorporated more large timbers than they were used to seeing, and the villagers had painted many of them bright colors to protect them from the finicky weather that played around the bases of the mountains. Many of the fields within sight had been planted in perfectly straight green and red rows that were flourishing with the promise of cabbages, beets, and various greens. They moved some distance from the road and set up camp close to the glimmering lake. Working together, they made short work of the job. Roald and Evin took the road into town to gather supplies and Harald began to gather wood to build a fire. Runa's head was aching, so she went to the tent to lay down. Alia and Inkeri went to get water, grabbing their containers and walking the short distance to the shore. The beauty of the scene was mesmerizing, and they decided to set out and explore the shoreline a little. Harald was concerned, but he knew the girls would enjoy the time alone, so he encouraged them to stay on this side of the lake away from the town. As they left, he returned to building a fire. The village was close enough to Alia's family home that she was able to share some interesting things about its history. Villages didn't often grow because people moved in from outside, but this one was different because the roads converged here, and it was the last stopping point for anyone wishing to head over the mountains. The lord of this region resided in the village as well, so the tribute from the surrounding villages poured in at the end of harvest to supply his needs. Excess poured over into the town, making it an ideal place to find extra supplies. Established farmers and merchants in the town were required to register each year so that it was easier to add new registrants when people decided to stay. As a result, the village had spread to occupy all the land on one side of the crystal-clear lake. They ambled along the water's edge, enjoying the view that dominated every direction.

They walked closer to the village but remembered Harald's words and didn't venture too close. From where they stopped, they could make out some of the people from the village working across the lake, which tapered into a wide, meandering river. Barges were being loaded for a trip south along the natural trade route created by the water. They stood, watching the faceless men work to load the boats, fitting the crates of goods on like giant puzzle pieces. Faces turned into the still-strong sunshine; they enjoyed a quiet moment. Alia's honey colored hair shone and stood out like a halo, braided around her head in a distinctive way. The girls giggled at how angelic she looked. Inkeri touched the braid carefully. "I've never been able to get mine to behave long enough to do this."

"My mom taught me when I was a girl. I can show you when we get back to camp."

"Speaking of that, we'd better head back before your dad worries about us." Inkeri started to turn toward camp.

A distant voice from across the lake stopped them and they peered across to see one of the men who was near the barges waving toward them. "Alia!" his voice echoed again. They both squinted in that direction but couldn't discern anything about him apart from general size and height.

"Must be Roald?" Inkeri questioned. They waved back and the man stood still, seeming to be satisfied with that interaction. Suddenly, he turned and disappeared into the crowd around the docks. "I hope they were able to find everything they needed."

"I'm sure," Alia said. "There is an abundance here." Her brow furrowed for a second like she was trying to remember something but she gave up and turned to saunter after Inkeri. The two continued the pleasant conversation on the way back to camp where they discovered Harald investigating his horse's hooves.

He turned, looking concerned. "I have to take this horse into Vatna and find a farrier. I noticed he was stumbling before we stopped and there's a problem with this shoe." He indicated the horse's right front leg.

Inkeri moved forward eagerly. "I wouldn't mind walking in with you if it would be okay? I would love to see the town a little more closely."

Alia held up her hand. "You two go ahead. I'm done with walking for the day."

Harald shrugged. "Sure. Maybe we'll run into the other two."

"One of them called out to us," Alia mentioned, "they were near the docks."

Harald lowered his eyebrows and looked a little confused, but he didn't say anything about that. Instead, he turned to Alia. "Will you stay right here with your mom? She isn't feeling well, and I would prefer not to leave her alone. Also, I don't want you to go off on your own. I don't expect any trouble, of course, but I would feel better if you promised to stay in camp until we get back. Should be well before dark when we all return."

"Of course. I'll stay put. I promise."

Satisfied, Harald grabbed the horse's reins and he and Inkeri set out down the well-traveled road into town. Inkeri related all the interesting things Alia had told her about the region and he confirmed and embellished the stories with a few of his own. "Things are a little 'wilder' here than they are where you're from," he concluded.

"What do you mean?" Inkeri looked genuinely interested, so he continued.

"The people ignore a few of the admonitions they've learned in the law. For example, you and Evin had never met before you married, right?"

"Right."

"That's the way it's supposed to be according to the law, but in many of the villages around here, the people tend to choose spouses for their children from among the families of friends, so they know each other, sometimes well before they marry."

"That might be nice." Inkeri smiled knowingly. "It would certainly help you be prepared for what you might see on your wedding day." She laughed.

"You seemed to make out okay," he grinned back at her, and then looked away. Suddenly his demeanor changed perceptibly. "Trust me, it's best to follow the rules." He seemed utterly convinced, and she got the sense he might be talking about Alia and Kai, but it was clear he didn't want to continue down that path, so she plodded along beside him quietly. They soon came in sight of town.

Inkeri exclaimed, "Look! Roald and Evin!" Sure enough, the pair was heading toward them on the path. They waved and met up just as the road entered the outskirts of town. Harald began to explain the situation with the horse's shoe, when suddenly he was grabbed and wheeled to the side. A young man stood panting in front of him with a wild look in his eyes.

Roald immediately reacted, knocking the man backward away from Harald several steps. He regained his footing quickly and looked dismissively at Roald. "You don't have any part in this, old man. Stay out of it."

"If you're going to grab my friend, then you make it my business." Roald replied gruffly.

Evin surveyed the situation and grabbed Inkeri, pushing her behind him. He was confused when he looked at Harald. The older man had paled by several shades and stood trembling and speechless, staring at his assailant with horror. "What in the world is going on?" The anger that Evin had been nursing all day found its way into his voice and Roald shot him a warning glance.

"Calm down, Evin. Somebody want to tell us what's going on?" Roald appraised the faces of the two men who were staring disbelievingly at one another.

Neither acknowledged Roald's question. "I saw her, Harald. Walking along the lake on the other side. I knew it was her. That hair. I called out her name and she waved." He looked disgusted and laughed, but it was not at all a mirthful sound that escaped his lips. "You lying, disgusting..." he moved again toward Harald.

"Hey!" Roald stepped forward and put his hand on the young man's shoulder, spinning him so he was facing him instead of Harald. "Look, kid. I'm confused as hell, but I'm certainly not going to let you attack this man, so stop trying."

The younger man stood fuming and pushed Roald away from him. "Don't touch me again." He looked dangerous. "This man took my wife." He spun back toward Harald. "You said she was dead. You..."

"Kai?" Inkeri stepped from behind Evin, looking upset.

Everyone turned together and looked at her with disbelief.

"How do you know me?" he spat. "Are you all in on this together?" Kai pushed his hand through his thick black hair and rocked back, looking at all of them incredulously.

"No one is in on anything!" Evin yelled, drawing the unwanted attention away from Inkeri. "We haven't the slightest idea what you're talking about, and frankly, I'm already tired of waiting for an explanation from you." Evin's young face looked menacing and disgusted. Inkeri looked puzzled at this drastic change in his usually easy-going personality.

Kai noticeably relaxed but kept glaring at Harald hatefully. "Last time I saw this guy, he told me she had died in an accident, and pretended to be devastated. He's a good liar, this one." He addressed Harald again. "She's pregnant, Harald. That means according to your precious law, she's mine." He emphasized the last part like a man possessed.

"How could any decent human...?" He stumbled over his words and looked like he might cry. "Are you planning to marry her off to let someone else raise my child? This is unreal!"

Harald finally came back to his senses, letting the impact roll off him. "Kai, I will not let you anywhere near her, and if you think you're going to even set foot in sight of her, I will kill you. I have been more than merciful to you because I love you like a son, but she thinks you're dead as well, and I mean to keep it that way."

Kai laughed again. "You have to be mad if you think I'm going to let you leave here without letting me talk to her. She has the right to know I'm not dead. Are you kidding? Dead? What were you going to do if I ever showed up very alive?" He narrowed his eyes. "What did you do to her to make her believe I'm dead?"

"You thought she was dead." Harald's words were haunting but not really an answer.

"Are you trying to convince me of your amazing skills of deception? I have no idea what role you played in any of this, Harald, but you're right. I thought she was dead! That is until I just saw her across the lake very much alive and very pregnant!"

"How could you even know what you saw? We were too far away to see clearly." Inkeri was clearly befuddled. "We couldn't make anyone out that far away."

Kai looked at her. "It's my job to look down the river for incoming barges and signal direction so everybody avoids each other. I use a glass that broke out of the bottom of a bottle to help me see further, and when I see people across the lake, I'm always curious." He looked at Harald. "Especially when their hair is the color of honey. I could see her hair, but not her features so much. But she waved when I called her name, and I knew."

Understanding was dawning on Roald's face, and he was suddenly eager to end this incredibly uncomfortable exchange. "Surely we can sit down and talk this out." He pleaded, not seeing any way this could end peaceably, but hoping he could at least keep these two from killing each other.

Kai looked at him like he'd spawned an extra head. "I'm through listening to anything this man has to say. I'm going to go get my wife, and I'm going to take her to our house, and I'm going to raise my child, and nothing short of death is going to stop me."

He moved to walk down the path and before anyone could react, Harald raised the hilt of his sword in the air and brought it down hard on the side of Kai's head. Kai crumpled in a heap, clearly not conscious. The others gawked at Harald, stunned not only by his speed and accuracy, but by his ferocity. He raised the sword as if to stab it into the younger man, but Roald stepped in quickly and grabbed his arm, stopping him. "I'm not going to let you do that."

Harald blinked at him and lowered his arm. "I don't think there is any other way, Roald."

"Leave him to us and go, Harald. We're not going to say anything to them."

Inkeri looked aghast. "Aren't you even going to tell her? This is wrong!" she stepped back in front of Evin, who gripped her arm to keep her from moving closer to them. She looked devastated on behalf of Alia. "She's mourning her husband and here he is!" Inkeri gestured wildly at the still figure on the ground.

"There's a lot more to it than you understand." Harald admitted defeatedly.

Roald gave Inkeri a warning look. She pulled roughly out of Evin's hand as if she might start a fight, and then she thought better of it and just stood uncertainly. "It will just take you a second to get this fixed at the farrier, Harald." He pushed the smaller man gently back away from Kai. "You should go do that."

Harald looked at each one of them briefly, and looking squarely at Inkeri, he said, "I'm sorry. I'm doing this for her." He grabbed the reins and headed toward town without a glance back. Inkeri sank to her knees beside the unconscious man and pushed him, trying to turn him over. Evin grabbed his shoulders and helped her roll him on his back. He looked dead, but his breath still came regularly. An angry welt rose just below his temple.

Roald looked at it expertly. "Wow, if he'd hit him just a little higher, he could have died."

"Good thing he's short." Evin quipped sarcastically.

Inkeri shot him a withering glance and looked around. "What do we do with him? We obviously can't get him back to camp. He took the horse." She gestured toward the place where Harald had disappeared.

"Camp isn't an option anyway," Roald reminded her. "Inkeri, you have to promise me you're not going to say anything. I know you don't understand that right now, but let's get him to the inn and we'll pay to make sure he's taken care of. When he recovers, we will listen to his side of things before we make any decisions. Sometimes the thing that seems the most obvious at the beginning isn't the best choice. We know where they live, and we know how to find them if we need to."

She looked distastefully at him, but she nodded grimly and turned her attention back to Kai. He was tall and built like Roald, which explained the fact that they had mistaken him from a distance. He had a shock of jet-black hair atop a kind and handsome face. He looked like he was sleeping peacefully if you ignored the growing knot below his temple. The other two men picked him up gently and the lot of them proceeded too slowly to the local inn, where they were pleased to find a room available in which to make sure he could rest and recover.

"I'm worried that he hasn't stirred yet," Roald sighed.

Evin looked at Kai. "That was quite a blow."

"If he doesn't come to soon, it could mean a much harder recovery. I've seen this a few times before." Roald's eyes looked sad, and his pronouncement was troubling. While they watched, Kai stirred a little on the bed, moaning lightly. "That's a good sign," said Roald. "Let's leave him in the innkeeper's care and we'll come back here first thing in the morning." They looked around at the room and then at one another. How could everything change so dramatically in such a short time? Evin paid the innkeeper extra and asked him to check on Kai occasionally, and then they hastened out of town, eager to make it back to camp before dark. As they arrived at camp, a light drizzle started, and they ducked into their tents quickly. Roald looked up and caught Inkeri's eyes, making a shushing motion before he ducked out of sight.

When they entered the tent, they found Harald sitting quietly on his pile of blankets staring into space. "You'd better give me a good explanation right now, Harald. I'm asking my group to keep quiet for you, so you need to talk. I need to know if I'm doing the right thing." Roald plopped down beside him and looked at him expectantly. Evin followed suit, sitting down on the other side.

"Well, this is a story I didn't want to ever tell anyone, but it doesn't look like I have a choice. I'm sure you've surmised that the man we met in town is... was my son-in-law. I'm sure you also know that those marriage bonds can be dissolved under the right circumstances. Thank you for waiting to hear my side of the story instead of just jumping straight to the conclusion that they should be together."

"I'm not one to force people to think like I want them to." Roald acknowledged. "On the other hand, it is also very clear they want to be married, so this better be a fantastic explanation."

Harald's shoulders slumped and he looked dejected. "I was telling Inkeri earlier that in many of the villages around here, people allow their children to know each other before they're betrothed. I'm sure you know," he indicated Roald, "that every village has a quota of goods to meet each harvest. An amount of goods and services to provide the lord of their region. Lord Arne succeeded his father five years ago, and he raised the quotas, but we had so much that it didn't really worry any of us." His head sank and his eyebrows knitted together.

He took a deep breath and continued. "Around that same time, Alia and Kai became close, and we allowed them to spend time together, because the families knew each other, and we felt like his family was good for our daughter to marry into. Every year, we've always had the crops to provide all the quota from our town. We've grown beautiful fields of rye for generations. For the last three, though, the rain was brutal and unseasonal, and over time, we used all our good stores and all the grain we could manage to grow to meet his demands. We requested at council he lower it while we recovered, but he came back and said he would be merciful to us by ignoring our disdain for the law up to this time. It was a warning for us to better enforce the laws. We would be expected to produce the full quota, and he anticipated that we would get better control of our people because he'd heard that they'd become lax under his father. He made it clear he would not be so easy to please. We planned for our harvest festival where, as is customary, we announced the pairings of young people that would be married in the following spring. Since rye is a winter crop, we knew long before the traditional fall harvest time that we were short of our quota, but we still expected mercy. For us, everyone else harvests while we plant, but it's customary for the quota to be gathered all at once from all the surrounding villages. We also have good vegetable crops during the summer, and we hunt, so we tried to make less bread than usual, but we didn't get as worried as we should have. We would supplement with some of those other things. We knew that there was the possibility that some of our boys would be taken as tribute to become soldiers to fill in the gap, but we expected to be able to choose who would go from among us if that should happen, and we considered that a big if. When we announced the couples that would be betrothed in the spring, we were thrilled to have our daughter and Kai on the list. It would be an honor for our family to contribute in this way to growing our village."

Harald paused again, as if he dreaded continuing the story. "A week later, the consort came to gather our tribute, and they insisted we provide our entire quota in rye, even though we offered other things. Of course, we were unable to comply. I'll never forget that day. They lined up all our unmarried boys who'd seen at least fourteen summers and looked them over carefully, like they were vegetables or haunches of meat. Then they called our council together, which included me, and gave us their decision. They would require three of the young men to make up for the deficit of rye. Instead of letting us choose, they pointed out the ones they would take, and unsurprisingly, Kai was among them. If I were trying to muster an army, he'd certainly be on my list. You've seen him." He looked down at the tent floor and spent a minute struggling to regain his composure. "It was like they'd chosen my own son." He balled his hand into a tight fist, white showing in his knuckles. "The youngsters were still lined up shuffling their toes around in the dirt like oblivious little boys. I begged them to give us the rest of the day, and we'd surrender the boys in the morning, so they could say goodbye to their families. They allowed it, since the day was already waning, and they had planned to camp near our village anyway. I broke the news to Kai and Alia that night in our barn. I had no idea that Kai would hatch his crazed plan and run off with Alia in tow. I mean, even though they were quite understandably upset by the situation, he'd always, always obeyed the law without question. When we woke in the morning, and we realized what had happened, we made haste to go after them. On our way out of town, we met the captain of the consort, and he was furious, having somehow heard what had happened. He informed me they would take two more young men to make up for the prize they'd lost, and they expected me to find Kai and bring him back to them within the year, or they would strip me of my status as an elder." He looked up. "Here we are more than half a year gone, and I'm returning without him. I'm returning without having been able to sow new grain in my soil, hoping someone else did. I'm returning with a pregnant daughter and a sad story, and I'm hoping beyond hope that it's enough. I spared his life, and now I fear that he's going to step into the middle of it again and end up becoming a soldier for Lord Arne. That would be the end of his life, you must understand. That would be what he did from now until he died, and I know that's not what he wants, so I am willing to make the sacrifice of my elder status to rescue him from that. I know he wants to be with Alia, but he has no right to put her in that kind of danger just to play married. I won't sacrifice her life for his comfort. That's where I draw the line. They weren't ever properly betrothed under the law."

He trailed off and put his head back against the side of the tent, letting the stiff material support the weight.

"By the gods." Roald looked stunned. "Well, that's a better story than I was expecting. I have some questions. How did you get them to each think the other was dead? What is to become of the baby?"

Harald spread his hands out. "This afternoon, the girls mentioned seeing you at the docks, and I thought that was weird, but I couldn't discount it, and when I saw Kai, I knew it was him. Alia was close enough to hear him call out." He shuddered. "What is he doing here? Lord Arne lives here! All it would take is one of the soldiers that came to our village to recognize him, and all is lost, yet here he is working at the dock. What is he thinking?" He looked at Roald. "We'll help Alia care for the baby until we can find a man to marry and care for her."

"I think I might know why he's here." The others looked at Roald, but he didn't elaborate. "You didn't answer the first question." Roald said.

"I'm ashamed to have done that, of course. It seemed like the only way. When we found them, they had set up camp to the north in Hvalr. It took us three months to find them. Kai had some friends in a village he'd visited sometimes with his father who knew a shaman that would provide marriage services for couples who wouldn't be able to take the time for the required training right away. This has sprung up in this village to the north of your own because of the fishing season. Men are betrothed, and, unlike here, where someone can tend the ground for them while they're away, the training is an undue burden. Every man is needed on the boat. Many choose to skirt the law and have the ceremony and then go to training when the season ends. Kai saw this as an opportunity to be married without the betrothal, so that's what they did. When we found them, they had a nice camp outside of town. Kai was even working on a house for them. There were cliffs nearby, so we hired some worthless men from the town to raid the camp in the night and drag the two of them away in very different directions under the cover of a very dark night. They followed instructions and left Kai in the forest, badly beaten, but alive. We took Alia, who would not calm down, back with us. After a couple of days, I went to find Kai, who had made his way back to his camp, to tell him we'd come to the village looking for them and had been directed to Alia's body being readied for burial. She'd fallen off the cliff trying to escape. We told her a very similar story about him, and then we took her and left, thinking he would continue his life there without her. We went straight to the holy site nearest your village, and that's how we ended up here. They took Alia in and gave her some training and helped her mind to calm. It was there she finally accepted he's dead. She doesn't even remember them dragging her and Kai from the tent. The shaman said our minds are eager to forget painful things."

"Of course, the shaman didn't know what had actually happened?" Evin asked.

"You two are the first to ever hear it spoken aloud."

The men sat contemplatively for a few minutes, trying to process the painful and trying story. Roald stood suddenly and began roughly readying his bed, muttering under his breath, obviously irritated. He tossed his pillow into place and collapsed into his spot without further ceremony.

Evin and Harald looked at one another and Evin shrugged. The two quickly followed suit, and soon the three lay still and listened to the drizzle on the tent, another night passing without sleep.

Chapter 9

There are few ways to describe the severity of the bad mood in the camp the next morning. Each person was unhappy for different reasons, and so it was with few words that the group parted ways. The women embraced, and Inkeri stood sobbing in the rain as Alia pulled away and left with her parents. Evin knew her reasons to be sad were much deeper than Alia knew, but now he was also aware there was no easy solution to the problem. He walked to Inkeri's side and placed his cloak on her shoulders, adjusting the hood to keep the rain from hitting her face. Still, moisture ran down her cheeks, and he didn't know what to do, so he joined Roald in packing everything up. Within a few minutes, she too had joined them, eager to go back to the town and see if Kai was okay. They threw many of the things that would have to be dried out in a haphazard heap in the cart and left soon after the other group. Town was quiet in the rain, which had been expected, so the work was done preceding its arrival. The group found a place in the barn to hang up the tent material and bedding that had gotten soggy and left quickly to see Kai. When they opened the door to the room, he was sitting up in the bed, a bandage wound around his head at an angle. A breakfast tray sat in front of him, the food untouched, and he was looking at it as if it had done him some wrong. He looked up at the three of them as they entered the room and furrowed his brow. "You must be the people who found me and brought me here. The innkeeper's wife said you were returning today. Thank you."

They nodded and looked at each other quizzically. "He must not remember." Roald said. Upon investigation, the bandage was revealed to be there in order to hold a poultice in place over the bruise. "He's been well taken care of." Roald seemed pleased. "Kai, do you remember why you're here? In this village?"

Kai squinted at Roald, and then looking suspicious, glared at Roald, looking him over from head to toe. He let his gaze rest on the others, and then looked back to Roald. "I presume you're the mercenary, Roald?" At Roald's nod, he continued. "Took you long enough! Guess it's a good thing you're the one that found me. Who is this?" He indicated the couple standing at the end of the bed.

Evin looked disgusted in Roald's direction. "Of course, there's more to this than meets the eye." To Kai, he said, "I'm Evin, and this is my..." he paused and looked sheepishly toward Inkeri, "...betrothed, Inkeri." He finally mustered.

Roald pulled a chair to the edge of the bed and looked back and forth at the two young men. "By the gods! I always make a bigger mess of things than I mean to. Okay, here's what we're going to do. Inkeri, will you go make arrangements for the three of us to join Kai here tonight? It's obvious he can't travel yet, and I want to see that he's well before we leave him. Take this," he handed her a pouch of coins, "and see we get some fresh food while we're here." He watched as Inkeri strode obediently from the room and then shot a look at Evin, who had moved to the window to stare at the rain. He knew that Evin was close to bolting, and he didn't know how to mitigate that risk. There was no way forward here except to tell the truth. "Evin, you know I'm not perfect. That's painfully obvious every day. I make impulsive decisions, and he represents one of those." He pointed at Kai. "I was tired of waiting around for a leader to rise up and lead the people to freedom. I was tired of waiting for your mom to decide it was the time to let me give you the training I thought you needed. Instead, she was happy to keep raising you in your comfortable life and wait for some portent that it was the right time for you. When she heard about Diederik, she felt like the time was right. I felt like I could see the signs everywhere before that, but she was never sure until then. There is a network of us, and I had some of them listening for any sign of opportunity. They told me Kai's story, which had unfortunately leaked into the village where it had happened. He was described to me as someone that might be a good leader for a rebellion, so I sent for him to meet me here. Age and strength are certainly on his side. The day after that, Lord Diederick had his fateful dream, and I was thrust into this other role with you."

Evin's lips turned up a little on the side. "I'm happy for you, Roald. It seems you've found your fearless leader." He shook his head and looked back out the window.

"I didn't agree to be anyone's leader." Kai sat up straighter in the bed. "Your messenger said to come and talk to you about rising up against the people that made the laws that ended up causing me to lose my wife." He furrowed his brow and pushed at the fabric bunching up over his eye. "I would do anything to have revenge against them for ruining my life."

"Wow, Roald, revenge is a great reason to get all fired up at someone." Evin rolled his eyes and continued with the sarcastic smile. "That's going to make for an exciting opening for your speech to your group of outlaws. Hey, this man broke the law, it backfired on him, so he's ready to exact revenge and he'd love your help doing that. Maybe some of you will benefit somehow from taking these drastic measures and also having your lives and families destroyed."

Kai ripped the bandage off his head and stood suddenly up from the bed, crossing the distance between himself and Evin in a second. He grabbed Evin by the front of the shirt and pushed him roughly against the wall, looking murderous. Evin was easily half a foot shorter and more than a year younger, but for the moment, they were face to face, Evin's feet dangling off the floor. "Yeah, instead you should definitely go for this pale, lanky runt to run things. He's got promise and a great attitude to match."

Roald pulled Kai back and Evin fell down on his feet with a thud, managing to balance himself against the wall and keep from falling. Kai backed off but continued mercilessly. "I had a real relationship, a real chance to have a happy life. It sounds to me like you're living in some kind of fantasy land hoping for the best to pan out in the end. You don't even know what it's like to care for anyone other than yourself."

Evin threw all his weight into a punch that landed squarely on the side of Kai's already injured head. He spun but held his feet, and then turned suddenly and ran to the wash basin, vomiting. Roald grabbed Evin roughly by the shoulders and pushed him against the wall. "Enough! You're acting like a spoiled whelp." Evin's jaw pulsed menacingly, and he pushed himself off the wall, but he stood still under Roald's disapproving gaze. Roald rushed to Kai's side to check on him, but a hand held up in his direction warned him off.

Finally, Kai collapsed on the bed behind him, grabbing his head and moaning. "Get him out of here." He said through clenched teeth.

"Take a walk Evin. Find Inkeri and see if she needs help." Evin brushed past the larger man without a word and slammed the door on his way out. Roald sunk down at the end of the bed and stared toward the stone fireplace that dominated one end of the room. What in the world was he going to do? He had two hot headed young men on his hands, one with an injury. The inn had one available room. Add to that an innocent young girl just trying to get used to being married and having to cope with staying alone with three strange men. The persistent rain and already wet materials made camping tonight sound like a miserable option. He stood back up, planning to go get one of the tents with which to partition the room.

Kai sat perfectly still on the bed. "At least he's got fight." Kai looked at Roald, smiled slightly, and groaned at the effort. "That hurt. I wouldn't have thought him capable of that." He rubbed his jaw and winced.

"He doesn't know what he's talking about, Kai. I'm sorry."

"I get it, Roald. Don't apologize for him. Let him grow up and do that for himself. I wasn't exactly nice to him either." He looked down at the bed. "He's good with hurtful words, that's for sure. Maybe he'll talk the enemy to death."

Roald couldn't help but laugh. He liked this young man. "Any chance you'd be willing to help us? As you can see, it's all I can do to keep him on an even keel right now. My fault. I waited too long to be completely honest with him."

"Start by being completely honest with me. I got the picture of an uprising against the lords and their injustice, but I can tell there's more going on here. All this talk of waiting for signs and picking a different leader. I get the impression something has told you he's the one. Where does that leave me? If I weren't nursing this injury, I would have been out the door already. I'm not sure I can follow him anywhere."

"He's the one El Olam has chosen." Roald said matter-of-factly.

"Oh, god's be cursed." Kai lay back in the bed. "I can't join some kind of religious movement, Roald." He rested his head against the head of the bed and looked asleep for a second, then continued with his eyes still closed, "I had an aunt. My mom's sister. She wouldn't let go of the idea of El Olam, and it ended up costing her life. I was a toddler. It was during the last war, but they made it clear where people stand who claim to believe in that god. My mom said she talked about him constantly, and it cost her everything. My cousin was about my same age, and he came to live with us after his mom died. It's kind of a family secret. It was like growing up with a twin brother. We don't even talk about El Olam for any reason anymore. It would be like profaning her memory."

"What if it would be like avenging her?" Roald looked hopefully in Kai's direction.

"I'd have to see some proof she was right and not just fanatical." He opened his eyes and peered in Roald's direction. "I didn't even know her, but she's not spoken of very highly in my family. Every time I hear about El Olam, it's derisively. If this god exists, he'd better act quickly before the last of his people disappear." Kai settled back into the bed. "Besides, if your leader is going to attack me every time we're together, it might not be a healthy place for me to be." He raised his eyebrows at Roald. "So much for compassion." He closed his eyes.

Roald sighed and turned. "You've got that right. We're running a little short on that right now. Just think about it. We could really use your help. We have to cross the mountains into the wilderness, and I'm worried. I'll go and let you rest. I need to get something to make a divider for Inkeri."

"There's the compassion." Kai muttered, and Roald left, tracing his hand along the rough wooden wall as he made his way down the steep steps. He returned quickly from the barn with one of the tents, now mostly dry. Inkeri and Evin were sitting in the inn at a table with mugs of warm cider and bread. They were both picking at the bread and not talking.

When Evin saw Roald, he stood. "I'm sorry, Roald. I was out of line." His jaw was still set in frustration, but he seemed to be much chastised.

"It's not me you need to apologize to, Evin, but it wasn't just you that was out of line. I think Kai would be a help to us on our journey, so I've asked him to join us. You're going to have to try to find peace with that." Roald turned, ignoring Evin's scowl. "Come with me, we'll make this room as comfortable for all of us as we can." He glanced at Inkeri and then headed up the stairs. They followed, and in the next half an hour, they had the bed situated on one side of the room with room beside it for sleeping, and a tent up for changing out of dirty clothes and getting as clean as possible. Each of them took turns, with Inkeri first, and before long, the days of grime from the trail were gone. Clothes were gathered and prepared for washing, which would need to happen before they left town. They settled in, insisting that Kai keep the bed because of the miserable headache he was dealing with. No one thought they'd be resting, but as soon as they were still, they each drifted off quickly. Too many days without sleep took their toll and the group was mercifully granted peace.

chapter 10

A gentle breeze blew through Evin's hair. He looked around with great pleasure, feeling the peace of his surroundings. He realized he was home, more because of the feeling of the place than because of any landmark. He was standing in a huge wheat field, and after careful examination, he realized it was just on the outskirts of the village where he'd grown up. He let the wheat run through his fingers and decided not to question how'd he'd gotten here. He could feel that this was his land and his wheat, and he felt pride swell up at the vast contribution he'd be able to make to his town's coffers. His dad would be so proud. He surprised himself by hoping Inkeri would be in a newly built house somewhere on this land waiting to welcome him home. Maybe his mom and dad would be visiting, and they'd all sit down for a warm meal together. He started walking toward the town, imagining the square he'd left weeks ago and longing to see his brother, Gunnar, lounging with the other young husbands that were sometimes sitting around the town center. He hoped suddenly that this was his reality, and that the nightmare was the last couple of days. His hair ruffled in the perfect breeze, and he sighed contentedly. This was exactly where he wanted to be. He started to turn and head in the direction of the village, but something in the distance caught his eye. Four men rode toward him on the most glorious horses he'd ever seen. The sight stopped him in his tracks, and he watched them approach. In the rear, three solid blood bay horses carried three soldiers in armor like he'd never imagined. Rippling metal shirts moved with the men like water. Over those, each man wore another cloth shirt with different emblems on them. He was astounded to realize the pictures they wore were representations of the shards of glimmering stone he kept in the pouch around his neck. His eyes moved to the man in the front. He wore bright gold armor and rode the most fantastic horse. Solid white and taller than the others, the animal had what could only be described as a royal bearing. The rider wore a similar cloth emblem, this one of the shards, but healed together in one beautiful whole. The men stopped the animals nearby, dismounted, and started walking toward Evin. He instinctively lowered himself to his knees on the ground and looked down. He touched the pouch around his neck and found it radiated warmth. He felt fear creep in that maybe they had come to take the fragments they seemed to have some interest in, and he closed his hand around the container protectively. The men stopped close enough that Evin could see the toes of the boot in front of him. He closed his eyes and waited to hear what they wanted. He feared for his life, suddenly realizing he had no power against these men.

"Rise, Evin." The leader's voice was as impressive as his appearance. The moment he spoke, the pouch around Evin's neck increased in temperature dramatically, searing the hand he had clenched around it. Evin jerked his hand away from it, but not soon enough to prevent a serious burn. Strangely, it didn't feel warm against the flesh of his chest. "Rise," the man repeated, seemingly oblivious to Evin's pain. Evin shakily rose to his feet, adrenaline racing through his veins. He gazed at the angry blisters forming on his hand, afraid to look into the man's eyes. Finally, the silence got the best of his curiosity, and he turned his eyes up to the man's face, leaving his head as low as he comfortably could and still see. The man stood patiently holding a goblet in his hand. "Evin, son of wandering, follow me."

Evin let his eyes move in the direction of the village where he longed to go, remembering his love for the people and the comfort that awaited him there, and paused. With timidity, he asked, "Where?" His mind immediately went to the boy in the barn just two weeks before who was clamoring for adventure, and he marveled at how quickly he'd come to desire exactly what he'd once feared.

Instead of a location, the man reached the goblet toward him. "Hold out your hands." He turned his hands palm up and held them toward the man, cupping them together when it became evident the man intended to pour the contents into his hands. The liquid poured slowly out of the mouth of the cup, moving like thin honey, but looking darker and shinier. The substance ran over his hands, pooling together. All the pain from the burn ceased the moment the honey-like draught touched it. "Drink." The man commanded. Evin obeyed, lifting his cupped hands to his mouth and clumsily slurping the sticky substance, floored by the sweetness and rocked by a sudden jubilation. He laughed, then continued to drink, slurping the last of the syrupy concoction. His hand began to sting intensely, causing the smile to leave his face. He grabbed it with the other hand and groaned, falling to his knees from the pain. As he hit the ground, the honey hit his stomach and he began to feel as if it would eat its way out of him from the inside. He doubled over and groaned, regretting following the man's command. After a time, he noted that the pain subsided slowly in his hand, and then grew less intense in his abdomen. He straightened back up and stood, swaying to his feet like he was drunk, trying not to let his weakness show. "Sometimes the healing is on the other side of the pain." The man's simple declaration seemed both insensitive and idiotic to Evin. "Follow me, Evin. Drink it."

The man reached out the goblet to Evin, beckoning him to take it. He was aware that if he chose to follow this man, this whole cup would be his, but for a second, he was still tempted. Then rage rose at the man insisting he be okay with the level of pain that was bound to bring. Without further reasoning, he reacted, swinging his arm wildly and knocking the goblet to the ground where the fiery liquid spilled across the dirt. The man stood unfazed, watching Evin with such love in his eyes that as he stared at him, Evin became painfully aware of the folly of his action. He heard someone nearby cry out and found himself unable to move his hands, and he fought the immobilization, desperate to understand and fix the situation. The scene shifted and the men and horses disappeared. He heard his name being shouted from a distance, and soon, he realized it was right beside him. Shapes seemed to reorganize and sharpen, and he became aware that he was still in the room in the inn.

"Evin, Evin. Get control of yourself." Roald's voice snapped him back into reality, and he suddenly ceased his fighting and allowed himself to relax. He opened his eyes to a bizarre scene. Roald was in front of him, holding his hands tightly and staring angrily into his eyes. Behind Roald, Inkeri stood bleeding from a cut on her eyebrow and Kai was holding her by the shoulders looking at the wound.

"Let me go." He struggled to free himself from the hold Roald had on him, but he felt inexplicably weak. "Tell that monster to get his hands off her. She's hurt. Roald, help Inkeri."

Roald looked puzzled, and then his face registered understanding. "He was dreaming."

"Some dream." Kai smirked.

"If you're not going to help her, Roald, let me go!" Evin struggled again against his bondage.

"I will let you go if you promise not to hit anyone else." Roald relaxed his hold a little but maintained control of Evin's hands.

"I haven't hit anyone, Roald. I..." Evin looked at Inkeri, and for the first time he saw the fear in her eyes. Inkeri reached up and touched her forehead, wincing from the pain, and stared back at Evin with eyes full of uncertainty. He realized the fear was directed at him, not Kai. He would have buried his face in his hands if the older man didn't still have a grip on his wrists. Roald slowly let go of him, realizing the danger he had presented had passed. "What did I do, Roald? Did I hit her?"

Roald walked to the fireplace and stood there looking into it and thought about it. "I honestly didn't see what happened. I was sleeping. You just weren't yourself for a bit there. What happened to you?"

Kai interjected. "Yeah, you hit her, but I think it was just because you were flailing around."

Evin leaned back and sighed. He gave Kai an icy stare. It must have been a dream. "Some man was trying to give me a cup." His explanation sounded comical enough to make Kai snicker. His eyes and voice suddenly filled with grief. "Oh, Inkeri. I didn't know. Please forgive me. I didn't mean to."

He moved over next to Kai and quickly examined the cut in her eyebrow. It caused him to experience emotions he didn't remember ever feeling before. Foremost was anger with himself, followed by a chilling fear that if this could happen once to him, it might happen again. Kai fetched a rag and mopped the blood from the wound. Roald stood across the room, watching the whole thing. He seemed to lose focus and drift away into his own thoughts. "Evin, did you say a man tried to give you a cup?" He sounded incredulous.

Evin seemed to shudder from deep within. "I'd like to try to forget that, Roald. It was only a dream."

He nudged Kai out of the way, causing the other young man to raise both hands and move back. "She's all yours, calm down." Evin reached up to touch Inkeri's eyebrow, trying to ascertain how bad the cut was.

"Only a dream doesn't cause the kind of reaction I just saw, Evin. You're still shaking all over." Roald moved closer and pointed to Evin's hands. "Look at your hands. What's that all over them?" He grabbed his wrist and turned it into the light. Inkeri gasped as he moved the other one in front of him and turned it palm up to match the first. The surface was covered with a sticky brown residue. Evin jerked away from Roald and clenched his hands shut angrily, squeezing his eyes shut to try to block out the memory. Instead, the sights and sounds that were last in his dream assaulted him again. The sticky liquid flowing into his hands and the ornate goblet falling to the ground appeared in front of him like they'd never left. His eyes flew open in panic and he stared at his hands, then stared in amazement at Inkeri, who was wincing and holding her eyebrow. He groaned an inhuman sound and bolted for the door like he could escape. Inkeri moved to follow, only to find herself restrained. Roald turned her toward the firelight and looked at her closely. On her forehead was the evidence of the blood Kai had been wiping away and a smudge of the brown residue, but no cut. In its place was perfectly smooth healed skin. He released her and backed a space away from her, still staring at her.

Kai watched, then moved closer and examined for himself, causing Inkeri to reach her fingers up and examine the spot. Fright registered on her face, and she whirled toward the door.

"It won't do any good to run, Inkeri. Whatever just happened isn't going away even if you run from it." Roald's strong hand on her shoulder was enough to hold her back. She trusted his insight even though she'd only known him a short time.

"I'm not running, but I do need air. If it's all the same to you, I'm going to wait outside for Evin. I need to try to understand this. This doesn't usually happen on happy wedding trips. I'll come back, I promise."

Kai turned to Roald. "I'm definitely traveling with you now." He grinned like a little kid. "My curiosity is piqued."

Inkeri frowned at him, and Roald moved his hand off her shoulder. She left the room with no further complaint from the men. She slipped down the staircase and through the darkened front room to the outside of the building. The air hit her face and took her breath in a cool rush. She stopped to gulp in the cool air. The coming summer would mean the colder air would soon be gone for a time. Inkeri stepped into the open and tested the air for rain with her upturned face. She was glad to find the persistent rain had finally stopped and a few stars peeked through the remaining clouds. Still, she couldn't see far into the night, so she lingered near the front of the inn, continuing to fill her lungs with long draughts of the mountain air. The town was empty, and the only sounds she could hear were of animals that made their way through the night. She made her way across the muddy ground, realizing too late she'd failed to put on shoes. She walked to the corner of the building and leaned against it, loving the solid feel of it against her back. The feel of the mud between her toes and the smells of wood fires reminded her of her childhood, and the memory of simpler times left her feeling much more at ease. She closed her eyes and took a tour of her house in her mind. She could almost smell the soft-baked bread and feel the soft blanket that her mom had embroidered with lovely pink roses. She let many happy memories filter through her mind and lead her back to a place where she felt safe and happy. As she wandered around her room in her mind, she was taken back to the morning of her wedding and her strange visitor. Once again, the apprehension of the unknown attacked her, and she began to shiver involuntarily. "Inkeri," she heard the warrior say again. "The man you marry today is no ordinary man." The memory almost made her laugh. He had looked very ordinary at their wedding, but the warrior's words had proven true. Inkeri groaned and whispered to herself. "Why must I be a part of this madness?"

"It is madness." The voice from the darkness beside her startled her and she nearly leapt from her skin. Before she could turn and run back toward the inn, the voice continued, "Don't run, Inkeri. I know I hurt you, but I didn't mean to. You have to believe me."

She peered into the darkness beside where she'd been standing until she could make out a dark shape seated leaning against the wall just around the corner. "Evin?" The dark shape stood and moved into the weak moonlight.

"It's me, don't be afraid of me."

"I'm not afraid of you, Evin. I just wasn't sure if it was you." Inkeri stepped up to him and grabbed his hand, turning it over to examine his palm. She touched it lightly with her fingers and held them up to the light to see the sticky residue that was still on them. What is this all about, Evin? I think I need to know what's going on here."

"So do I, Inkeri." Evin grabbed Inkeri's fingers tightly. "Is your eye ok?"

"It seems you've healed it. There's no cut."

Evin leaned in closer and looked at her face in the weak light, then rocked back on his heels. "Well, okay. In the dream or vision or whatever that was, I also had an injury healed by the stuff." He laughed "I wish this made any sense! I promise that as soon as I put some of this together to share with you, I will. If I told you what I know now, you'd be as confused as I am. That wouldn't do anyone any good." Evin relaxed his grasp on her fingers and lowered his eyes to the ground. "Maybe another day will shed light on this whole mystery, Inkeri. Something tells me we should wait and see." She could feel his hand still trembling underneath her fingers. She remembered her vow to herself to keep her distance from him and she begrudgingly let her hand fall to her side. "Thank you for staying." She didn't know what to say to that, so she just continued to stay, standing hopelessly in the moonlight. In a few minutes, Evin indicated they should walk toward the inn. "Let's go get some sleep." He said, and she noted that his breathing was finally steady. They made their way back up the rough stairs to find the others sitting and waiting. "Back to bed," Evin encouraged, as he washed his hands off in the basin, indicating an unwillingness to talk right then. "We've got a lot to do to be ready for the next part of the journey."

Chapter 11

A week passed as they waited for Kai to heal from his injury. They had plenty to keep them occupied while they waited. Inkeri adjusted to life without another female. They chose which supplies they would need for the journey. Kai woke feeling a little better each day, his headache abating enough for him to begin to feel like himself again. The group decided to split the last day's tasks in hopes of getting back to the trail early the next morning. Evin seemed to want to pretend the vision hadn't happened, so the others didn't mention it. He went about business without his former warmth, but that seemed understandable enough for the moment. Kai and Evin settled into an uneasy truce. Roald decided to trade the cart and extra goods to get a horse more suited to riding, so Kai could make the trek over the mountain with them. He planned to look for packs to use on the animals that had been pulling the cart so the group could carry supplies. Kai decided to go with him to take care of those things while Inkeri and Evin found a place to wash the clothing that they had used to this point. After a brief conversation with the innkeeper's wife, they found the perfect spot in the crystal lake to get things clean, far enough away from the village to provide privacy.

The weather was warmer, and the beautiful setting was idyllic. All the stress of the days before melted as they worked on the simple task together. To this point, they hadn't spent much time in conversation, and at first it seemed that it wouldn't be any different today. They washed each piece of their clothing carefully and laid the pieces in the sun to dry. They worked quietly at their task until each one had been done, then sat by the shore to await the arrival of the others who'd agreed to meet them here once business was done. The water lapped in short ripples that ran only a short distance onto the millions of tiny pebbles that populated the shoreline before sinking back into the stones and receding into the body of the lake. The sound the water made was like a wash basin for the soul, and as the almost married strangers sat quietly with faces turned into the sun, they both felt more peace than they had for a while. The stones gleamed in the sunshine as the water washed over them. Evin picked up several of them, confounded that as they dried, they reverted to the dull colors that could be seen on any normal rock. He found a few that maintained their beauty even as the intensity of their wet color faded, tumbled as they had been in the surf for years unmeasured. He was content to sit here alongside Inkeri and dig into the stones. A couple of times, he cast a glance in her direction, but as usual, none of her emotions played across her face. She had that enigmatic look that always kept him wondering what she must be thinking. It wasn't long before he found out. "No one has told me why we haven't mentioned Alia to Kai. We're just all going on like nothing happened, ignoring the fact that his memory is bound to return sometime soon. You and Roald know something of the situation you haven't shared." Evin felt the prick of shame he'd been suppressing threaten to come back to the surface, and he resorted to finding larger stones among the small ones and flinging them out into the water while he thought about what things it might be best to reveal to Inkeri. He knew that all pretense of a normal wedding trip was past, and he was frankly amazed she hadn't demanded to be taken home. On the other hand, he didn't have all the information himself yet, and he didn't want to feed her the pieces he did have for fear she'd leave. It struck him that he was playing the same role in her life that Roald was playing in his, and suddenly his distaste and shame grew. He stopped throwing the stones and looked into her earnest face. Why was she sticking around for this craziness? He opted to start with the easiest truth, telling her the story that wasn't theirs. He related a condensed version of the tale he and Roald had been told. She sat quietly listening, but a few times he saw tears well in her eyes, and he knew it was having an impact on her.

"We've always been told since we were little that those laws are in place for our good," Evin said "and you and I have experienced first-hand the results of living under them. Apparently, Kai is what happens when you choose not to."

She looked through him like she could with those piercing eyes. "Do you think he should have just gone with them? No one talks about the guards, Evin, unless they choose to be one, like your brother. Even he knew that he was giving up a life of marriage for a life of war, but your family can celebrate that because he's making that choice to deal with his grief. What if he didn't have the choice? Would you feel differently?"

Evin thought about her question. He remembered his dad explaining to him why young people didn't have choices. It was for the older people in their lives to make the decisions that would lead the whole group to experience a more fulfilling future. Until his marriage, he'd never been impacted by the parts of their society that sounded disquieting when spoken aloud. He didn't personally know anyone that had been conscripted into lifelong servitude, but he struggled with how that would be different than having everything else chosen for you. Your life was never yours to make decisions about, but instead was a carefully crafted story woven together for the good of the community. The community needed people to enforce the laws. It needed people to create the goods. It needed people to farm the land. If each person accepted the role that they were expected to fill, then the whole thing would work, but if they bucked against it, you would end up with chaos. "I would be sad," he concluded, "to see him have to go like that, but I would recognize that he had been given his part to play. I'm supposed to farm and lead. Othniel could have stayed and done the same if he'd wanted. Someday Gunnar and I will be elders, like our dad, and we will help ensure the people in our village work together to grow and meet our quotas so our whole country can thrive. A good elder does whatever it takes to make sure his people don't face the negative consequences of the law." He turned his head back to study the lake, unsettled by his own answer and its implications. He was ashamed to have inadvertently accused Harald of being at fault for everything that had happened. He sounded just like his dad. He wanted to rise and choose for himself, and he was struck by the absurdity of his emotions. Again, silence left him to wonder if Inkeri agreed with him or if she was just appalled by him. Roald had completely thrown him off kilter with all the talk of an uprising, and even though he'd loved his mom's stories as a child, he was blown away that people were willing to die to be able to usher in chaos. He'd had all his choices upended and he had people making most of them for him, and he was surviving. He felt trapped much of the time, because now he was painfully aware he couldn't go home, but he was doing his best amid the madness.

The two sat in stillness for a few more minutes before a voice behind them ushered them back to reality. Kai and Raold strode up and took their places on the rocky shore near them. "Wow," Roald sat back and looked out over the lake. "You guys found a prime spot to wash everything." He smiled in their direction and Inkeri gave him a wan smile in return. Evin just kept staring out over the lake, ignoring their arrival. "Well, you two are obviously having a party." He chuckled and joined them in soaking in the sun.

"Enjoy it," Kai said. "Soon, if we're lucky, we're going to be seeing quite a bit of rain."

"Are you a farmer?" Inkeri asked.

"No," Kai smiled at the thought. "I know enough about it, for sure, but I'm glad we weren't farmers. I don't really like doing that kind of thing."

Roald glanced at Evin, and finding his eyebrows raised, decided to just let the conversation play out.

"My dad was responsible for trading goods from our village with other villages. He'd take the leftovers our village had and trade for goods from other villages. You've probably all seen him at some point." He smiled at the thought. "I always thought I would enjoy following in his footsteps. I liked it when he'd let me go along on longer trips. I learned a lot in other places." He looked introspective and followed the other's examples, turning his face into the sun and looking out across the lake. His face went still, and he looked like he was trying to remember something. Evin looked back at Inkeri and saw that she was watching Kai intently. Kai continued in a minute. "One thing about being a trader is that you get to do a lot of training with weapons and what boy doesn't like that? I'm a fairly good fighter." No one asked the obvious questions, because they already knew the answers. "I guess you know that didn't really pan out for me." He got quiet again. "What part of my story did you hear, Roald?"

Roald rose and walked to examine something on the shore, trying to surmise which parts he remembered from the messenger who came to tell him about Kai, and which parts only Harald would have known. He didn't want to inadvertently reveal any of those. He told a brief account that included hearing the boy had panicked upon being chosen to be a soldier in his region and had fled with a girl from his village, whom he'd married. He'd lost his wife in a raid and was ready to fight for a cause that would allow other young people to not have to make such devastating choices. "It's good to hear you know how to fight. We might need some of that." Roald finished, and satisfied, perched once more on the stones.

"My wife," Kai added, embellishing the tale to provide context, "was a light in this dark place. She and I knew everything about each other. She believed in me and trusted me even when that seemed really illogical."

Thoughtlessly, Inkeri said "That sounds like Alia." Immediately when the words left her lips, she gasped and put her hand over her mouth, looking back and forth at Roald and Evin with fear in her eyes, aware that once words were said they couldn't be taken back.

Kai looked confused for a minute, sitting up tall on the shore and then glaring at Inkeri. "What did you say?" His voice sounded both hurt and astounded.

"Nothing, I didn't mean to say anything." She struggled to understand how to quench the flames she'd released.

He sat for a second, his eyes moving wildly back and forth while his injured brain tried to make the connections he needed to make sense of Inkeri's declaration. "You were with her. On the shore." He touched the still tender side of his head as if that would help. "I remember seeing you." He suddenly stood to his feet and crossed the distance to Inkeri, pulling her to her feet in front of him. He wasn't rough, just urgent. "She's alive. Gods, where is she?" He grabbed Inkeri's shoulders and stared into her face. She shrank away from him, overwhelmed by his sudden intensity.

Before even a moment had passed, Roald was gently prying the young man's hands off Inkeri. His other hand was held out in warning to Evin, who was standing looking alarmed and angry a short distance away. "Sit down, Kai. We were waiting for your memory to start coming back on its own. We don't know where she is. Sit down and tell us what you remember." Kai looked disgusted at the idea of inactivity, but his face was still robed in confusion as well, so he did as he was told.

"How is she alive?" He looked at Inkeri again. "Is she well?" he thought about it for a second and then concluded. "She was pregnant when I saw you. How long ago was this?"

"Ten days." Inkeri seated herself again and looked at her lap, afraid to say more, already mortified for having spoken out of turn.

Kai's hand moved through his hair in much the same way it had when he'd found them on the road the first day they'd met him. He brushed back the dark locks that were threatening to fall in his face and looked at the ground, still reaching for connections. Finally, he looked at Roald. "Tell me what happened." He gestured to his head, indicating he was having no luck remembering how he was injured.

Roald grimaced and shot Inkeri a withering look, clearly dreading revealing unwanted news to yet another young man in his company. He looked at Evin, who stood scowling as he seemed to do far too often now, acutely aware that he had caused Evin's angst. "This is so much harder than hunting someone down and exacting revenge on them." He shook his head as he spoke and Evin turned away from the group, clearly annoyed by the situation. Roald told Kai all that had happened on the road, watching him carefully for unwanted reactions. Kai sat still instead, listening in disbelief to the tale. "I had no idea until I heard your name from Inkeri's lips that you were in any way connected to our fellow travelers. Purely coincidentally we ended up in their company for the trip here." He finished.

Kai looked to the sky for a few seconds and then jumped to his feet, putting the pieces all together again for himself. "This means he looked me right in the eyes and lied to me. He told me she was dead, that they'd already sent her body home to protect me from the pain of seeing her like that. What the hell have they been doing for the last several months?" He looked astounded. "They should have made it home in a matter of weeks."

"They took her to the chapel in our region. To settle her nerves and help her get over your loss." Evin interjected.

Kai whirled to look at him. "She thought I was dead too?" Kai put both hands in his hair and paced back and forth, uttering every curse he could muster on Harald. "Why did you let her go? Didn't she want to see me?" He looked again at Inkeri.

Inkeri's cheeks colored at the memory of wanting to tell Alia and being unable to. She stared at the stones, letting them tumble carelessly through her fingers.

"On my life!" he exclaimed. "No one told her?" He looked at all of them as though they'd each betrayed him.

"That's a lot to ask of people who barely know her and don't have the whole story, Kai." Roald spoke softly. "We wanted to hear your side of it. Harald would have killed you if I hadn't restrained him. It seemed unwise to proceed without some context. Disturbing a very pregnant woman without good cause didn't seem like a good plan. We were as rocked as you were by the whole thing."

He stared at Roald for a second, and stopped pacing, positioning himself between the water and the three of them, scanning the shoreline behind them. "I didn't have a choice. I was going to be taken the next morning. I've been around. I've met a lot of soldiers, and they only talk about serving their masters and doing their job. They live for it. It's unnatural. I don't know how it's accomplished, but a soldier is single minded in his devotion to his lord. I gave Alia the choice whether to come along, and she chose me. She chose me!" Anger flashed in his eyes. "How dare they take that away from her!" He resumed pacing. "We went straight to Hvalr, because once when I traveled there with my father to trade, I spent some time with the children of the fishermen. Several of the boys were nearing marrying age, and I distinctly remember them talking of marrying without the requirement to go straight to a chapel afterward because they would be going to sea shortly after the wedding. Of course, they still went to the chapel, but they were lax about when that happened. It seemed like a good opportunity for us to be married, and we were taken with the simplicity of life in the village while we were there. They didn't really have an established tradesman, so I saw an opportunity to use the skills I had acquired to provide something to the community. We chose to settle along the coast there, and I started building us a home. We established a base camp and every day we worked alongside one another to build a life. We missed family, but we knew when we left we could never go back. That lasted a couple of months before we were attacked." He lowered his eyes, reliving the painful memory, then looked up and continued. "I was dragged away into the forest, beaten soundly, and left there to limp my way back to our homesite. When I got to camp, there was no sign of Alia, and two days passed. I searched everywhere. Town, shore, forest; she was just gone. Then out of nowhere, Harald materializes and tells me he's discovered where we are right after we were attacked. He and Runa recovered her body from the shore where she'd fallen trying to escape and had already paid to have it taken home." He looked stricken. "I believed him, because he was like my own father. He'd never given me reason not to believe him. On top of that, he said he and Runa wouldn't reveal my location to Lord Arne, so they could save me from my fate as a soldier. They said payment enough had already been exacted from our village. I got the impression that if they'd found the two of us there before we were attacked, they would have been satisfied that we were well and would have left us to return home." Anger washed over his face again. "Now I wonder if they might have planned the whole thing."

Roald glanced at Evin only to find him staring back, the weighty knowledge that they shared eating up the space between them.

Kai continued. "I had no idea she was going to have a baby." He thought about it for a second, then allowed himself a grin. "That was fast."

"She didn't know either at the time." Inkeri eased his mind with her words.

"I wish I could have found out about that from her." He wrestled with it for a minute. "I guess I kind of did." He smiled sadly. "She just doesn't know she told me."

"A lot could hinge on your next decision, Kai. I implore you to think carefully about what you want to do." Roald pleaded. Evin shot him a murderous look, which he ignored.

"Oh, I know exactly what I want to do." Kai assured him. "I'm just not sure what I should do."

The group resumed their repose on the shore, but very soon the sun that had dominated the morning began to recede behind the clouds, and Inkeri went to check that the clothes had dried. She affirmed that was the case and they headed back to the inn to configure the remaining stuff they would need in packs. Kai went out to walk and clear his head, and Roald followed shortly, afraid he would leave without a word. The rest of the packing went according to plan. Evin and Inkeri worked well together, and he enjoyed the snippets of conversation they had as they worked. At one point he caught himself just watching her as she stuffed tent material in a bag while she animatedly told him a story about her and a cousin trying to fish one day. He couldn't even remember how the topic came up, and he didn't care. Instead, he reveled in the fact that she felt comfortable enough to laugh with him about it.

After they finished laughing, they fell into a comfortable silence for a few minutes, tying the tops of the filled bags shut. Inkeri finished the last one and turned to Evin. "I have to tell you something, Evin. At least I think I can tell you." She lowered her eyebrows and thought for a second, then shrugged. "Only one way to find out." She walked to the edge of the bed and sat down, urging him to sit across from her. "Normally, I'm really a spoiled little girl who would never stick around for more than a few days of this foolishness."

"I don't believe that." He countered. You've been here for over three weeks."

"I said normally, Evin." She looked insecure, biting her lip a little, then continuing, "this is not normal."

"Tell me about it." He muttered.

"The day we were betrothed, I was very unsure. You were very young, and I was having a hard time imagining our life together. My family assured me that you were from a very strong family, and that I would be lucky to have you. I decided to accept that, and I was going to go through with it, for all these selfish reasons. I wanted the status that being married to you would bring. I wanted the nice house and the big fields, and I never even thought about you." She looked into his eyes, and he felt his cheeks color. It was weird having someone talk about you to you. "My mom called me down to have breakfast that morning, and when I went to walk out of my room, I found that I was unable to leave. A strangely dressed warrior stopped me at my door and told me that you were no ordinary man. That's the first time I thought much about you." Her eyelashes batted downward for a minute. "Except to worry about whether you'd be handsome." She looked back at him. "He warned me to tell no one, and when I tried to tell my mom, I was unable to talk for the rest of the morning. I'm not sure what exactly is going on here, but he told me that day that I should work alongside you and not abandon you. He said you would find the truth about El Olam." She let that sink in. "So here I am. I'm going to stay here no matter how weird it gets. This is the first time I've ever been interested in something that wasn't about me."

Evin sat on the bed across from her, enjoying the moment to just look at her without it being weird. "I would have laughed in your face a month ago," he stated, then curiosity sprang to his face. "What did he look like. Can you describe him?"

Inkeri thought for a second and then carefully described the warrior. She described his shiny armor and broadsword and Evin listened intently. Then he described the symbols he'd seen in his dream, and she remembered seeing one similar on the chest emblem of the warrior to whom she'd spoken. "We've seen members of the same army, Inkeri." Evin gasped. He thought about what that could mean, but when he couldn't immediately figure it out, he switched subjects. "Roald has given me some outrageous news. I promise I'm going to tell you, but I think this all has to do with these visions and the god that we hear whispers about. That sounds unquestionably ludicrous when I say it out loud."

She looked as apprehensive as he felt. "I'm not sure what to make of it either." They sat staring at each other as if they might find some clue in each other's eyes.

Just then, Roald and Kai walked through the door together and stopped as soon as they saw the couple. "Whoa, getting a little close there," Kai quipped. "Might want to back it up a couple of feet." The two of them leaned further apart, but didn't move, giving the intruders their full attention. Kai smiled and moved aside, taking inventory of the fully packed bags. "At least they packed everything first."

Roald rolled his eyes and stepped further into the room. "Kai decided to go along with us on one condition. I think it's worth hearing him out, because we're certainly going to need his help on this trip up the mountain."

Evin looked at Roald, ignoring Kai. "Why wouldn't we just sail to the other side of the mountains? It seems to me that would be a much easier way to get there."

"It would seem so, yes." said Roald patiently. "It's a much more treacherous way to go that finds you in a wasteland on the other side. There are no settlements within a comfortable reach of the boats. Fjall is situated at the top of the mountain on the pass, so we would still have the climb, just from the other side. Storms can come out of nowhere on the sea. Let's leave the sailing for when we absolutely have to do it.

"Back to Kai, then." Evin said impatiently. "What's the condition?"

"I want to go see Alia before we go up the mountain."

Evin stood up, his fiery temper once more showing in his flashing eyes. "Are you a fool? You're going to get yourself killed! You're going to destroy the peace she has now." All the reasons he could think of tumbled out. "You're going to endanger all of us."

"Relax, Evin," Kai said. It seemed he was getting used to the outbursts. "I don't mean talk to her. I mean see her with my eyes. I want to see her and decide for myself whether I can leave her for the moment. Roald says it would be a lot of help if I were to go along. When we come back, she will have had the baby, and soon after that I'm sure Harald will be looking for a husband for her. I'll see if she's still interested in the one she's already got." He looked decisive.

Evin calmed a little but lashed out with his words. "You're not even really married to her, Kai. Maybe you should fix that first." Roald and Kai both bristled, and Evin thought better of his statement. "Sorry. I shouldn't have said it like that. I mean, Inkeri and I are still following all the laws that you guys seem to have complete contempt for. It's a little hard right now to know where I'm supposed to stand."

Roald sighed. "You might see a lot of things you don't understand, Evin, but you have to let go of this stubborn insistence that everyone you meet lives up to your standards, or you're not going to get very far."

He looked at Inkeri, who was intently listening. "It seems my mom forgot to mention the fact that I should try to be more of a miscreant when I'm all grown up. It doesn't matter. Let's go chase down Alia. Is there a plan for how to see her without actually seeing her?"

"We're hoping to use Inkeri as bait. You and I can say Inkeri was really struggling when Alia left, and we can set up a meeting for them in the town square. Kai can watch from some distance.

Inkeri can ask about how she's doing, and he can feel reassured that she's fine." Roald seemed satisfied with the plan.

"I just don't feel good about this," Inkeri piped up. "I feel like she's been through a lot. She wouldn't want to be kept in the dark. I think you need to tell her you're still alive."

Everyone stared at her as if they were waiting for the punchline. "I'm serious. She's dealing with a lot of the consequences of you dying and leaving her alone. I think it would make it better for her to know that you're alive and coming back for her. It will also give her the fuel she needs to fight being betrothed to a different man while she waits."

Evin looked impatient. "I just want to get where we're going. I don't really care what you decide to tell her, but this is going to add a week to our travel time. Are we sure it's worth it?"

Kai took a turn to look disgusted. "I'm going with you because I believe your ill-conceived scheme might be the only way for me to ever have a home with the woman I love. I'm going to check first and make sure I'm not leaving her in a bad situation before I go. If you want my help, you'll have to make the little detour." Evin started to say something, but Roald looked at him in a way that indicated if he said the wrong thing, he might not live to regret it, so he didn't say anything else. "We're only two days from my village. We might even be able to make the journey faster without the cart." Kai seemed excited.

"Let's go down and enjoy dinner in the inn this evening. Then we'll get some rest and leave with the sun in the morning." Roald stretched and moved toward the door. "I'm glad I'm working for a wealthy family." He winked in Evin's direction. "You're buying." He stopped at the door. "When we get finished with this mission, I've set up a meeting for you before we head across the mountain. I want you to hear something." With that, he made his way down the stairs.

Chapter 12

The trip to Selby took only a day and a half, and by the time they'd made the journey, Kai had decided to tell Alia he was still alive. Because of this, he would sneak into town himself under cover of darkness to try to figure out a way to contact her. He used to knock on her window to get her attention, and he hoped she would still answer. They found a good campsite just out of sight of the town and waited for nightfall. Kai left with a wave and trotted toward town, unprepared for the emotions coming back to this town made him feel. He carefully avoided wide open spaces and emerged without ceremony at the house where he'd spent so much time with Alia. Creeping to the window he knew had always belonged to her, he angled himself to see inside. He was rewarded with a good view of the bedroom. When they were younger, they'd sit at the window and talk for hours. Eager to wake his sleeping lover without raising the rest of the house, he tapped lightly on the glass. He repeated the attempt when no motion was detected, and then had a moment's panic. What if she wasn't there, or what if they'd switched her room? For a minute, he couldn't breathe, wondering what his next move would be if this didn't work, but then, a form rose from the bed and looked toward the window. Hoping against hope that this was her, he waved into the room. She moved quickly to the window and slid it open noiselessly, looking down at him from her slightly higher position. He hoped the trauma of seeing him wouldn't make her do something stupid. "Kai?" Her voice sounded sleepy, but beautiful. Her brow was lowered in confusion. "A dream, "she stated.

"I'm not a dream, Alia. It's me. I have something important to tell you." She still didn't react like he'd assumed she would, instead she rubbed her forehead, muttering about a strange dream. He reached in the window and took her hand. "Alia, wake up, it's me." She looked confused again, so he tried to clarify. "I know it's hard to understand what's going on, but I'm alive. They lied about me being dead." It was clear from the look on Alia's face that she was trying to understand something her brain couldn't process. He decided to try another tactic, and reached through the window, pulling her close and caressing her face. Then he kissed her. At first, she didn't react, then she melted into the embrace and relaxed.

She eventually pulled back and stared at him. "A good dream." She smiled lazily in his direction, and he got the distinct impression that she still wasn't awake. It was imperative he do something to help her understand the truth of the situation. He considered what might work, and while he was thinking, he reached down and touched her belly, suddenly astounded by the life growing there. He leaned in and kissed it gently.

"It's me, little one. I'm your daddy." He lingered for a moment, placing his hands firmly but gently on both sides of her swollen middle. He looked up and smiled at her, only to see the consternation he'd expected registering on her face.

"Kai, you have to be a dream." She kept repeating herself, but with every second she seemed less sure. "You can't really be here." She blinked her eyes a few times, and all the color drained from her face.

"It's really me, Alia. I swear. They lied to you." She looked confused by that, and he moved his hands back up to face and looked into her eyes, willing her to understand. Her eyes seemed a little vacant again, so he moved his hand back to her belly, and watched her eyes refocus. It was the strangest experience he'd ever had, like she couldn't comprehend him being real for her, but he could be there for the baby. He kept his hand resting there, and took her other hand, holding it close to her side so that both of his hands were making contact with her. He just let her process while he did the best math he could in his head, wondering when the baby would be due to come. Two months? He gazed at her, and tears streamed down her face. "It's ok. Look at me." She obediently locked eyes with him. "I'm going to come back for you and for the baby." She still looked unsure. "I'm going to come back and get you." He was very confused by her strange behavior, but instead of focusing on that, he worked hard to overcome her confusion. He told her how he'd seen her across the lake. He told her how up until then he'd thought she was dead. He knew he didn't have much time with her, and it was obvious that this was taking a toll on her as she made every attempt to wake up to the idea that he was alive.

"When we married and went to Ellerton I was so happy. What happened to you?" She didn't look like she expected an answer, but Kai was struck by the absurdity of her statement.

"We didn't go there, Alia. Remember Hvalr? We started building a house together. We married there." He was earnest, willing her to remember. "Our campsite was attacked..."

She lowered her eyebrows and concentrated, a tiny spark seeming to ignite in her eyes, and then snuffing out. "That seems like a really familiar story."

He stared into her eyes for a minute, watching her wrestle with her memory. He was reminded of his own struggle. "Did something happen to you, Alia? He raised his hand to caress her head, watching for any discernible wincing or other indication she'd had an injury. She just gave him a weird look. He was suddenly filled with sadness. Something was wrong here. He lowered his head, resting it against her midsection, amused to feel the baby wiggle away under the pressure. He rested there for a second, trying to memorize the feeling of her. He tried to breathe in deeply enough to remember her smell. She was cared for and secure for the moment. His heart ached each time he thought of walking away, but he knew he would have to leave now.

She raised her hand and ran her fingers over his brow. "I love you, Kai."

He would take that, he thought. It might not be the jubilant reunion he was anticipating, but it was all he needed. He stretched up and kissed her as though he might never see her again, and this time she was immediately receptive. "Don't tell anyone I was here." It was so difficult to let her go, but he did. Encouraging her to try to get some rest, he moved away from her window.

Distracted as he made his way through the field and then back to the town, he was not as careful as he was on the way in. He made it just to the edge of town before he tripped over something on the path. He hit the ground hard, knocking the breath from his lungs. Before he could rise, he was yanked to his knees by unseen hands and forced to stay there. He started to yell, but a cloth was forced into his mouth and secured, stifling his cries. He was dragged, still on his knees, across the rocky ground and his hands were bound around a lanky tree. He knew what was next, and he began to struggle and beg his unseen assailant to no avail. He'd seen this punishment doled out for serious criminal offenses before. "We've been watching for you," stated a gruff sounding voice.

"If he survives this, he won't be back. Are you sure he was heading into town and not out of it?" Another voice queried.

"Yeah, I'm sure. He turned to run the other way when he heard us."

Kai was momentarily filled with relief. Whoever they were, they didn't know he'd made it to see Alia. The sudden ripping of his tunic jolted him back to reality, and he began to wildly struggle, prompting the men to secure the ropes more tightly that bound him to the tree. His cheek pushed against the rough bark of the tree, causing scratches with each movement. He stilled himself, terrified, waiting for the punishing blows he knew would soon come from the straight leather whips that were used for this purpose. The remnants of his shirt were yanked from his back unceremoniously. A gruff laugh filled the air along with the sickening whistling of the whips swinging through space. His attempt to plead through the filthy rag in his mouth was met with more laughter. The whip's singing intensified, and Kai's body was wracked with searing pain. Almost immediately, another strike and another led him to understand that both men were taking turns whipping him from opposite directions. He couldn't draw the breath he needed, and the rough bark against his cheek made the search for more air an agonizing experience. When the lashes hit just right, they cut deeply into his skin. Ten lashes... eleven... twelve. He imagined they intended to kill him as the beating continued. Mercifully, shouting and confusion erupted, and the beating ceased. Kai slumped against the tree, willing himself stay conscious. He listened as blows were exchanged. A whip sang through the air again and a yelp arose, then a different singing, of metal cutting the air, and another thud. In seconds, the cords binding him to the tree were cut and the gag was removed.

"Careful." A familiar voice encouraged. He winced in pain as he was set on his feet, and his arms were draped over the welcoming shoulders of his campmates. "Can you walk with help?" Roald watched him expectantly. He nodded. They moved as quickly as possible back to the campsite, which was blessedly nearby. They seated him quickly on a stump and hastily began gathering all the supplies and readying the horses. "We have to get out of here as quickly as we can. One of those guys might not survive that fight. We need to be as far away from here as possible by morning."

Inkeri moved behind him, squinting in the moonlight to see the damage to his back. He knew from the sharp intake of breath that it wasn't the best case. He could feel blood trickling down his back. "He has a couple of nasty looking cuts. How many times did they hit you?"

"I lost count around fifteen." His voice was hoarse and thick with pain.

Inkeri watched carefully between helping the others to ensure that the bleeding would stop. "I think a couple of them might cause some problems."

"We don't have the time to worry about that now." Roald used a stick to scatter the remaining embers and poured the leftover water on the coals, dousing the light. He looked at Kai. "You're going to have to ride. Now." He mercifully helped Kai climb on the horse and left to get on his own. Finally mounted, they rode north. They were forced to move more quickly than was comfortable, but the occasional moans from the middle of the pack were the only complaints they heard.

~~~~~

The sun rose and moved to the middle of the sky before they stopped. Roald chose an isolated copse of trees by a stream that would provide a solid hiding place. They could carve out a small campsite near the rear of it and see the road from the south clearly. Roald helped the injured man from his horse and lowered him on to a blanket he'd stretched on the ground, resting him on his stomach and encouraging him to drink several draughts of water from his water-skin. Kai lowered his head and was almost immediately asleep.

The other two men worked on the camp, situating it so that it was as invisible as possible. They made a small fire at Inkeri's request. She gathered plants she knew to have medicinal properties and steeped them into a poultice to dress the wounds. She was grateful that she had paid attention to her grandmother, one of the village's midwives, when she'd stirred together her miracle cures. Unfortunately she was missing some of the ingredients, and she was left to hope they wouldn't be too critical. When she walked over to begin working on his back, the others joined, hoping to assess the situation and discover just how bad it was.

Roald whistled when he took the time to finally examine Kai's new stripes closely. "Looks like we showed up just in time. I knew one of those guys. We've..." He paused for a second, thinking through his next words, "...worked together before. That means they were men for hire. That could be good for us, because I imagine they've completed the job they were paid for. I can't really see a reason for them to follow us."

"I thought you said you killed one of them." Evin looked surly, then examined an angry red welt on his forearm.
~~~~~

"I said might have." Roald looked at the welt and commented, "Good thing that wasn't your eye."

"Wouldn't they come after us if we killed one of them?" Evin asked.

"Not likely. We're kind of a disposable commodity."

"Gods, what are you doing?" Kai's sudden exclamation brought the two men back to attention.

Inkeri quickly rested a reassuring hand across the man's mercifully uninjured shoulder. "I have to help you, Kai. It will sting, but it's important you hold still. Too bad we don't have some of that honey stuff you had on your hands, Evin." She continued working, leaving Evin to wonder if she was serious. She cleaned each wound with water she'd boiled and combined with some herbs. Kai winced and groaned a few times but managed to hold relatively still while she moved the damaged skin as close together as she could and applied bandages made from Kai's torn tunic soaked in the herbal mixture she'd created. Satisfied, she stood and turned to the other two men. "I know we're all exhausted, and Kai needs to rest as well. I think we should rest for the remainder of the day, and then at dinner this evening, you two are going to explain everything you know about what is happening." With that she turned and disappeared into the tent.

Chapter 13

The trees were well situated to be able to see in three directions, with the camp out of sight among them. Roald, used to living a life punctuated by long periods without rest, and feeling anxious about the coming talk, had wandered the area surrounding the camp to have time to consider what to say. He returned just as the others were stirring and stoked the fire, then settled near it with his back leaned against a tree. Kai moved across from him, lowering himself to the ground gingerly and sitting cross legged, looking at him through the smoke. The others joined and after adding a pot to the fire, settled in close enough to both listen and tend the cooking meal.

"I think if anyone was coming after us, we'd have seen them riding." Roald said reassuringly. "How are you feeling, Kai?"

Kai dropped his gaze, stirring the dirt in front of him with a twig he'd found. "I'm very sore." He touched the scratches across his right cheek and then examined the remnants of the bruise on the side of his head. "It's been a rough couple of weeks in more ways than one." He looked back up. "They've also been some of the best weeks of my life." A smile lit his face, replaced quickly with seriousness. "Thank you for rescuing me. I'm sorry to put you at risk." His eyes went back to his business with the twig.

Roald looked around at the group, noting their accepting nods and quiet demeanor, and for the first time he liked his chances of uniting them around something bigger than themselves. "I've thought a lot this afternoon about how to tell you what I know in a way that will make sense to you. Because each of you is so young, you cannot remember our history as a people. I think that's the place to start."

"What of the stories our clans told us as we grew up?" Kai looked a little defensive at being told he was ignorant. "How is a history lesson going to help?"

Roald continued. "You have doubtless heard the near history of your village from the elders. That history is not even as old as I am. Not as old as your parents. Does anyone speak of anything that came before?" He looked at each face and when he was satisfied that they had understood his meaning, he went on, "We were once a group of fishermen, with their wives and children who lived to the far west on an island. That village was strong and many people sailed in and out of our home village with all kinds of news and trade. We lived among many other people like ourselves, content to pass our generations quietly on our shores. People from other lands visited and some brought news of El Olam. They told of him and his son, who was promised to come and rescue us through his sacrifice. He was to permanently replace the animal sacrifice that some peoples still hold to. It was a beautiful story, full of power, and some among our ancestors believed it, and turned to worship the new everlasting god, in time abandoning our old gods. They continued in this way, living peacefully with one another, learning from the priests of the new faith that had carried it to them. They built chapels and worshipped El Olam. Most in their village turned to the new god. It is said the priest who had come to them was trusted because he had a history with our people. The things he said made sense, and they readily accepted them. I don't know anything else about that, but I do know that our people lived on a small island situated among other islands, some smaller than our own and some much larger. Some of the tribes on the other islands grew hostile. Our people were competent sailors, and their village had several large boats that they used for trade. They heard many rumors that some of the tribes around had become discontent with the changes made by the priests who'd come to tell them about god, and that some tribes were killing them or running them out. They didn't think too much of it because, as traders, they were at peace with their neighbors. They felt like the other tribes needed them. One day, another priest rode in carrying a book he'd received from their homeland that told the whole story of El Olam. He was beside himself with excitement to share what it said with us. He was to start translating it for us to hear first thing the next morning. That evening, a tribe from one of the other islands attacked as the sun set. It was said to me that they rose out of the sea like sand, swarming over their small island without warning. Word reached the village that they were coming when they were almost upon the people. Since trade had been their strength, they were clearly no match for such an enemy, so as the murderers marched into one end of their settlement, they fled out the other, grabbing whatever they could as they made their way to their ships. Their vessels would have held much, but each person came with only what they could carry, and many times that was a smaller person. They were herded on board as quickly as possible, but in the confusion, many were unable to make it to the docks, and most of the villagers were being cut down by the sword and fire of their enemies. Their men of fighting age made a line against the assault, and fighting valiantly, they provided as much time as they could to allow survivors to get away. The priest ran out of the village with the book containing all the truths about El Olam. He pushed it into the hands of one of the boys in the boats, admonished him to care for it, then turned and joined our men to fight alongside them. It was said of that battle that our people were valiant. The men raged back against the destruction and saved many from the clutches of death. Some on the boats watched as husbands, fathers and brothers were chopped down where they stood. Finally, the men that remained turned and fled in the face of complete defeat, and their families rowed as they fled, pulling them onto the boat as they moved away, sails filling. Several of the boats were reached by the enemy as well, because they had waited just too long to save as many as they could. As a result, they lost many more. As they left our home, the village burned, not a building left untouched. The chapel that had stood on a hill was said to be like a beacon of flame reaching into the sky. The boats that the enemy torched sank around them, and they pulled more people onto their vessels as the few remaining boats plowed out to sea." Roald paused here, looking at the expectant faces staring in rapt attention at his tale. It was almost as if he'd been there, so many times had he heard the tale and repeated it to keep it alive.

"Go on." Evin urged, looking enraptured by the old history brought to life.

"The sounds and sights were said to have been the most horrible thing. They heard screaming people and shrieking fire and enemies shouting in victory. It was a long time before they sailed out of sight of the blazing fire, and as the sun rose, they discovered themselves to be three trading vessels left of the six that had been at the docks when the melee had begun. All were overfilled with people and lacked adequate supplies, and they drove east away from home, unsure what would happen to them. Their ships were designed for shorter trips along the coastlines of the islands they'd called home, and had seldom sailed this far. Thankfully, the sea in which they found themselves was peaceful and for a few days, they continued sailing east until a gale caught them in the night and drove their ships against the rocks west of here. One of the ships completely disappeared in the gale. Miraculously, the other two ships were badly damaged but managed to run aground close to shore, and the people on them emerged into this place." He gestured around him. "They landed in a desolate land compared to what they'd left, but in spite of the fact that they couldn't grow things the way they always had, they were able to find sustenance from the sea. Eventually some of them moved further away from the shore when a scouting party found a forest in the northeast. There, they were able to cultivate crops from the seeds they'd saved from the destruction. Those two groups thrived, and though the book proved useless to them because of the language, they held it in high esteem. They told the stories the priests had shared constantly, afraid to lose touch with the god who they came to understand had saved them. The people used the pieces of the ships they'd sailed here to establish homes for themselves on the shores along with stones in the surrounding desert. To the north, timber was adequate for the task, and so that settlement also established a strong community.

Over time, the villages grew, and began to explore more of the surrounding land. In the wilderness, the people lived on the shore and fished the surrounding waters with great success. The land was difficult, but livable, and the sea provided a wealth of resources. For what they were unable to grow they were able to trade with the forest group. The mountain pass was found, and some groups of our people poured over into these fertile valleys and rich hillsides. At the same time, the people from the other boat were found to have settled in the south. They had encountered a tribe of people already living there and had integrated with them, accepting all their practices and forgetting quickly El Olam who'd saved them. The people that were already here were nomads, and the other group adapted quickly to a new wandering lifestyle. Last I heard of them, they still move from place to place instead of settling. Tensions ran high between the southern group and our wilderness brothers. Our families to the south had forgotten god. They abandoned the worship of him for the worship of nature. The people born here had not heard of god, and their worship was very like that of our ancestors before we came to him. There was no reconciliation to be had. Our brothers had so successfully intermingled with the native tribe that they were unrecognizable, and they were hostile to any attempt to change their mind about god. If we stayed to the north, they were content to carry on in the south, so peace reigned for a time. Likewise, our people who crossed the mountain pass found native populations with which they lived peaceably and eventually intermarried. Those tribes were accepting of their loyalty to El Olam, and their worship melded together, gradually becoming something different. They were able to teach the nomadic natives the cultivation techniques our people knew and helped them settle into villages. In the west, where they'd landed first, their faith remained pure, and the stories they remembered about El Olam were told more often than across the mountains. The difficulty of traveling back and forth meant our people were separated more and more in all the ways you can imagine. It was at this point in history when the annual councils started so we could stay one. The land was divided in three districts on this side and two on the other side of the mountains, and a man set over each of them to lead each settlement. The lords of the regions still come once a year to the council, as you know, but now each is lord over many settlements. By then, our people had ceased to think about home and had made new homes here. To the west lay the small island where your mom was born, Evin, and the settlements in the wilderness and the forest, where we may find the help for which we're searching. There is a hill place in the northern wilderness that has long been called the Holy Mountain or Viberg, because there our ancestors built a vault in the stone to protect the holy book. Since it could not be read, we thought to preserve it, so it was placed in a dry vault and sealed with heavy stone doors. An intricate precious stone seal guarded the entrance. It had to be activated somehow to open the doors. There is a tale that describes the stone being given to the people by god instead of crafted." He looked at Evin. "When your mom and I were children, the people of the south grew restless and revolted against us, hoping to take what was ours. Raiding parties struck mercilessly, sometimes destroying whole settlements. Masterfully, they would strike fast and run away quickly.

They hated our insistence in worshipping El Olam, and on one of their more successful raids, they made it to the Holy Mountain. It is said that their chieftain tried for half a day to access the vault, and then in frustration, raised his sword hilt and struck the seal. Light radiated from it, and it broke into three smaller, less colorful shards." He stopped for a minute, looking straight at Evin, trying to decide what to say next, then continued. "The chieftain was still unable to get in, and after some more destruction, he and his men rode home with their latest haul, leaving the broken seal behind. The people no longer had access to the vault and the book they'd venerated. Finally, the anger of the people to the south was suppressed through negotiation and the raids stopped. It was during those raids that Evin's mom lost her family and came to live on this side of the mountains with her aunt. For some years, there was uneasy peace, and the councils continued to meet. The people here to the east of the mountains developed the law over time. They explained and taught the law to the westerners, but who knows how well that took root. It seems it has, because they drop in at counsel every year still. On this side of the mountains, many of the worship practices of the natives remained because they had never been discouraged, and many here had already forgotten the true god, even though they still worshipped him in chapels. Quietly, the leaders became intoxicated with the power of controlling the masses using the laws, which had initially been intended to give the people a framework inside of which to seek the truth of god. The only thing standing between them and total control was the priests we had placed in the chapels. They would teach the people that only god has the right to be in control, and that they were free inside of their faith in him. The priests reminded them of the promised deliverance that El Olam offered his people. Why that would be such a great threat is still beyond me. With our limited remembrance of god, our worship of him had always been difficult, so we clung with desperation to the things we knew to be true of him, and those things were not convenient to the lords of the regions. They sent our men to war against the very faith that had sustained us in our journey here, joining ranks with the enemy to the south across the mountains to ensure the destruction of every chapel we'd built and the death of every priest and anyone who was stubborn enough to stand up to their claim of absolute power. That happened the year Evin was born." Roald looked satisfied that he'd finished his history. "You know the new stuff. Remember, obey, serve. For the good of the community." He waved his hand dismissively.

"How do they manage to convince an entire country to do whatever they want?" Kai wondered. "Why don't the people just revolt against that if they have a problem following the rules? I mean, I know I haven't followed them exactly, but if they'd continued to work for me, I might not have ever questioned them."

"That's the key, I think." Roald said. "Initially, living within the laws was easy because they were made to ensure safety and freedom, but when our leaders discovered they could amend them and use them to become wealthy and build their own armies, then they began to become oppressive. Larger quotas are insisted on and more and more sons are required for service. I think it has been so gradual that the people have become used to providing much of what they have 'for the good of the community' as they are told. They are even encouraged to be proud of their contribution."

Kai thought about it for a minute. "I still feel like there's more to it, though," he concluded.

"What about the people over the mountain? Do they have the same laws?" Evin was curious to learn if Fjall would have different expectations of them.

"Now, we only hear from the region over the mountains at council once a year. We assume they also lost their chapels and got new priests. Fjall hasn't changed in my lifetime. I know this because occasionally some fool boy picks the chapel at Fjall for his wedding, and I've been there a few times as a guide for Diederick when he goes to council." He smiled at Evin, who was staring thoughtfully into the fire. "We have to go past there to find out if there's anyone left there to help us." Roald let the last part sneak in, hoping to get away with finally getting to the point Inkeri was waiting for and saying so little.

Inkeri stood and busied herself stirring the stew she had boiling in the pot. "So," she drew her words out like she was deciding how to ask her question. "What you're saying is that after a stop at Fjall, Evin and I are going over the mountains where almost no one ever goes so that Evin can look for other people who believe in a god that I've never heard him claim to believe in himself? So, little of this has to do with our wedding."

The group sat quietly for a minute, then Roald looked at Evin. "I think he should answer that."

Evin looked up at Inkeri, standing and pretending to still be interested in the food. "I didn't choose to go to Fjall." He watched her face carefully, but only saw a slight rise in her eyebrows, so he continued. He related his mom's story about leaving her home and how she'd insisted he go to Fjall to find help. "I definitely intend for the time at the chapel to be about our wedding." She still stared into the pot, her expression unchanged.

Kai asked the question Evin was sure Inkeri was thinking. "What made your mom think you're the one to go and do that, and why in the hell would she drag her into it?" He pointed at Inkeri.

Evin shrugged slightly, as though he really didn't understand that part himself. "I don't know what to believe about all of this. Inkeri is right to say I don't know how to feel about the sacrificed son Roald was telling us about, but I've heard the stories of El Olam since I was little, and they are remarkable. Also, apparently I was born grasping a shard that I assume must belong to the seal in Roald's story. Then there's the matter of the dream I had that somehow crossed over into reality. Obviously, something outside the normal is happening."

"What?" Kai looked more than incredulous. "You were born with a shard of a seal in your hand? Who told you that?"

"Both Roald and my mom told me the story at different times." He shrugged again. "Of course, I don't have proof of that, but I do have the shard."

"And Inkeri? Why is she here?" Kai reminded Evin.

This was the hard part he wasn't ready for. He thought of brushing it off as coincidence, but he knew neither Kai nor Inkeri would go for that. "Apparently, my life is in danger, and my handfasting is the best way to sneak me out of my village safely." He said it quietly, and you could tell from the tone of his voice that he was still experiencing raw emotions about it. He felt a weight lift off his shoulders with the confession. He walked to Inkeri, who hadn't changed her countenance at all, but had stopped stirring the food. He reached out and lifted her chin with his fingers, until she was looking him in the eye. Then quietly, as if to her alone, he said, "Inkeri, I want you to know I knew nothing of this until the day before we ran into Kai. When I found out, I was angry, and I wanted to take you home, but that wouldn't have worked for so many reasons." She just stared at him, so he continued. "I just realized how much I really want you here, but I promise you that I will not hold you to our marriage if you choose not to go through with the ceremony. That will be your choice." He dropped his hand to his side. Feeling awkward, he looked down at the food.

Inkeri leaned in to get a stick and moved the pot off the flames to a place where it could cool a little to be served, and as she leaned close to Evin, she whispered for only him to hear. "Thank you, Evin."

He was dismayed, thinking perhaps she was being sarcastic, but when he looked at her, he could see tears threatening to spill over her eyelids and he realized she truly was grateful for something. Was it because he'd told her the truth? Was it because he was giving her a choice whether to stay with him? He just nodded at her, unsure if she even saw and moved to sit back where he'd been.

Kai adjusted himself painfully and Inkeri handed him a wooden cup full of the stew she had been cooking. He thanked her and looked back and forth between Evin and Roald. "Well, this saga just keeps getting more interesting. I think you could have maybe told the people you're traveling with that you're in mortal danger, especially if any of that extended to us as a result."

"It doesn't, Kai. They're after me, not you." He tried to keep his irritation at being questioned out of his voice.

"Well, this is a fine mess." Kai spooned the hot liquid into his mouth and stared at Evin.

Roald interrupted. "It is fine, Kai. You should finish that and rest. We need to get you back in riding condition so we can get underway. We have a meeting to get to."

Kai sat the cup down and stood carefully. "I'm going to that meeting with you, Roald, and that's where I'm going to decide which side of this I'm on." He turned and strode to the cot and lowered himself back on it.

Roald looked at Evin. "That was brave. I'm glad you decided to do the right thing."

"I'm not sure what the right thing is, Roald. I'm here and I'm going to stay for now. Kai's right. This is a fine mess." Without eating, he stood and walked into the trees.

Chapter 14

He wandered aimlessly, not really wanting anything but peace. He walked through the glade, drawn to the top of the hill, where the trees looked different. When he reached them, he realized the conifer dominated landscape gave way at the crest of the hill to a perfect circle of straight, beautiful aspens. He stepped into the center, looking out the circle at the top into a solid blue sky. He was glad the sun dominated the sky today. He sat down at the base of one of the aspens and continued to stare into the sky. He felt slightly dizzy, so he closed his eyes and kept his head back. He drifted off, but in a minute something awakened him. He was very puzzled at first, but then realized he was hearing a newborn baby crying. He leapt to his feet and looked around frantically, aware that there were many dangers for a baby out here. When he turned back to face the center of the glade, he saw a man standing there. The man moved back and forth and gazed into his arms with interest. Evin rushed over, and looked as well, relieved to see the infant in the man's arms. "Oh, I was worried."

The man looked up, unsurprised. "Hi Evin. I have a gift to give him. He's going to need it when he's older. Will you help me?"

Evin was caught off guard at the use of his name, so he looked more closely at the man. He was the same man who'd tried to give him the cup. This time he was dressed in fine clothes. These were not the clothes of a warrior, but instead the clothes of a very wealthy king.

"I think I need to leave." Evin turned to walk away.

"You need to stop running, Evin." The man's voice was kind and calm.

Evin wheeled around, incredulous. "Maybe you need to stop chasing me!"

"You asked for answers. I'm here to provide them." He seemed unfazed by Evin's attitude. "Here." He reached out his hand to Evin, beckoning him to take something from him.

Evin didn't make a move. "Is this going to be like last time? That was quite painful."

"Also, quite sweet. A lot like life." The man smiled with a little sadness in his eyes.

"Oh, why not." Evin leaned forward and let the man drop something in his hand.

"It is one of three. From an object uncrafted." The king watched as Evin uncurled his fingers and gazed at the shard.

"I already have this one." Evin stated, trying to appear unfazed. "Do you know where the other shard is?" Evin asked. "I'm going to need it, I think."

"Yes, definitely you are." He smiled again. "Your father has it. He'll give it to you in time. This one's not for now." He pointed to the baby. "It's for then so you can know beyond doubt." Evin looked carefully at the baby now resting quietly in the man's arms. "Give it to him."

Evin looked confused. Surmising that the baby was meant to be him, he said, "What of time? I am here and I can't also be there." He pointed to the child.

"What is time to the everlasting God, Evin?"

Evin shrugged, and smiling in disbelief to himself, moved closer to the sleeping baby. He raised the child's right fist and looked his arm over carefully. As he expected, a distinctive birthmark stood out on the baby's forearm. He looked at the man and found him studying him. He pushed the tiny fingers aside and seated the small fragment in the little one's fist, carefully closing the sleeping fingers. Then he shook his head slowly and gazed upon himself seventeen years ago. He knew he was dreaming. He would be left with no sign that this had been anything more than that, he was sure, and it was fascinating to imagine, so he didn't fight it.

"Time to give him to his mother." The man turned and walked to a basket on the ground, bent and placed the baby within it. Another one appeared next to it, and the man came to stand beside him again, this time holding an older baby. The child lay completely still in his arms, and at first, Evin thought it might be sleeping, but soon realized that the child was either extraordinarily ill or already dead.

"Gods," he exclaimed, "Do something!"

"The gods can truly do nothing, Evin."

"I didn't mean... forget it, you already knew that. Can you do something?"

"Do you believe I can do something?" The man stared at Evin.

Evin narrowed his eyes at the weird question. He looked closely at the little one; the face was beautiful, feminine. She looked like she'd been dropped from heaven. Her cheeks were red, and she moved listlessly as though in pain. She looked familiar. He looked back to the warrior king. "I don't know you. If I knew who you were, I would know whether I thought you could save her." He touched her cherubic cheek and discovered it to be burning hot. "She's going to die if you don't help her." He made a decision and looked back to the man's face. "I believe you can heal her. Please help her. Help me believe!"

The man smiled. His dark eyes crinkled into the most genuine smile Evin had ever seen. "You remind me of someone else." He said. Then he lay his hand across the child's chest, and lifting his eyes heavenward whispered something indiscernible over her. "There is a much more important healing every man needs," he admonished Evin. Immediately, the child's eyes fluttered open, and she looked at Evin and then at the man holding her. Her eyes were the most striking icy blue. She frowned but didn't cry about her unusual circumstances.

Suddenly, recognition dawned on Evin. "Inkeri?" He looked closely at her, lifting the edge of the blanket, where embroidered pink roses stretched in beautiful rows. She reached and grabbed the edge of the blanket from his hand and began playing with the delicate row of flowers. He peered at the man suspiciously. "El Olam?"

"I'm his son, and him. I came to be the healer." Evin wrinkled his brow in confusion at this idea, and before he could decide for sure the baby was Inkeri, the man stated, "Time to give her back to her family." He walked again to the baskets, and as he placed her in her basket, another appeared. Evin craned his neck to try to see a baby appear inside but saw nothing. The man raised up again and brought a third little one to Evin. This one was smaller than the others. He handed the child to Evin. He'd only ever held Gunnar's son before holding this baby. He looked the tiny boy over carefully, noting a bright red birthmark atop one of his toes. The child slept peacefully, making an occasional jerking movement each time Evin moved. "He's almost ready to meet his mom, but I'm keeping him a little while longer." The man watched Evin hold the baby for a few minutes, then took him back and smiled. I knew you'd like to meet him. He put the baby back and no more appeared.

He straightened up once more beside Evin and they looked at one another.

Then he turned and sat something on the ground before he walked away. "Can you drink it, Evin?"

There on the ground sat the goblet he'd seen before, and he promptly spun and ran away from it, tripping over a stone and sprawling headlong into the clearing, where things seemed to shift and wave back to reality. He stood and brushed off his clothes. Then, checking that the pouch was still where it belonged, he ambled back to camp.

Chapter 15

Evin was ravenous when he re-entered the camp and was thrilled to find that someone had put the rest of the stew in a cup for him and sat it on a rock. Inkeri stepped from the tent followed shortly by Roald. "We helped Kai get in there. Tomorrow, we'll change those bandages and see how he's doing. Now he should be able to rest all night," Roald informed him.

"Did you have a nice walk?" Inkeri asked expectantly.

"Very nice," he stated. "Interesting." He picked up the cup and sat on the rock where it had rested and began eating too quickly. The sunset cast beautiful colors across the sky behind the trees, causing a breathtaking display of beauty. "The Healer is also an artist."

Roald looked at him. "What did you say?" He crinkled his brow in Evin's direction.

"Well, we're not hiding anything from each other anymore, right? I'm fairly sure I talked to El Olam in the aspens, or his son. I think he seems like the kind of guy that would love to make beautiful things."

Inkeri looked concerned. "Did you find mushrooms in the aspens? This is the right time of year for them."

Evin looked disappointed. "No, Inkeri. I certainly did not find any mushrooms. I just sat down for a minute, and I guess I fell asleep. Probably just a dream, of course. It seemed really real."

Roald just stood looking at Evin. "By the gods, Evin. What is going on with you? I don't think you could stand face to face with El Olam and be this nonchalant about it."

"I'm not nonchalant about it, Roald. I feel insane inside. I've decided it was just a dream. See, there's nothing on me I brought back from the other side this time." He gestured at his chest. "The best thing I can do is just be calm. If this is going to keep happening, I'm going to have to make a decision not to act maniacal about it."

"What happened in there?" Roald asked.

"Well, I gave baby Evin the shard of the seal that was in my hand when I was born. Then, there was a baby that looked like Inkeri, only this one was really sick. She had a raging fever and was super listless, like she was in pain, but he healed her. He told me he came to be the healer, so I'm going to call him that."

Inkeri looked at him sharply. "Did you say she looked like me, but a little baby?"

"Not exactly a little baby. I'd say a little under two summers. Then I held another baby. The Healer said he was keeping that one for just a little bit longer, but he knew I'd want to meet him. Don't you think that's the craziest thing you've ever heard? I think this whole experience is just making me insane."

"I'm not so sure." Inkeri said. "That actually happened to me when I was a child. I had a dreadful fever and I was only getting worse and not better. My mom liked to tell the story, so I've heard it often. She said I was so sick one night she thought for sure I would die, so she sat up with me and begged every god she'd ever heard of to save me. I would assume since she was alive before the chapels were torn down that list would have included El Olam. I was the only child she'd been able to have for some reason she never told me, so she was terrified to lose me. She said near morning, my fever just melted away and I sat up and opened my eyes and looked around like I was looking at something a little scary. She said I wasn't seeing her at all, and she thought it was something from my fever. Then she said I looked at the hem of my blanket and started playing with the little pink roses she'd embroidered there, then looked at her and smiled. She said the pink roses were my favorite from that time on."

Evin just stared at Inkeri, and the color faded from his face. He remembered the little girl in his vision taking the blanket from his hand just as she'd described. He had brought something back from the dream. This time a memory that belonged to someone else had traveled away with him from the vision. He'd been there when his future wife had almost died, and he'd watched her be healed by this man who kept asking for his allegiance. He continued to look at the beautiful young woman standing before him. In his mind's eye, he saw her going about all the tasks she had for the weeks he'd known her. She was patient, gentle, and smart. She provided a peace and a comfort that this mission desperately needed. He was immediately filled with this incredible debt of gratitude to the Healer for preserving her life. The gratitude helped, but he was still shaken by the irregularity of the experience. "Inkeri, I'm the one who handed you the edge of the blanket. Rather, you grabbed it out of my hand. God knew we needed you here. It's not just a scheme that brought you here, but he intended for you to be here." Evin was filled with conviction as he spoke the words out loud. She wasn't just a pawn in some story that didn't involve her. They needed her, but they just didn't know it yet. She just looked at him impassively. He told them exactly what he'd seen when he was with her in the vision, and it lined up exactly with the story she had told. The three of them just stood together for a time, taking in the implications of what was happening to Evin, then they settled around the fire and told each other what they knew of El Olam.

Roald had the most to say, telling them story after story of remarkable events he had witnessed in his days that always pointed to the work of god in his life and in that of others. He told of Evin's grandfather, and how much he had loved El Olam. For the first time, Evin was able to hear in detail some of what his mom's life was like when she was a child. For the first time he learned that she and Roald had grown side-by-side in the seaside village of her youth. Roald had hidden during the raid and found his way to the same chapel as Sanna when he'd emerged to find the village destroyed. "I think you're like your grandfather, Evin. He was considered a prophet among the villagers where we lived. It was as if he had dinner with god every night or something. People joked that he spent more time with El Olam than with us. He knew the stories about him better than anyone I'd ever heard tell them. People said all kinds of things about your grandfather. One of them was that he was descended from the boy who had been given the book as we were driven away from our homeland. He certainly did his part to keep it alive in our village." Roald watched Evin carefully as he spoke, noting as his face moved through the various emotions that he was experiencing. He knew he still had a lot to share with this young man in time, and he thanked god as he watched him soften Evin's heart and make him receptive to the truths he'd only been allowed to hear in small doses as he grew.

"You have said to me that you don't know how I know so much of your family, Evin, but I have been around. You just don't remember. Do you remember the trip to the sea that you went on with your dad? Certain elders of your village and others were chosen to go and investigate whether a sea passage would be possible between the east and the west of our country because the passage over the mountains is difficult. The south is dangerous because of the lawless ones, so they thought maybe the sea to the north would provide the sought-after passage. I was chosen by your dad to be one of the guides. We discovered the sea to be the home of a mountain of floating ice, and it was decided to be too dangerous to go near in our vessels, because of the danger of running aground on some invisible part of it. Going around it would take more time and resources than continuing over the mountain."

"I do remember parts of that trip." Evin interjected. "The color of the iceberg was one I'll never forget." He gestured toward Inkeri. "It's the same as her eyes."

"Yes, you and I didn't interact much, but I remember how awed you were at that iceberg. Everyone there was amused at your amazement."

Evin smiled at the memory. "It was astonishing."

"So, who was the third baby, if the first was you and the second was me?" Inkeri wondered.

"Well, it seemed like he wasn't born yet? The Healer said he wasn't ready to meet his mom." Evin looked thoughtful.

"Maybe Kai and Alia's baby?" Inkeri wondered. "Why would you want to meet him?"

Evin shrugged. "I'm learning not a whole lot is going to immediately make sense right now."

Roald laughed. "Look at him growing up in front of our eyes." He beamed at Evin, who smiled back at him. It was the first time since Roald had shared the truth with Evin about his betrothal that he'd spared a smile for the older man.

Evin looked away and stared at the ground, basking in the silence around them. They had sat until well after the sunset, and now the sounds of crickets and frogs surrounded them, and the stars stood out in bold relief against the ink black sky. The moon was new, making no appearance, and light from the fire played across the camp like a million sprites. Evin thought of the reverence for nature that he'd grown up seeing in his neighbors and friends, and even his father. The beliefs he now understood had been a part of this land for all the time humans had walked here. Ancient and unyielding, the faith of these people was in their landscape and in themselves. They believed there was a god for everything, and they worshipped in the open fields or in a copse of trees like the one where they were currently camped. His ancestors had come from afar and brought another faith, but instead of supplanting the former, at least on this side of the mountains, it had merely become a part of what had always been here, somehow losing its power in the process. Also, men had begun to use the washed-out power of the combined religion to control the people they had been given lordship over, claiming what suited them best from each. Evin began to see that to leave these people in this state without hope would be wrong. A system that seeks to control the people who walk in it isn't better if it claims the reason for that is any god. Still, aside from Kai and Alia's story, he was too unaware of the true plight of the people to understand why so many were discontent with living the way they were. He realized, though, there must be more to the story than he knew right now, and he was learning to be more patient while he waited for the answers. He thought of his mother, glad now that she had told him the stories she knew of El Olam, but he began to see how the training even she had experienced had been woefully inadequate because of the circumstances that brought them to this place. They were a people without complete truth, and without roots. The roots made him think of the worship of the people born here that had in some ways become all of theirs over time. He knew the gods that were responsible for everything from fertility to night. He knew there was evil to be blamed for the chaos that sometimes happened in nature and through illness. He had long considered this god his mother worshipped as another one of those gods, but he was coming to understand that there was more to this story than he'd been allowed to see before. There was definitely something different to be said about this god, or there wouldn't be any reason to squash the worship of him among the other gods. He stood and stretched to the sky, and he remembered doing the same in a ritual dance just over three weeks ago as he beseeched the goddess to grant him and Inkeri a long and fruitful marriage. Now, he stayed in the pose, stretched to the heavens, and realized that there wasn't even a goddess to speak to. The god that could indeed work wonders was there but largely unknown to him. He imagined reaching for him and thanked him silently for the direction he was being given to help him find the truth. Then he relaxed and headed toward the tents, leaving the others staring into the fire.

Chapter 16

Four days of watching and tending Kai's wounds passed before it became evident that they would heal without further issues. He would forever be marked with the memories in the form of large unsightly scars, but all of them cut straight across and none were in joints where they may have caused him mobility issues. He'd been able to spend much more time working with the others without pain, and finally it felt safe to move on. It was with a heavy heart he had to move further away from Alia, but he knew he could never go back. Instead, he would have to wait patiently for freedom to pave the way for him to come back to her.

They set out in the early morning of the fifth day. The company didn't have too far to go to the meeting place Roald had designated, but they set up a camp nearby before they rode to it because he expected the meeting to go late into the night. He'd ridden out a few times to talk to contacts and determine the best time and place for a gathering. He explained to the trio that they would meet several of the people who had been close followers of El Olam who had been forced to move their faith completely out of sight as the laws had been made to suppress their worship. They would be able to hear their stories and determine for themselves if they believed the plight of these villagers warranted their help and if so, what would be the best way to accomplish that. They rode due west, into the foothills of the looming mountains, marveling at the way the mountains began to fold into secluded valleys at the base. One after the other, they provided perfect hiding places, especially when no one was looking for you. Their camp was in a beautiful glade near a large stream, ready to come back to later in the night, but without fire. Evin marveled at Roald's navigation skills. He imagined that if he had to find the way back there, he would be lost forever. They rode even further into the forest, weaving back and forth several times until they reached a large clearing where several people already milled around. They joined the people they found there in gathering a pile of firewood. "Won't we be likely to be found out if we have a fire?" Evin wondered aloud.

"No." Roald bent to grab more dry branches from the ground. "We are so far from any settlement that it is very unlikely we will be seen, especially since we will take care with the size of the fire. If anyone did happen to see it, they would assume it was in worship of one of the gods. If they decided to investigate, we would offer them a drink." He winked and smiled, continuing with his work.

"What is that supposed to mean?" Evin looked flabbergasted.

"I'm going to assume he means we'd offer them a goblet laced with these, among other things." Inkeri bent and pointed at a leafy dark green plant growing at the edge of the glade. "If you know what you're doing, the person you offer it to isn't going to remember anything in the morning."

"Oh, gods! That is diabolical! Who would do such a thing!"

Roald laughed. "Well, I've never had to do that, but a few of our people, like Inkeri apparently, are well trained in the uses of the plants and what they can be used to accomplish. It's good she had that knowledge to help Kai. Besides, it's a better idea than killing them, because that would raise too much suspicion."

"Well, and they'd be dead." Evin stated.

"Yeah, and there's that." Roald grinned again and walked off to carry his bundle to the waiting area. Evin shook his head, finished gathering, and followed him. Over the course of the next couple of hours, more and more people appeared until at least forty were packed together in the clearing.

Evin, Kai, and Inkeri stood at the edge of the crowd watching as the people came together. "What could have brought all of these people?" Kai queried.

"Do you think they are all just people who didn't want to live under the law and thought their own way was better?" Evin asked the question innocently enough, reverting to his life-long understanding of the goodness of the law.

Kai turned to him and narrowed his eyes. "What does that mean?"

Evin looked into Kai's angry eyes. "I don't know. I only know your story, and I know I can't completely understand everything you've gone through, but it seems to me like everything would have gone much smoother for Alia and her family if you'd followed the edicts that were handed down for you."

"I thought we were through with this, Evin." Kai growled, turning to face him, looking menacing. Inkeri watched with big eyes. He moved until he was mere inches from the shorter young man and bent until they were almost nose to nose.

Evin stood his ground. "I'm tired of you belittling decisions that I had to make under pressure you have never felt. I will not apologize for my marriage that you consider illegal. I will not apologize for my child that you consider illegitimate. I will not apologize for my freedom that you apparently consider ill-advised." He stabbed his finger roughly into Evin's forehead, moving him backward a few inches. "Today, I am here to preserve everything about me that you hate, and if you're going to continue to think like this, you and I are only going to be enemies."

Evin held up his hands, recognizing too late he had hit a nerve. "Look, Kai. I said I don't understand, ok. I'm trying, here, but I can only see things the way they have always been for my whole life."

Kai lowered his hand but continued to glower at Evin. "Your whole life is an unbelievably short time, Evin," he sneered. "You barely even have experience being alive, so don't push that nonsense on me."

Roald approached and Kai turned away from Evin, still fuming. "What's going on here?" He looked back and forth at the two of them but neither offered an explanation. "This isn't the right place for this. We'll talk about it later. Evin, you come with me. I need to introduce you and then I'm going to let them tell their stories. Kai, you and Inkeri come and stand with me."

Kai looked disgusted but followed with Inkeri at his heels.

Roald gave the waiting group a brief synopsis of Evin's life so far and the journey that brought him here, then said finally, "I need him to hear what you have to say. He has grown up with knowledge but without understanding. We must help him understand our plight. We must come together to impart to him the wisdom god has given us." He paused here, watching their faces. "We must do this for Evin, because as I have already mentioned to as many of you as I have seen, and as you have no doubt shared, his life is in danger. I had hoped you'd gather to help me protect him and you did. What you do not yet know, but might have suspected by my urgency, is that Evin was born with a shard of the seal in his hand." At this declaration, the crowd erupted into questions and moved in closer, jockeying to try to see the young man. It was some time before Roald was able to calm the crowd and get them settled into a pseudo peace. It was as if the air was buzzing. Roald called forward one man after another to tell his tale. Each told of some way the law had been used against him and his family, creating a devastating tapestry of what life looked like when you didn't walk the line exactly the way it had been scribed. Evin could feel dismay rising in him as he realized the black and white thing he'd made of obedience and disobedience was not a reality. He still felt himself struggling to hold on to his preconceived notions, because they were the last comfortable thing he had left, having let go of all his expectations for his own life.

A man told of his mother, who had been beaten to death because she had shared her food with a family who had been accused of the worship of El Olam. The village had been told to leave them on the street to die after everything they had was taken away. His mom had been unable to watch them starve to death, but when she'd offered them food, someone had turned her in. One of the guards beat her in the usual fashion, with the same kind of whips that had been used on Kai, but she was much older and endured more lashes. She was unable to survive the aftermath. She had been widowed, and her death represented a line that had been crossed. In time past, the whips would have never been used on a woman, much less an older one, but because there was no man to take the blame, she bore the full brunt of Lord Arne's anger. The son had been away when the offense had occurred and punishment had been meted out, and he returned to hear the story from terrified neighbors. He was understandably incensed, and his anger rose as he spoke, the story less than half a year old. "I watched in terror with the rest of our village as that family died one by one. The guards prevented them leaving and prevented us helping." When he finished, he was trembling. Evin glanced at Kai to find his visage mirrored that of the man. Evin realized that Arne would be the lord under whom Kai would be forced to serve. He realized that he would be forced to enforce all this lunatic man's ridiculous punishments on his people. His eyes were opened to the fact that there was much more Kai had to consider than just whether to submit to be a soldier in a peaceful country for the rest of his life. While that was already daunting, he would also face being put in a position to mercilessly punish the people he longed to walk among as one of their own. He sat in the middle of the gathered assembly, exhausted and saddened by their stories. There was in his own country a group of people needing rescue and they thought him the rescuer. He sat cross-legged, having long ago sank into a seated position. Now, he nearly bent double with his head resting on his lap. His face was safely hidden from the assembly while he listened, so that he wasn't worrying about what these people were thinking of him, but instead just concentrating on what they were saying. He felt an abject sense of ineptitude and unworthiness as more stories flowed forth. He could not be some sort of savior for them.

"Everlasting god. Healer." he whispered into his legs. Over and over, he whispered the only names he had for the one who was calling him to this. Finally, he switched his mantra. "Please help me." He began to rock slowly back and forth, losing any sense of time as the stories continued, and then silence. He sat still for as long as he dared, and then, afraid they might think he was asleep; he stretched his back straight and looked around. Dozens of pairs of eyes stared at him full of questions. Crickets and frogs provided the only noise for a couple of minutes as Evin wondered what was next. Roald stood off to the side of him, hands hanging clasped in front of him, and head bowed. He didn't move, and his eyes were closed. Evin began to panic, thinking that perhaps the next move was supposed to be his. Into his uncertainty stepped an old man, perhaps the oldest Evin had ever seen.

He raised his hands and began to speak. "Ours is a tale new and old." he said.

The gathered men answered. "How new, and how old?"

"We are newly thrown together here, far from home and family. We are an ancient people with ancient stories. Will the generations forget them?" the old man replied. Evin realized these must be old words, from when they first found this home.

"Thrown together and all alone. Our village is gone. Our people are gone. Where are we?" the men began to sway as one, hands clasped in front of them in the same manner that Roald's were. Evin settled back on his heels and watched with wonder as he seemed to disappear from their memory. Peace settled on him as he listened to the ancient words.

"Far from home, nothing to go back to. Who will rescue us?" the man's voice sounded reverent.

"The King of Glory!" The men's voices rose, coming close to a shout.

"Who is this King of Glory?"

"The LORD, strong and mighty, the LORD, mighty in battle! The LORD of hosts, he is the King of glory!" All of them shouted in unison, and then a hush fell over the group again.

The old man's voice once more issued forth into the glade. "Who sees our misery? Who watches as we wait for our rescue?"

The answer came, more subdued, full circle. "He is the King of Glory. He is El Olam. He will send a rescuer."

Silence settled with the words, and all motion ceased. For the first time, Evin heard where the name had come from, used in words that had apparently been repeated for generations. El Olam, he thought, and as the words came into his mind, he felt a rush like a refreshing wind lift his spirit. He felt jubilant and something akin to powerful. He felt a long sigh escape his lips, like his soul was releasing a great burden, and for the first time since he'd become aware of his purpose, he felt capable. The feeling was such a powerful rush, that he held still, letting it settle over him, afraid the slightest movement would bring him back to reality.

The old man continued. "Long years, we've cried out as we become fewer. Now these remain who remember. Who will rise up to rescue us?" This time there was no answer. "Who will rise to preserve the truth? Who will rise to crush our oppressors?" Still not a sound from the group. The old man's voice changed tone.

> "We are beaten.
> We are defeated.
> Day and night, our enemy laughs at us.
> They scorn us everywhere we turn.
> They lay on us a joyless burden.
> They lace it with joy and present it as a gift,
> and more and more take it and forget.
> Let us not forget, El Olam!
> Rescue us! Rescue us! Remind us!"

The man's hands were still aloft, reaching far into the night sky. The hands of the others in the assembly now rose in a similar fashion, and Evin squeezed his eyes shut, suddenly feeling like he was in the middle of a private conversation, unsure what to do.

"The seal of our fathers protected us.
We worshipped in peace.
We came to the holy mountain.
We could not read the words.
We didn't even try.
We settled on the shores.
We caught the fish.
We camped among the groves and planted seeds.
We built houses, strong and mighty.
We built houses to god, and houses for ourselves.
The seal remained in place, miracle of the wasteland,
Guarding our secrets, holding the truth until we could discern it.
Dark night arose.
The sword shattered the seal.
Dark night settles, and only shards remain.
We cannot worship our god!
We're forgetting his face!"

The men whispered, "Only shards remain."
The old man continued,
"From the west, a young girl comes, broken pieces in her hand.
The seal is shattered to three, broken shards remain.
One with priest, one with warrior, one unseen."

"Where will the third be found?" The men ask in unison.
"In a baby's hand, the shard will be revealed." The old man answered.
"Who will make the three pieces one?"

Evin knew the answer before he heard it uttered, and he suddenly couldn't handle the weight of the glory he'd been basking in while he listened. The energy-filled rush was too strong, and he felt himself moving, perhaps trying to escape.

"The baby grown into a man will reunite the shards to one.
The man will seek them.
He will fuse them.
He will make them one."

The men around him took up the verse.

"He will bring truth that will destroy our enemies.
His words will ring true.
He will reestablish peace.
He will lead us home."

As suddenly as it had begun, the prophecy was over, and Evin opened his eyes. He was standing in the place where he'd been sitting, in the center of the glade, surrounded by the small company of mostly older men. These men had seen the demise they whispered about but had so far been powerless to stem the tide of the oppressive darkness. These were, according to the verses they'd spoken, the last of the people who were desperately trying to remember a god their ancestors had learned about on a distant shore. They had for a time had a book about him that they could not read, and when they were on the cusp of hearing the truth of it, the only people who could decipher it had been killed. He began to see the reasons for their desperation and the familiar powerlessness he'd lived underneath for days returned. One by one, the people left, melting into the woods to return to their homes and camps before the light did. The fire was extinguished and the four of them moved back to their camp in the same manner, heavy with the stories of the night and the responsibility that none of them felt equal to. In addition, the recent tension between Kai and Evin threatened their peace. They didn't talk, but instead settled into a blessedly uninterrupted sleep.

chapter 17

Roald looked menacing when they stepped from the tent the next morning. Inkeri excused herself to go about readying the camp for the day, but Kai and Evin understood the scowl on Roald's face was meant for them. "When I sat out on this job, I knew it wasn't going to be easy. I knew I was going to be doling out some shocking news and making some tough decisions, but one thing I did not know." Roald lowered his brows, looking angrier if possible. "I lay awake half the night thinking about all of the names I could call the two of you for being willing to let your little feud get in the way of everything we need to accomplish to save some of these people's lives. Some of them will be discovered and murdered while you boys push each other around. I haven't been over those mountains since I was a boy myself, and none of us know what to expect. We will come to Fjall quickly, but we must go beyond that and that's almost unknown territory. We're going to need to be focused." His eyes bored into Kai. "Kai, I know that Evin is young. I know that he's going to be making decisions that are going to impact a lot of people, and I know he isn't ready for that, but I think you're smart enough to be able to see at this point that he has been called to this and he needs our support to even have a chance to accomplish any of it." He looked at Evin. "Evin, I know that you heard enough last night to convince you that the laws aren't what you thought they were. It's time to start seeing them for what they are and stop holding Kai to some standard that shouldn't exist." A fire played in his eyes that neither one of them had seen before. "Since I was a young man like you," he jabbed his finger into his palm, "I have given everything to work for this goal. I have worked for this moment in history. This is the one chance we have to see anything change for these people. It is too late for me to have what I wanted in my youth, but I will keep putting one foot in front of the other to help. I expect the same from the two of you. Let go of the foolish idea that this is about you alone and move on."

Kai did a good job of mirroring Roald's anger. His voice was loud. "I didn't ask for any of this. I just happen to have survived long enough to be an asset to your ploy. I believe in what you're trying to do, but it is absolutely about me for me. I have a responsibility to Alia to get back to her as quickly as I can, and I am decidedly through with him" he pointed angrily at Evin, "acting as if none of the decisions I made had any merit just because they go against the law that, if I'm understanding correctly, he's supposed to be in charge of destroying."

"Forgive me for being given one understanding for my entire life, and then being whipped around in an instant and expected to have a different opinion. You have already pointed out more than once that my whole life is so much shorter than the one you've lived, even though you must only have two summers on me. In addition to all of that, I have to at least pretend to walk perfectly inside of what the law has laid out for me, while you traipse around ignoring all of it." Evin clenched his fists, trying to remember the things he'd realized the evening before.

"Is it jealousy that you're holding on to, Evin?" Kai tilted his head and stared at Evin. "Are you jealous of the fact that Alia and I chose to be together and that we have something personal to fight for?"

Evin's hands unclasped, and he stood thinking for a minute. "I won't lie. I think that if I had some reason to be more connected personally to this mission, it might make more sense. As guilty as I am of downplaying your right to fight for your relationship, you are just as guilty of pretending I don't have anything at stake. Yes, I've been thrust into this, but I'm starting to see that it isn't right to leave people like this, and if god chooses to use me to work out the solution, I'm willing to do that."

"Oh, it's so brave of you to be willing to be the hero. This isn't like running through a field of poppies, Evin. My aunt disappeared from my life when I was too little to remember her because she clung to this god whose name you throw around like it's a normal, everyday utterance. You know what it is, Evin? A dangerous game! You need to learn to keep your mouth shut and stay inside the lines you love so much for the moment and see this for what it really is." He gestured around them wildly. "There are some really bad guys here who want to control everything for their own benefit, and we're trying to find an army to help us go against them. That means a fight, Evin, with real weapons and real death and your head is in the clouds. You are completely unprepared for anything like that. What do you think you're going to do, plow over them?"

Roald stepped forward. "That's not fair, Kai. Evin has been dedicating time every day to getting better with his weapons. He's good with them, a natural. He's right, too, that he was flung into this rather suddenly, and that he has to worry about Inkeri and the impact this is all having on her." Roald stole a glance at the fire where Inkeri was bent over working on something and pretending not to listen. "You might think nothing of the part that god has to play in this, but that is the most important thing Evin has to figure out right now. He hasn't said anything to endanger us."

"Believing in El Olam is dangerous, Roald." Kai pushed back. "I'm here, and I'm going to stay, but I am not convinced that letting go of one controlling idea and grabbing hold of another one is the way to free anyone."

"Surrendering control is the only way to be free." Roald's voice had lost its angry edge.

Kai laughed out loud. "That is the most ridiculous thing anyone has ever said."

"Regardless of how you think it sounds, you will come to see the truth of it in time, I believe." Roald looked at the pair of them for a moment, taking in the looks on their faces and their proud bearings. "I know that god has brought this group together for a reason. Kai, you might not even believe he exists, but that doesn't matter. Evin, you might only have an inkling of the power that he has. Still, despite these differences, we must work on becoming united in our belief that now is the time for things to change. That has to start here. You both need to change the way you think about one another and learn to work together. There is the potential for the two of you to use your strengths to build a great foundation for the changes that need to happen here. Can we move forward and concentrate on the job at hand for now?"

Kai shrugged. "I'm here, aren't I? I don't intend to leave, and I'd love nothing more than to make quick work of this."

Evin nodded. "I can agree to stop focusing on your faults. I apologize for belittling your choices. I didn't understand the full scope of them until last night."

"Good." Roald spun and started to walk off to care for the horses. "We have some plans to make. Start packing stuff up. We move on today."

That night another campfire provided a space to talk, and Roald spent more time telling them the stories he remembered about god. Inkeri especially had questions, having never heard any of the tales the other two had at least heard about. He explained that god was in three parts, but one, like the seal, only unbroken. El Olam, aware fully of the plight of his people and ready to step into history to rescue them. His son walked the earth to somehow effect that rescue. The third part is in communication with our spirits, to bring the truth. "Important parts are missing, I'm sure of it, but we have worshipped him as we were taught, and he has never failed to meet us where we are. In time, we will know all we need to know about him. Right now, we just have to survive long enough."

The next day, the group wound through the hill country, passing back through the town where they'd stayed with Alia's family, and that evening once more occupying their small room at the inn before moving away from civilization for the mountain pass. At the top they expected to find Fjall and the chapel where Evin and Inkeri were supposed to be headed to complete their marriage ceremony and begin their training in the laws. That process had begun to take on a whole new meaning as they had wrestled with whether it was being used to help control the population. Each couple left for training, each soldier was sent for training, and very few people managed to elude the ever-increasing push to be subjected to the trip to a chapel. Evin's mom had warned them that something seemed amiss about the process to her. Now, it seemed, someone was pushing to have people report to training centers even earlier, often choosing soldiers from the younger people in a village and encouraging the people of the villages to pair off their youth more quickly. Inkeri and Evin were no longer unusual among the people who were marrying and settling into their expected lives. It seemed that part of that was a push to increase the working population faster to increase production, but there seemed to be a missing piece. They'd discussed a lot of scenarios as they'd sat in camp in the evenings, but it felt as if they wouldn't be able to know for sure unless they could see for themselves. For that reason, the group decided before they moved through Fjall, they would send Evin and Inkeri into the chapel to begin their training and report back what was happening. It had been their intention until very recently to continue with the supposed reasons for their trip, so it seemed a natural part of this leg.

Inkeri sat staring into the fire on the evening before Roald thought they would get to Fjall, trying to quiet the emotions that she wasn't sure what to do with. She knew she was brilliant at keeping the things she was feeling off her face, but that didn't mean she wasn't feeling them. She assumed she wasn't typical. She knew one girl in the village who would cry over everything unanticipated that happened in her life. Inkeri not only didn't show her emotions, but to some degree she didn't feel as deeply as she assumed others might. She thought about what they were facing tomorrow. They would make it to the place where she'd always assumed she and Evin would finish the marriage ceremony that would make them husband and wife. Now, it felt as if that wasn't a clear goal of their time there. She struggled with how she should feel about that. While she was pondering, Evin wandered over and sat down beside her. Though he no longer felt like a stranger to her, she had not allowed herself to get close to him in this process. There was too much at stake, and there was no guarantee that he was going to survive this. He was staring at her, so she looked back, locking eyes with him but keeping her thoughts as hidden as ever. "We need to talk about tomorrow," he said the words she was thinking.

"That would be a good idea, yes." She smiled, glad he'd brought it up.

"I have learned a lot in the time since our handfasting." He seemed to struggle with how to say what he was trying to say. "Learning that our betrothal was just a way to save my life was clearly the most devastating news for me. Had I had the choice whether to involve you or not, I wouldn't have chosen to drag you this far from home." He looked down, still saddened by the thought. "However, I have come to understand that you are supposed to be here as much as I am, and although I don't fully know why yet, you have become a strong strand of the rope that is holding us all together. Who knows if Kai would have survived without the care you were able to provide? Those wounds may not have healed as well or at all." He looked back up at her, finding her still looking at him. "I appreciate the fact that you always keep a cool head, even when things are bizarre. I know that I am younger than you, though not by much, and I know I don't look as imposing as Kai or Roald, but I hope you have at least come to the point where you could see that being promised to me might not have been the worst fate to befall you." He grinned with that unsure boyish grin that always made her almost forget her vow to keep her distance from him and continued, "I wanted to tell you, though, that I've been thinking a lot about it, and I don't think it is fair under the circumstances to ask you to follow through with the ceremony that will bind us for eternity as husband and wife. That is to be your decision, not one that you need to have made for you." He reached up and removed the necklace she'd handed him on the day of their first ceremony. Before she could protest, he slid it over her head, moving her hair out of the way to let it settle into place.

She looked down at the simple silver pendant and then into the fire, letting her fingers play over it. "What does that mean for what's going to be expected of us tomorrow?"

"We'll have to finish the ceremony to have a place in the training at Fjall, but I wanted you to know beforehand that unless you want it to be real, it doesn't have to be. I will not hold you to any of the promises we will make." He grasped his hands together and stared at them. "I mean, I couldn't imagine a better match for me. I think my parents chose very well, and I could see spending forever with you, but I'm not going to pretend that I still have the right to expect that with everything that is going on." She was overwhelmed with the wave of emotion that threatened to invade her calm. She closed her eyes, willing the tears she could feel trying to surface to stay buried. She only half succeeded as she raised her eyes once more to look into the earnest face of the man beside her. Tears welled but didn't spill out, and she considered that a victory. That is, until he reached up and touched her cheek. "Don't cry, Inkeri." It was simple, but it seemed like a dam had been released on all the emotions she'd been bottling this whole trip and she began to cry in earnest. He pulled her into a hug and sat there holding her close while she sobbed in the most undignified way. After a minute, he pushed back and looked into her face. "That was supposed to make you happy." He smiled at her with a tinge of sadness.

"It's not that. I'm just not sure what to do at this point. It's all too much, and it would almost be easier not to have choices to make. One thing I do know," she moved to take the necklace back off, "I meant to give you this, and I meant all of the things I vowed to you the first time I saw you." She placed it back over his head. "No matter what happens tomorrow, I want you to have that." She gestured at the necklace. "Maybe I just wish I'd known you my whole life, like Alia knew Kai. Maybe I wish I'd had the chance to learn what you're like when you're not under immense pressure. Maybe I wish your life wasn't endangered and you didn't feel to me like an idea or a vapor instead of a reality." She held her face in her hands, regaining her composure, then looked at him. "I certainly don't feel like marrying you will be the worst fate to befall me." She looked back down. "Losing you so soon as I might, could be." At that moment, she realized she had not managed to keep her distance like she'd imagined. She had no control over the rush of attraction she felt for him that she'd been squashing for days, but she sat staring down, wrestling to kill it again.

He leaned back staring into the stars. "Well, that's good to know." He laughed, and his voice sounded free of all the tension that had inhabited it for weeks. "I promise to give you the space to discover those things for yourself, Inkeri. We have plenty of time to learn everything about each other and hopefully life won't always be this tumultuous. Tomorrow is a good time to make the commitment to spend a lifetime getting to know and love each other, and it doesn't have to be anything else. We can focus for now on what we're trying to accomplish here and when I miraculously survive, I will work on winning your affection." He grinned into the sky and turning his attention to her, reached out and took her hand. "Thank you."

She looked at their joined hands and decided to leave them that way. “You’re welcome.” She wasn’t sure exactly what she’d done, but he seemed pleased.

Kai strode up to the fire and plopped down surveying the situation. “Congratulations on the impending wedding.” He smiled, gesturing at the joined hands. “Does this mean we’re going for the real thing?”

Evin smiled, graciously ignoring the comment he may have once taken as bait. “We’re going to try to survive the apocalypse first, but real intentions, yes.”

“Well, good.” Kai looked genuinely pleased. “You two deserve each other.” Again, the snarky grin. “I mean that in a good way. You do seem to belong together.”

“Thank you, Kai.” Inkeri was genuinely pleased that he had positive thoughts about the possibility of she and Evin deciding to finish their marriage ceremony in the midst of all of this craziness.

Roald walked up, holding a bunch of plants, oblivious to the situation he’d just walked into. “Inkeri, there are tons of this stuff. It seems like there are millions of weird plants growing here.” He’d been impressed with her knowledge of the vegetation and had been having her point out the plants that had different uses. She’d been teaching him how to use the ones that were safe and warding him off the dangerous ones. He already had a great base of knowledge on which to build. She let go of Evin’s hand and reached to take the plants he’d brought back to her. One was the plant from the clearing where they’d had their big meeting. “I already know that one, but there are so many of them here. It’s pretty insane.”

“Yeah, I wouldn’t try to use it if you don’t know how. It doesn’t take much of it to kill someone.” She cycled through the remaining few that he'd brought for her to look at. "This one is good to eat," she said, holding up a broad leafed one. "Nothing, nothing... oh, this one will make you see visions!"

"Evin must have been eating that one." Kai laughed.

"Not that kind of visions," Inkeri corrected him. "Like unrealistic things. Sometimes it used to be used in worship." She looked at the group. "There was a group of shamans who could combine some of these to great effect. They got very good at understanding how much to use of each one to reach the desired impact, but my mom said they were from the old unadulterated religion and had died out. I didn't understand that historically until I heard you speak, but I think the faith in El Olam that you talk about must have had something to do with suppressing it. I think there's been some resurgence of that. Must be since the original chapels have been destroyed." She looked at Roald. "My mom had a great need to understand how all of these things worked together in her job as a midwife, so I think she was glad to see the chaplains gone who'd insisted they might somehow be evil. She was only trying to help save people, and I think she felt pressured by them to abandon her use of the things in nature because of people's tendency to worship them. Still, none of the things she used to try to heal me worked, so they only have so much power." She handed the plants back to Roald. "I'm going to have to watch you. Those can be very deadly if used incorrectly."

"Warning taken," he smiled. "Generally, in my line of work death is the desired impact. I promise not to try any of them without seeking advice first." He stood. "If we get an early start tomorrow morning, we'll make it to the chapel before dark. It's mostly a climb tomorrow, so be ready for that." He looked at Evin and Inkeri. "Are you two ready for your mission?"

Evin looked at Inkeri and smiled "I think so."

"Full of confidence is always a good place to start." He smiled at them, then sighed. "You have two goals. Find out what the training is going to involve and learn as much as you can about the lands on that side of the mountain." Roald paused.

"Maybe finish our wedding ceremony too?" Evin looked at Roald.

"Yes, and that." He slapped the younger man on the back. "You can thank your parents for making a fine choice for you. We'll decide on the way tomorrow how we'll communicate when you're in the chapel. I mean, you won't be prisoners or anything, so it should be pretty easy to set up a meeting occasionally." With that, he turned and went to the tent. The others followed closely behind, and as Inkeri slipped in she tried to push aside her growing uneasiness. Something about this situation seemed more dangerous to her than the others seemed to be letting on.

Chapter 18

The journey up the mountain was a lot of winding, a lot of rocks, and a lot of stopping to rest. The path was severe and single file, and it became apparent why people didn't often travel this way. It was almost a whole day of this climbing, but finally when it started to seem impossible to go farther, they came to a fork, one path leading up and the other down the other side. They went up, turned a final corner, and found themselves situated in the most spectacular view they'd ever seen. To the right, a stone structure rose from the rocks, insisting they look at it first. A circular tower rose in the front, the first thing everyone's eyes saw. Then, the view opened, showcasing the barren, rocky landscape that resided on the other side of the mountain. To the left, a series of gardens carved into the soil among the rocks produced a profusion of vegetables and flowers. The air was much cooler than it had been when the day had started, but still warm enough for the garden to thrive. Inkeri dismounted and walked among the rows, surprised at their careful cultivation. The others dismounted and looked at the chapel.

"This is the furthest I've been since I was a child. They didn't burn this one in the last war, they just replaced all of the chaplains who were here." Roald said. "Usually, the chapels were situated among larger towns in the different provinces, but this one seems to be the only building here. I think the idea of rebuilding it up here with no audience to be appropriately terrified kept them from destroying it. I'm pretty sure that the only people that live here are here for the chapel itself. It serves as a stopping place for getting over the mountain, and sometimes it is used for the council to gather. They rotate provinces each year, and this one serves for both the provinces over the mountains."

They stood for some time taking in the view and enjoying the moment off the horses. "They will recognize me here, most likely, because I have always served as one of Diederick's bodyguards and guides when he makes the trip here. It would be odd if you turned up without guides, so Kai and I will serve as those. Generally, the guides camp in the plain behind the building because there are many staying inside at council time, so I would like to do that. It gives us a good meeting place. You can come out and easily give us updates. We'll know how long we need to stay once you guys figure out how hard it will be or how long it will take to get the information we need. Because you're supposed to be here for several months, it would be weird if we hang out too long, but I can easily buy us a few days to make a new plan if we need to. Hopefully you can get what we need and then make the decision to relocate closer to home, and we can leave together." He looked at Evin and Inkeri. They stood quietly, looking nervous. "Are you ready?" They nodded assent and the four of them moved to the front gate, where Roald found a servant and sent him to care for the horses. Then they continued through the open gate and across a wide expanse of yard with several benches and other structures all of which were positioned to take in the excellent view. Flowers bloomed here and there in carefully thought-out patterns. The main door stood beside the tower that initially caught their attention. Two small doors made of heavy wood stood open to either side, welcoming them into a vestibule with a clean swept gray stone floor.

As they entered, a plump, bustling man approached, smiling from ear to ear. "Welcome!" He took a quick look at them and surmised the situation. "A wedding party, I presume?" At their agreement he smiled even bigger. "Delightful! Only a few couples make the trek up here a year, but I think they've made the best choice. I see you have one of the best guides. You must be from an important family."

Roald bowed slightly. "Evin is going to be an elder in his village." He clapped Evin on the back. "He's excited to learn all he can to lead his people well. If it is ok, my trainee and I will camp in the plain out back for a few days before we head away. We'll come back for them after the prescribed time."

"Of course. That's perfect. Get some rest and replenish your supplies. We're having a great growing season up here. More rain than usual, and many of the early vegetables are ready for enjoying. I'll send some out to you."

Roald looked pleased. "Thank you!" He touched Kai's arm and moved back toward the door. Kai took a last look around and turned to follow, nodding at Inkeri and Evin before walking out. The two of them emerged back into the glorious yard and Kai wordlessly followed Roald around to the back of the massive structure. Down a set of large steps, a large grassy field followed the ridge of the mountain back away from the chapel. It was positioned so that it was shielded from the winds on the mountains and was the perfect place to camp.

"I can't help feeling very anxious about this." Kai looked troubled. "I can't put my finger on it, but something isn't right."

Roald, unpacking things to make camp, looked up surprised. "It's fine. We'll see them tomorrow to hear how it's going. We can bolt if we need to for some reason then." His words, meant to be reassuring, rang hollow, but Kai stooped to help.

While they worked, a servant worked his way across the rows of plantings across from them, carefully choosing certain plants. Roald waved as he came near. He balanced two baskets, then sat one near the plantings and approached with the other. "Vegetables for you, as promised." He smiled and they accepted a basket filled with a few fine specimens of spring growth. "I'll go finish gathering for your young people." He moved away to his other basket, filling it before moving away toward the chapel. Finally, camp was ready as evening drew near, and with wood provided for making fires, the two cooked their fresh goods and waited for news.

Evin and Inkeri were immediately led away from one another to separate chambers where they could ready themselves for the ceremony that would seal the vows they had made to one another in their village. Their travel-worn clothing was taken away to be mended and cleaned for their return trip and they were visited with a timeline for the rest of the day. No time would be wasted. The wedding ceremony would be held first, and then a celebration dinner would be served to the two of them in a central dining chamber during something called the law bringers ceremony. Then they would rest to start formal training the next morning. A woman came into Inkeri's chamber with a few embellishments for the simple dress she had brought with her. She laid them across a table in the room and smiled at Inkeri. "You're already lovely, but I brought some things you might want to choose to wear as well. We keep them on hand because the journey here doesn't usually allow for people to bring their own things from home. Sometimes this helps." She busied herself sorting through the pile and laying them out for Inkeri's inspection. "Tell me about the young man. Are you looking forward to spending the rest of your life with him, or are you wondering what your parents were thinking?" Her face was kind and genuine.

Inkeri walked over and examined the pile of things. "I think they chose well," she said simply.

"Glad to hear it, my dear. I've seen a few girls here who weren't too happy." She lifted a belt from the pile. "This would look lovely with your dress." She reached around Inkeri and secured the belt, standing back to admire her work. "Perfect. May I help with your hair?"

Evin stood in the chamber looking at the few things he had on hand for the coming ceremony and feeling inexplicably nervous. This seemed far more imposing than the ceremony in their village. The chubby man entered with a couple of other things to add to the pile he was considering. "What an exciting time!" he looked carefully at Evin. "You seem nervous. Do you like this girl?"

"I don't guess that matters at this point, does it?" Evin smiled.

"Oh, it matters, trust me." The man waited for the real answer.

"She's everything I could have ever wanted." Evin told the truth to the stranger, figuring that there was no reason not to.

"Splendid." He seemed genuinely pleased. "Here's hoping she feels the same way." He helped Evin choose the perfect additions to the simple clothes he'd brought for this purpose, and then the two of them went to the meeting chamber where they'd wait for Inkeri and her attendant.

He stood once more in a circle waiting for his bride, but this time, he knew who to expect. This time, he would be promising to look after her in front of the shamans, a more formal and more legally binding ceremony that would have them recognized as husband and wife by everyone. He remembered his promises to Inkeri, and he centered his heart on El Olam, knowing that even though his name would not be spoken aloud in the ceremony that it was he that Evin wanted to seal their marriage more than any man. He closed his eyes and recalled the Healer's kind eyes and gentle bearing. Hastily, he breathed a prayer that he would be able to be like that for Inkeri. He was struck once again with regret that he had not been able to accept the cup the Healer kept offering him in his visions. He was sure he was missing out on something important and necessary, but it was a burden he hadn't been ready to accept. A commotion in the room caused him to open his eyes, and he saw Inkeri coming up to stand beside him. He took her hand and gazed at her, just as blown away with her beauty as he had been when he'd first laid eyes on her. This time, her hair was swept up and secured with silver pins that glinted like jewels. Her waist was encircled with a belt studded with silver and stones that caught the emerald color of her dress and enhanced it. "Wow." He whispered to her, and she smiled.

The plump shaman shuffled in and stood in front of them. "This ceremony is in recognition of the fact that the two of you have promised in the presence of your friends and families to cherish one another and to be bound together under the laws of our land to present yourselves to your community as servants of your lord and loyal subjects of our land." Thankfully, he required no response to that one, because Evin wasn't sure anymore that he could promise those things. "The law we now live under has brought peace out of chaos. It has united us to thrive together. It is our obligation to remember. It is our obligation to obey. It is our obligation to serve." Both had heard these oft repeated words, but now they had an ominous feeling. "By coming here today, you show that you are uniting yourselves together to uphold and protect it." Finally, he finished droning on about the law and turned toward Evin. "You have been given this woman by her family to care for her and to protect her and to love only her for the length of your days. Are you prepared to do this?"

Evin looked at the Shaman. "I am."

He turned to Inkeri. "You are given to this man to be the greatest gift he ever receives and to be his strength, and to be beside him and only him for the length of your days. Are you prepared to do this?"

She smiled and replied. "I am."

He continued to Inkeri again. "Join hands in remembrance of your betrothal." They turned to face each other and complied. "What has your family given as a token of your promise?"

Inkeri indicated the silver pendant Evin already wore. "This pendant, passed down through many generations and blessed by the gods to provide peace and prosperity is my sign to Evin that I have been given to him in good faith."

The shaman turned to Evin. "Wear this symbol always."

Evin nodded.

"Fjall is a humble jewel in the crown of our country. Here we worship the gods in thankfulness for their blessings of rain, fertility, health, and all other good things, for which they are responsible. In their names, and in the name of Lord Thorvaldr, who the people of Fjall are blessed to serve, I give recognition to your union among our people. May your home be filled with children and your fields with crops. May you unite to move our people forward into a future of promise." He beamed over them, seeming genuinely pleased with the work he'd accomplished. "It is done. We will celebrate with a feast, where we will tell the story of the law bringers." He indicated they should move through a door, so they stepped out of the circle they'd inhabited and moved through the door, still holding hands. A large table filled the center of a small room. Tapestries and rich cushions filled the space and the chairs sat close. The space felt intimate and luxurious and was a welcome change from the evenings on the ground around a campfire. They were seated at the near end, and others from the chapel filtered in to join them in their celebration.

Evin found himself wishing that Kai and Roald could join them, and he was surprised that despite the animosity he had felt toward them, he had also grown accustomed to their presence and even desired to be in their company. The table was also covered in rich cloth and beautiful dishes were crowded with wonderful smelling food, some of which Evin couldn't identify. A man gave a revolting speech about the history of the law bringers in which he told a tale in complete opposition to the one Roald had told them about their histories. The lords of the land were represented as descendants of a group of men that had seen the disarray of the people and out of their own wealth and benevolence had united the country together under the rule of the council. Then they had risen up against the monsters that sought to keep them from coming together, squashing them completely. Stamping out beliefs that threatened unity, they had ushered the people back into faith in the gods of their fathers. Evin managed to chew and swallow appropriately during this speech, but he must have looked quite stricken.

Inkeri reached out and touched his cheek, turning him to face her. "Focus on me, Evin. Focus on why we're here." It seemed a logical request.

Evin smiled. "Sorry, Inkeri." He said quietly. "I have asked the blessing of El Olam on us too. He..."

She placed a finger on his lips and smiled, but her eyes held a warning. He turned to the side and saw a servant filling goblets right behind him. The man's face didn't indicate he'd heard anything, but Evin was reminded afresh that he needed to be more careful here to stay within the boundaries.

The servant stepped forward and handed the goblets to Inkeri and Evin. They were the largest cups in the room. Each was a beautifully carved piece of wood filled with an amazing smelling spiced wine. The man bustled out of the room, his job apparently done. The shaman appeared in the room just as they were presented with the goblets. "I see you have your mulled wine. Drink up. Ours is the best in all of the world." That boast seemed a little unlikely, but he seemed to believe it. He seated himself in an empty seat across the narrow table from them. They spent the next half an hour sampling incredible foods from the region and hearing tales of how fantastic the growing conditions were here thanks to the interesting situation of the mountains. All the while, they sipped the truly wonderful drink they had been given. The spices were carefully mixed with the strong and sweet wine that was common in the country, but which neither of them had ever had the equal to. It seemed the man's boast about the goodness of it was perhaps not as much of an exaggeration as they'd first thought.

Evin had drank his fair share of wine in his life, and he was aware of the point when he needed to stop. The goblet was only half empty, but he was careful to remember he needed to keep his head about him, so he only pretended to drink after a time. This wine was unbelievably strong, but by the time he realized that he'd had enough to send his head into a pleasant spin. He could still think clearly, though, so he just decided to enjoy the evening off from the stressors of the last several weeks in the company of his new bride. He leaned over and whispered into her ear. "This is strong stuff. Be careful." She nodded like she too had figured it out, and he felt proud of their ability together to recognize a danger and not press into it.

The shaman watched as their eating and drinking slowed and leaned forward. "Give me your hands." He held his hands out, resting them on the table in front of them, and they each placed a hand in one of his. "You are bound by your words and your promises. You are bound by your devotion. Lastly, we will bind you by your blood." He smiled and a tiny knife was brought close and presented to him. They must have looked alarmed. "Don't worry," he chuckled. "It's a bit of old symbolism that will leave you with a tiny cut on your hand. We treat it carefully to avoid the risk the cut will hurt you. It's a beautiful way to end your evening of ceremony." Without any more explanation, he picked up the tiny knife and starting with Evin, made a small cut in the pad of his right hand. Evin watched in amazement as blood flowed into his palm. He turned and did the same to Inkeri's left hand, then signaled to the servant, who stepped forward with a small bowl of some strong-smelling tincture. "This will ensure your safety." He rubbed a cloth filled with the liquid onto each of their cuts. It stung for a minute and then dulled into a strangely pleasant ache. Then he pushed their hands together, indicating they should clasp each other's hand tightly. "Now the two are one soul, one life, one blood." He waited a minute, watching them expectantly, then nodded at the servant. The younger man took Inkeri's elbow and indicated they should stand. "Repeat after me," the shaman continued. "It is our obligation to remember. It is our obligation to obey. It is our obligation to serve." They both did, although not with any conviction. "We are united to serve a greater cause. Our lord holds our allegiance. Good gifts are from his hand."

Evin's head began to swim, and as he heard the words and began to repeat them, he knew he could not mean them, but they seemed to have a stupefying hold over him. He thought of the lord to whom he was swearing fealty, apparently the same man who wanted him dead. Weirdly, the juxtaposition didn't seem too difficult to overcome. He felt an enhanced sense of meaning flood him, and before he could process it, he felt the words the shaman was speaking seem to become his own thoughts. He must have repeated more, but by the end of them all, he was grasping desperately to hold on to any sense of his own restraint. Within minutes, they were led away and ushered into a beautifully simple bed chamber.

"Rest." The servant looked at each of them and repeated. "Rest well." He turned on his heels and seemed to melt from the room, closing the heavy wooden door behind him.

Evin turned to look at Inkeri and found her standing with a hazy gaze, looking around the room with a relaxed curiosity. He was flooded in an instant with an intense desire for her that he couldn't deny. He sought refuge in his mind but found nothing there to restrain him. He took in her slim figure under the emerald gown. Positively breathtaking. He crossed to where she stood and put his hand on her cheek. Her skin seemed like silken fire under his touch, and she looked into his eyes and smiled. Her smile was more intoxicating in that moment than all the wine at the table over the course of the whole evening. He held her eyes and tilted her face until they were inches apart. Something nudged at the edges of his consciousness, but before he could entertain it, she reached out and touched his arm, still smiling in his direction.

She leaned close to his ear and whispered. "I love your grin."

It was hardly the sultriest thing she could have said, but the effect was immediate. Her closeness and the scent of her and her welcoming attitude combined with the effects of whatever had been in that wine moved him irreparably outside of the boundaries he'd been so proud of before. He pulled her into his arms, and she didn't resist, instead giggling. He could almost feel how uncharacteristic the exchange seemed, but there was no way on earth he could care in any way. Keeping an arm around her waist, he pulled each of the silver pins out of her hair and watched as it cascaded down her shoulders in what seemed like slow motion. Her face was flushed and beautiful and he bent to breathe in the intoxicating scent of her, kissing her neck under her ear eliciting another giggle and drawing in her presence like he could hold onto it forever. He untied the belt that circled her waist and tossed it aside. She pushed back a little and moved her hand to his face, pulling him close and kissing his lips gently at first and then with passion he couldn't have imagined was underneath her almost always cool exterior. He closed his eyes and squeezed the lids together, trying to remember something. Trying to make sense of something he knew was there somewhere. The shaman's words about the law were all he could muster, and those were a desperately unwanted intrusion right now, so he pushed them aside and gave himself over completely to the growing unbelievable rush of emotion and pleasure that he could not have previously imagined existed. The look on her face was a welcoming one he'd never seen before. Her fingers played exquisitely across the back of his neck, pulling him toward her. Then they moved down his back and under the hem of his shirt, moving up his bare back. He tugged her dress up and over her head, tossing it aside. Then he scooped her off her feet, moved to the bed and finally surrendered completely in his mind to the idea of her. She was, in that moment, the only thing in the room that he cared about.

~~~~~

Roald and Kai sat by the fire, listening to the gentle crackle and thinking. Finally, Kai broke the silence. "Do you feel like this is an entirely safe place, Roald?"

Roald thought about it. "I've never seen anyone come to harm during a marriage trip. I have guided a few of the sons of the lords on marriage journeys, and they always need a guide back. If anything, they seem incredibly happy."

"That's almost what worries me." Kai still looked unsettled. "The incredibility of it. When I saw Alia, she didn't remember our story. She had a new story that involved a legitimate wedding trip to Ellerton and a weird memory of our time at the chapel there. What are they doing in there?" He motioned to the chapel.

"Sanna has questioned the ceremonies, too. I think she warned Evin before we left to be careful. I'm sure he's on his toes."

"I don't think you can be on your toes about everything." Kai stood and rubbed his hand in his hair in agitation.

Roald thought about it for a minute, then stood too. "By the gods, Kai. They said they were picking things for Inkeri and Evin's dinner over there." He pointed. "The only things growing over there are decidedly not foods."

Just then, a figure approached from across the yard and both of the men drew swords. The figure held up both hands and stepped into the ring of the firelight. One of the servants appeared before
~~~~~

them, his face ashen. "Please. I mean you no harm. I need to speak to you of your..." he tried to find a word, "...people in the chapel."

"They are our friends after our journey." Roald sheathed his sword, indicating Kai should do the same once they were satisfied the servant was unarmed. "What of them?"

"Forgive me, my life is in your hands. If I should misspeak, this may very well be the last thing I say. I am casting my life into your grasp." He bowed his head and they stared at him.

"Spit it out. You don't need to fear us." Kai was growing impatient, dread realization gripping him.

"I fear for your friends," the man said. "I have watched many ceremonies, but tonight when I poured wine for them, Erik, I think is his name was talking quietly to his bride and he mentioned El Olam to her. She hushed him, but if that name is heard spoken here, he will be killed."

"It's Evin. Why didn't you tell?" Roald eyed the stranger curiously.

"I hope to have time to tell you my story, but that is not a luxury we have right now. Suffice it to say, I have known El Olam for my whole life. If you believe in him, please get your friends out of here as soon as possible. They are already being fed the laws in a very" he emphasized the next word "orchestrated way. The truth they believe will come out to be replaced, and I fear they will not survive it."

Sudden understanding flooded Roald's face. He pointed to the patch of plants he'd watched another servant pick from earlier. "They drug them?"

The servant nodded.

"Gods be cursed!" Roald exclaimed and began pacing, eyes racing back and forth. He looked wildly at Kai. "What in the hell have we done?"

Kai held his hands palm up and glared back. "I told you..."

"No time for that." Roald looked impatiently at the man. "Can you help us?"

"I will help you get them. I know where they are. But you must take me with you. I will surely die here, and I have been praying for an opportunity to leave for my whole life."

Roald clapped the man on the back. "Looks like your time has come. What's your name?"

The servant looked pleased. "I'm Johannes. I'm responsible for getting their travel clothes back to them in the morning. I think it would be best if you came then and we left. I don't think it would be wise for them to go to breakfast."

"What happens at breakfast?" Roald still had a look of unbelief on his face.

"Let's just say that the herbs work best in slow and steady doses after the initial dose. A first powerful dose and then continued smaller and smaller doses to wean them off it before they leave. The morning will be the second dose. Any more and the withdrawal will be severe. That's why they're here for so long to learn a few laws. The drugging combined with almost constant repeating of a few key points, and you end up with a couple of happy citizens."

Roald looked stricken, "I really did not see this coming. I can't even imagine."

Kai looked angry. "They did this to my wife." He looked like he might punch the servant for lack of someone better to attack.

Roald touched Kai's arm. "Calm down. We have to get them out of there without letting our emotions get in the way. Let's work on a story that makes sense."

The servant nodded. "You get that settled and I will finish my duties and prepare. Come to the vestibule as the sun rises, and you can tell Shaman Njal your story and I will lead you to get them. Just make it believable." We will only have a little time until they discover I'm missing, and I will have to steal a horse, so they may decide to come after us."

"Is there any place in the chapel where they can see which way we take at the mountain pass?" Roald asked.

"No, we're tucked off to the side of the actual crossing, and it isn't clearly visible from here."

"Good," Roald said. "They'll be going the wrong way."

Johannes looked puzzled, but dipped his head and turned, melting into the night.

Chapter 19

For the next several hours, Roald and Kai devised a plan they thought would work, carefully thinking over details and taking into account that they couldn't be sure of the mental state of Evin and Inkeri. Instead of resting, they packed and readied everything so that it would be a simple matter of getting the horses and going. The sky finally began to lighten. The reality of what they'd learned dawned with the sun, and they were both feeling desperate to escape the place that had once felt at least a little safe. As the sun broke the plane of the horizon, the two of them strode into the vestibule with purpose. A few people already moved around in the weak light preparing for the day. Their entrance caused everyone to look up and within minutes they stood before the chubby shaman with the kind face. It was a struggle to keep emotions in check and pretend to be his friend. Roald put his hand on the man's shoulder. "I'm sorry to disturb you so early, but we've had a difficult word in the night from Evin's village, and we have to take him home right now. It would be best if we leave immediately."

Njal's eyes narrowed, and he looked at the two men. "What kind of news makes its way to our mountaintop?" He was clearly suspicious.

"Evin's father has unexpectedly died. One of the men from the village rode here to tell us. He's giving his horse some food and rest and as soon as we grab Evin and Inkeri, we will head back. Evin will need to be there as soon as possible to take his place as village elder."

"Their ceremony is done, but their training will have to be completed." The man looked uneasy with the idea, but somewhat more settled.

"Of course. The chapel in Ellerton is near Evin's home, and it will be better for them to train there since the circumstances have changed. I'm sure you understand."

The shaman still looked uneasy at the unusual circumstances but decided to believe them. "Okay. Since they have been a short time here, everything should be fine. You will need to take it easy on them today. They may have enjoyed a little bit much mulled wine last night."

Roald was appalled at how easily the man lied to him, but played his part perfectly, smiling. "I'm glad for them to have had a good night before I have to deliver such news to Evin. He was very close to his father."

"I'm sorry to hear that." Njal turned and called out. "Johannes?"

The servant materialized at his elbow. "Yes, Shaman Njal?"

"The new couple must leave unexpectedly. Can you get them their things and make sure they are ready to depart?"

"Yes, Shaman." Johannes said without a look at Roald and Kai.

Roald stepped forward. "I will come with you. Evin will want an explanation. He's been very excited to be here and complete his training." Roald looked at Kai. "Go help make sure the horses are ready."

Kai turned and walked out.

Johannes motioned for Roald to follow and moved down a windowless hall back into the dark. Roald followed closely behind him, stopping at a large wooden door. Johannes knocked and waited. Roald felt the electricity of the situation. He stood ready for anything, willing the time to move them through this most dangerous part as quickly as possible. He prayed to god that Evin wouldn't say anything that would jeopardize their mission. He really didn't want to have to fight his way out of here.

The door opened a crack and light from a window behind Evin flooded out, keeping him mostly hidden in silhouette. Roald moved so he could see his curious boyish face and his tousled sandy hair, but the rest of him was hidden by the door. He looked at the two of them and confusion came over his face. "Roald?"

Johannes shoved a package toward the door. "Please get dressed and come quickly. Roald has news for you. You have to leave." Evin looked confused for a second, then took the offered clothes and closed the door.

Roald was amazed how well the man stayed in character. Apparently, he'd had years of practice pretending to be someone he wasn't. They stood in the close passageway for a few minutes, and then the door opened again, revealing a pair of very tired looking young people. Both looked dazed and slightly ill, so Roald stepped forward and grabbed Evin's arm, looking into his eyes. "Evin. There is bad news from home. We need to leave." He hoped beyond hope the boy would fight him a little on it just in case anyone might be in earshot who would think it odd if he left without a better explanation. Evin didn't disappoint.

"What about our training? We haven't really started yet." He didn't look convinced he wanted to start and stood rubbing his forehead mindlessly, obviously confused.

"It's your father, Evin. Something has happened. I will fill you in on the ride."

Evin's eyes focused on Roald for the first time since he'd stepped into the room, and he furrowed his brow. "What do you mean?"

"Just come so we can get on the road home. I will tell you the rest then." Roald looked around the room, taking in the untidy bed and the clothes strewn everywhere and gave Evin a mystified look. "Gods, boy, you didn't waste any time." He grabbed things he could identify as Evin and Inkeri's.

With help from Johannes, he left the things belonging to the chapel laying across the bed, stuffing the rest into a bag. "I told them to rest before I left." Johannes surveyed the room, then shrugged. "When I saw them in the circle, I knew that wouldn't work." He shrugged. "It was worth a shot."

Finally, they steered Evin and Inkeri through the chapel and out the front door, past the other servants and Najl. Roald smiled as they walked by the man, stopping briefly in front of him. "You weren't kidding. We'll make sure they're taken care of today. Thank you for your service to them and our country."

Njal seemed pleased to be recognized, puffing his chest out and smiling.

Johannes stood with Inkeri, who still looked half asleep. "I'm going to help her get to her horse and then I will take care of the stables since I'll be out there."

Njal nodded. "Peaceful journey, my friends. Maybe I will see you at council this year."

"Most likely." Roald agreed and moved quickly out of the door, recognizing that they had limited time before Johannes didn't reappear inside and they started asking questions. They moved quickly to the stables where Kai had managed to gather all the bags and supplies and was in the middle of getting the third horse saddled. Roald sat Evin and Inkeri down on the pile of gear and rushed to help Kai and Johannes finish the other two horses they'd need. Then he pulled the couple to their feet and roughly grabbed Evin's face, forcing him to look at him. "Can you ride?" He shook Inkeri's shoulder, making sure she understood the question was for her too.

Evin looked at him with a million questions on his face, then looked at Inkeri and back at Roald. They both nodded, so Roald and the others pushed them into the saddles of their horses and positioned them in the middle of the pack, starting off at a quick clip.

Evin sat forward in the saddle but maintained control of the horse. They moved quickly out of sight of the chapel and around the bend that wended back down the mountain. After a very short time, the path split, and the five figures made their way away from home. "What's wrong with my father?" Evin still looked completely confused. "Who is this?" He motioned to the man riding between him and Roald.

Roald turned in the saddle to look at him. "Nothing is wrong with your father, Evin. We just needed to get you out of there. This is Johannes. He saved your life."

Johannes smiled in his direction. "Pleased to meet you."

"You're the servant with the goblets." Evin appraised the exceptionally pleasant looking fellow in the light of day. He'd shed the brown wool vestments that all the chapel servants wore and was now donned in clothes for traveling like the rest of them. Red hair was swept to the side away from his forehead, and his strong chin supported a well-trimmed beard. "Well, thank you, I guess."

The rest of the day was spent riding back down the mountain away from the chapel and everything they'd ever known. Roald remembered some of his first trip over the mountains, but now they only had the hand drawn map that Sanna had given Evin. The mountains blocked the rain that benefitted the other side, so much of the land around them was arid and rocky, supporting very little in the way of valuable vegetation. By late afternoon, they had left the mountain behind and were in the foothills. Evin suddenly stopped his horse and launched out of the saddle, landed on his knees beside the horse and bent over breathing deeply trying desperately to keep from vomiting. Roald jumped down beside him and touched his shoulder. Then he looked up at Johannes. "Is this normal?"

The man nodded. "It can be. Especially after the first big dose. Some people don't handle it very well when they're coming down from it. It's a very strong combination of several things, so the impact varies from person to person. It wouldn't have happened if he'd gotten the next dose." He looked at Inkeri, who had yet to say anything. "How are you feeling?"

"I'm not sure. Sick, but more like I need to sleep." Her eyes had lost some of their hazy unfocused look.

"We should make camp as soon as we find a safe spot." Kai interjected.

"Who knows where a safe spot is around here." Roald looked at the miles of rocks and scrub brush with decided distaste. "At least we'll be dry."

Evin barely managed to climb back on his horse, and it was evident they needed to stop and let them sleep off the rest of the effects of the drug mixture they'd had. They steered to the left among the foothills, looking for fresh water to camp nearby. There was little to be found at first, but before too long, they happened upon a stream trickling out from the rocks and gathering into a small pool. Some grass grew around the pool for the horses, and they were able to set up a decent campsite. Johannes had brought another tent, and it was decided that Inkeri and Evin would take one and the other men would share the other one. It was also agreed that from now on, they would take turns keeping watch at night, since they were completely unaware of any dangers in the place.

Evin spent a wretched night stretched out on the ground in front of the tent, too sick to spend any time in there before he'd need to be out again. As he came to himself more, he also became sullen. Thankfully, by the wee hours of the morning, he was able to sit beside the fire and sip water.

Roald, who had the last watch, emerged from the tent to find him staring into the fire. He glanced at Kai, who was moving toward the tent to try to catch a little rest from his watch. "He's been like that for about an hour now." He shrugged and disappeared.

Roald threw one of the empty bags on the ground with a good view of the surrounding area, sat on it, and stared across at Evin. "Why don't you go get some rest?"

"I can't sleep." He looked down into his cup and took another sip. "My head feels like someone is smashing it between two rocks. You guys put me in a tent alone with Inkeri."

"Is there a problem with that? She shouldn't be alone, and you seemed the logical choice. She is your wife."

Evin didn't respond, he just looked dejectedly into the fire.

"Did something happen, Evin?"

"I promised her, Roald. I sat down with her and I held her hand and I promised that I would give her the space and the time she needed to choose whether or not we should be together. She was worried about something happening to me and

I promised her we would take the time to get to know each other and learn to love each other after all this craziness had played out. Then, they put us in a room together and I pretty much attacked her."

"Attacked her?" Roald looked alarmed

"No, no, not like that. I was just... insatiable." He struggled "I couldn't even remember the promises I'd made. I wanted to be able to honor her in this whole experience and give her the choices she didn't get to make that she deserved to. We're trying to make changes and free people and I played right into the same formula, and I desperately wanted her to know she could trust me to be different." He grimaced and held his head in his hands. "I wasn't able to protect her from any of whatever happened back there, and I wasn't even able to protect her from me." He leaned back on his elbows looking into the stars. "What did happen back there? I remember everything, and nothing makes sense. Now we have this new guy, and I feel like I fell off the earth."

Roald watched him. "I'm sorry I let that happen, Evin. I had no idea until last night. You did find out a vital piece of information, albeit accidentally. They use the plants Inkeri and I had been talking about, apparently rather expertly, to create a powerful drug to control the whole experience. You mentioned Johannes. He hasn't had time to share his story, but he heard you mention El Olam to Inkeri, and he has been secretly following him his whole life. He knew you would die if you mentioned that to the wrong person, so he kept you from getting your next dose and in return, we brought him with us."

"I'm glad he was there, but I wish he'd worked just a little faster." Evin sighed. "I'm such a fool, Roald. I don't know how to even say a word to her when I see her today. I don't think I can. It's like she's all I can think about, and I don't think it's in the healthiest way."

"It isn't unhealthy to think of your wife that way, Evin. You should talk to her. It sounds like the drugs had a few more effects, at the very least removing all your restraints. Even enough wine will do that. Did you have a lot of that?"

"No, I stopped and warned Inkeri to stop drinking that as soon as I realized how strong it was. I was so proud of us." He laughed derisively. "Little did I know."

"That's exactly right, Evin. You didn't know."

"It doesn't change anything that happened, Roald. I still failed her in the worst way. I let my own wants make decisions I wanted her to make in her own time. I know that wasn't her time."

"Well, I think she gets to have the final say about that. You have to talk. I don't think she's going to hold you completely responsible. I think you're probably seeing this as a much bigger issue than it is."

"I think she's going to hate me forever." Evin looked years older.

"Evin, you need to rest. Go to the tent with the guys if you need to and get some sleep. I'll keep watch over Inkeri. We'll need to move on in a few hours."

Evin pushed uneasily to his feet and stumbled into the men's tent without another word.

Chapter 20

They managed to pack up the camp and move on several hours later. Both Inkeri and Evin had horrible headaches, but aside from having some new information about the law inexplicably memorized, they seemed no worse for the wear. They traveled further into the wilderness as the day went on, everyone keeping company with their own thoughts. Roald told a few tales of his childhood on this side of the mountains. He explained that as they neared the coast, the land dipped lower to the sea, and they would begin to see more vegetation again, though primarily the brushier, heartier kind. Here, they were technically in their own country, but they had no idea what it was like to live on this side of the mountains now. The landscape was different than anything some of them had ever seen. It was a land of big gray stones and short grasses and other hearty plants. Rain was scarce, but there did seem to be ground water, so some plants and even the occasional tree managed to survive. Evin rode in the back most of the day, avoiding company and nursing his bad mood. They stayed close together, aware that they were highly visible from any viewpoint. "This is the most vulnerable we will be to attacks." Roald told them.

"What exactly are we expecting to attack us?" Inkeri asked.

"People." Roald looked around at her. "Feeling better?"

"People? Why would anyone attack us?" She considered his question. "I think I'm almost mended. My brain still feels a little fuzzy. They were expert at mixing that stuff together," she stated.

Johannes, riding behind her, asked the obvious question. "How do you know about that?" The group had yet to broach the subject of the drugs Evin and Inkeri had been forced to take.

"I figured it out, based on my experience of the last two days and the way you were talking about Evin when he first got sick. First, they gave us super strong wine with a lot of spices. I'm pretty sure that had something else in it too, because both Evin and I sat and let them make a cut on the palm of our hand without fighting, which he proceeded to swab with something much stronger." She pointed at Johannes. "I realized when I was thinking about it this morning based on how hard it hit us and how fast that it must have been introduced through the cuts. Whatever combination they used enhanced our memory instead of making us forget, so much so that I can remember the patterns on all the materials I saw after that. It was like an awareness awakening."

Johannes smiled. "Smart girl! It awakens all of the senses."

"That's for sure. Every time I've seen strong plants used for whatever reason; the person doesn't remember anything later."

"They use ancient recipes." Johannes elaborated. "They can manipulate the situation so the memory does what they need it to do in that moment. Any mention of the law is attached to fantastic memories. When they find resistance in a person to any of the teachings, which is common for everyone, then they use a combination of different compounds and negative experiences."

"Negative experiences?" Kai, who had been listening quietly, was suddenly very interested.

"Nothing too heinous." Johannes said. "They'll do things like keep the couple separated if they want to be together and have them take a series of exceedingly boring lessons while they are drugged in which they destroy all of the arguments that they may have had against the way things work. When they wake the next day, they've forgotten all of that, and the negative experience of feeling goes with it over time. Sometimes takes a lot more than one session."

"What part did you play in all of this?" Kai was gripping his horse's reins with white knuckles and clearly fighting his desire to kill someone.

Johannes continued, oblivious. "I've been there for so many years, that I can really do any part of it I need to. For Evin and Inkeri, I was responsible for serving them. So, I basically took care of their needs and brought them things they needed, cleaned their travel clothes, showed them where they needed to be next. That sort of thing. I understand the different plants and how to process them and how much to use, so I can do that if I need to, but that generally wasn't my responsibility. I did unfortunately do the administering as part of the serving for Inkeri and Evin."

Kai moved his horse beside Johannes'. He stared at the older man. "You mean to tell me that you've spent however long you lived there manipulating the minds of countless young people so that they believe they are free, happy citizens of benevolent leaders, or loyal soldiers fighting for a just cause, and you can just talk about it like you've done nothing wrong?"

Johannes coolly examined the obviously angry man beside him. "I'm going to guess that this is personal for you, Kai, and I'm sorry for that. I heard you say something about your wife when we were at the chapel. You have to understand I was surviving in the enemy's camp for long years, and I did what I needed to do to make sure that it never occurred to anyone in that chapel that the servant needed to have his memory altered. Almost all of the people who came to our chapel did not need any significant convincing, because they already had parents and family telling them the same things we were telling them. They were happy to go home and live oblivious to what's going on. It was different for many of the young men who were to be soldiers, and it was heartbreaking, but I prayed daily to the god my parents had taught me to revere that he would free me and allow me to be able to fight for them. Here I am. Are you on my side?"

Kai's grip on the reins lessened some and he looked away from Johannes' convicting gaze. "I am most definitely on your side." He rode quietly for a minute. "It is also most definitely personal for me. Maybe this god you all like so much will show you a way to reverse this brainwashing?"

"Maybe, Kai. I would love the opportunity to work on that." Johannes watched as the other man dropped back into his place in the line.

They kept moving quietly for the rest of the morning, only taking a brief break for rest and food.

In the afternoon, a man approached from the west. His clothes were different from the usual clothing in the east. He rode his horse steadily and slowly toward them, and as he drew close, they stopped.

"Hello!" He called out. "Don't mind me. I just saw you across the plain. I didn't mean to cause you alarm. Just wanted to make sure that I knew who else was out here before I set up camp. Sometimes you can come across unsavory people. I usually wouldn't travel alone, but sometimes it's unavoidable."

Roald looked him over carefully, sizing him up as he pulled even with the group. It seemed he was doing the same to them. They exchanged cursory greetings with the stranger. He looked carefully at each member of the party, letting his eyes linger longer on Inkeri than the others. Evin moved his horse between her and the man, shooting him a menacing look.

After a minute, the man raised a hand. "Good journey." He turned and rode off, continuing the way he'd been going.

Roald watched as he drew away. "I didn't like that at all. Something weird about the whole thing. We're going to need to be careful how we choose our campsite tonight."

As they rode on, they watched the land change and flatten. The last of the hills gave way to big barren plains. Every strike of the horse's hooves on the ground brought forth a puff of dust and before long they became aware that the giant plain was going to have to serve as their campsite for the night. Roald was exceedingly unhappy to discover there was little variance in the ground that might provide some protection from at least one side. Most of the ground was maddeningly the same. Finally, they realized they would have to set up camp or risk running out of light. It was decided that there should be two lookouts at a time for the nights from now on. They pitched the tents close together and secured everything as well as they could. Evin and Johannes took the first watch, one on either side of the tents. Evin watched Inkeri move quietly into the tent and wished he could afford a few minutes to talk to her. Tomorrow, he would make that his first priority. For now, it made the most sense for the least experienced fighters to be the first watchmen because they would be fresher earlier. Also, the night would grow darker once the moon disappeared, so it would be better to have more experienced men guarding then. The moon shone brightly, and the two men stayed on opposite sides of the tents, ever vigilant. Halfway through the night, they traded places with the others and were asleep within minutes. Kai and Roald took their positions, watching uneasily as the moon sank below the horizon, leaving only dark in its wake as time crawled toward dawn. After a time, the horses started stirring. They were wide awake and jittery, scanning into the night.

"Wake the other two. Something isn't right." Roald said to Kai, reaching for his sword.

As Kai turned to move to the tent, an unearthly yell stopped him in his tracks and brought him whirling around. Suddenly the light of several torches burned around the camp, and the yelling continued. Temporarily blinded by the sudden light, the two men put forward a valiant effort, yelling the names of the other two as they hacked at anything that came near. Their vision returned just as Evin and Johannes stumbled out of the tents, disoriented but ready. They each held their ground masterfully. Abruptly, Evin was brought to his knees as a whip struck out and wrapped around his legs. His sword skittered away, and he was immediately swarmed by at least five men who dragged him out of the circle of light. He could still be heard fighting, but it was evident he wasn't going to be successful. Whoever was attacking rode around them on horses, and they were wildly outnumbered. Still, they took every opportunity to fight back. Within moments, the enemy had expertly disarmed them using the element of surprise and the skills they possessed with their long whips. Each man had succumbed in turn to being bound hand and foot and rendered powerless. Roald was the last to go, hacking and circling expertly. He pulled one attacker off his horse and made a quick end of him, but then he too was incapacitated. They watched in horror as the bandits turned their attention to the tents. Inkeri's screams brought new life to their struggles against the ropes that bound them. Evin yelled fruitlessly in the direction of the tents, and within seconds that seemed like an eternity, three bandits emerged from the tent carrying Inkeri, now bound in a similar fashion to them. She was struggling so much that it took two of them to carry her. Confusion erupted once more. Dust stirred up by the horses' hooves blocked any view of what was going on. Evin strained at his ropes even harder.

A torch approached them, bobbing happily along until a familiar face appeared in the ring of light it created. The stranger from the afternoon smiled at Evin. "Thank you for bringing a beautiful woman into the wilderness. A gift straight from the gods." He laughed and turned on his heel, striding to his horse.

The only clue to Inkeri's whereabouts were her screams. Evin inched forward painfully toward them until they suddenly stopped. The silence was much more disturbing than the screaming had been. Tears streamed down Evin's face as he continued to drag himself forward, yelling at the man to bring her back. Within seconds, all the horses began to move away from the camp, including theirs. Evin eventually reached the edge of the tent, and as the last sounds of the hoofbeats died he positioned himself against a rough wooden tent peg and began to work the rope back and forth across it desperately. It was clear that they weren't intended to loose themselves. The others did the best they could to find similar ways to work on getting free. It was exhausting work, and twice Evin almost let feelings of hopelessness overwhelm him, but adrenaline rushed through him, keeping him going. As the sun made its appearance, Evin finally felt the ropes go slack around his wrists. He moved quickly to free the ropes that had been cutting off circulation from his feet and then freed the others.

When his hands were free, Roald grabbed Evin's wrist and turned it over, exposing ugly cuts from the tent stake. "These need to be cared for, now."

Evin jerked his hand away. "Leave it. Help me figure out what to do next." They wandered the camp, looking at the scene for any clues to what should be their next step. Evin stooped in front of the tents, examining the dark stains on the ground. He touched them and brought his fingers up, examining the dark red smear.

Roald watched. "Blood. Probably from the one I took down." He was eager to reassure Evin.

"It could be from Inkeri, right here outside her tent." Evin said, then sank to his knees on the ground. He pitched forward and planted his forehead on the dry ground, sobbing inconsolably and trembling from head to toe. "Please, god, no!" He shouted into the earth.

Kai moved closer and touched his shoulder, hoping to comfort him.

Evin looked up and narrowed his eyes at Kai. "You! Don't come near me with your fake sympathy. I know this is what you've wanted from the day we met. You couldn't stand the thought of anyone around you being happy. You probably prayed to your gods that something like this would happen." Evin once again buried his head in his hands, trying to regain his composure. He couldn't understand the well of emotions he was drowning in, but he felt as if his heart had been ripped out.

Kai stood still as a stone for a moment, his face registering several different emotions, the most prevalent of which were anger and disbelief. He ran his hand through his hair, trying to think of something to say to counter the appalling accusation. He squeezed his eyes shut trying again to block out the screams in his mind, first Alia's and then Inkeri's. He let his fingers play delicately against the cuts and bruises on his face. All the anger he'd felt suddenly welled to the surface. He grabbed Evin's shirt and dragged him to his feet. Evin looked bewildered and frightened by the assault. Kai grabbed Evin's shoulders and brought his face inches from his own. Johannes started to move forward, but Roald shook his head and put a hand on the man's shoulder. Kai breathed out. "You listen to me, 'cause this is the last time I am going to explain myself to you. I might not get along with you very well all the time, and yes, I will admit that I have been jealous of you getting to see your wife every day, but I will have you know one thing. I wouldn't put my worst enemy through any of the things I've been through. Last night, I stood there beside you in front of those tents and I tried to stop you from suffering the way I have. Every one of these marks on me is one I took for your wife; one I took for you. I will not have you questioning my character anymore. Your wife is a precious treasure to you. I know that, and last night, I took another beating to try and help you keep her. I did not want us to lose that fight, and I would do anything to keep you from knowing the hell I've been through firsthand." Evin had luckily found his feet beneath him and when Kai let him go, he remained standing. The two men stood inches from each other breathing heavily. Evin stared defiantly at Kai for a second, and then his head dropped, and he shook it back and forth slowly. His tears fell into the dust, each one making a mark at his feet.

"I'm so sorry, I'm sorry." Evin cried.

Kai relaxed his body and reached out his hand putting it on Evin's shoulder, this time a lot more gently. "No, Evin, I'm sorry. I never wished for this to happen. I never prayed for this to happen. I never wanted you to know this kind of horror. We'll find her, no matter what. If she's alive, we'll find her."

Evin looked into Kai's eyes, for the first time seeing past the laws the other had broken and meeting the ally that had been waiting there. "I'm so sorry to have said that, Kai. I wasn't trying... I'm just so upset."

"I understand, Evin." Kai muttered, and Evin knew he did, better than anyone else.

Roald relaxed his hold on Johannes's shoulder, glad he'd trusted his instinct not to interfere. Evin rubbed his cheeks roughly, smearing blood and dirt through the tears on his face. "Where do the tracks head, Roald? We have to try to find her." He walked back toward the tracks, motioning for the others to follow.

Chapter 21

They spent the day following tracks here and there across the ground, the real direction of the assailants hidden among the hoof-prints that were woven together in every direction. Spots of blood they found punctuated the hopelessness of the situation. The bandits did not intend to be found. The days and nights melted together as they searched on foot, and Roald was careful to move them in the direction of the nearest city on the cloth map. He carefully took account of the provisions they had left, and on the sixth night of the search he approached Evin with the news that the young man dreaded hearing the most. It was time to move on, or they would die in this wilderness. At this point, that sounded like the best thing to Evin, but the others knew the importance of hope, and they tried to no avail to bolster Evin's. The evidence they had found in the wilderness did not mean his wife was dead, and their best chance of finding out what happened to her lay in places where they could talk to other people. They were weary to the bone as the four of them gathered around the fire that night. Roald had taken the map from Evin, who didn't seem to care what direction they were headed in, and he studied it, trying to match the limited landmarks in this godforsaken place with what he was seeing on it. Kai and Johannes busied themselves with portioning out the last of the food they had with them. Evin sat staring into the fire in much the same way he spent every evening, completely despondent.

Johannes settled down beside the fire. None of them had been doing much sleeping since the attack, and all of them felt depleted. He looked over at Kai, who stood warming his hands. "Roald says he thinks we'll locate a city in the north of the country tomorrow. I think I would like to hear your stories before that happens. Can you tell me?"

Kai smiled weakly across at him. "That's going to make for a long night."

"It's ok, we're not resting much anyway." Johannes said. "I am praying about what's next for me. I am away from Fjall for the first time in my known life, and I want to be in the place god has for me next. Maybe that's with you?"

Evin kicked at the edge of the logs, pushing them further into the fire, making it crackle and tumble around, but he said nothing. Roald moved in and sat beside him.

Kai and Roald took turns filling Johannes in on the journey so far, telling him almost everything they had experienced. They told of Evin, and the prophecy. They told of Kai and Alia. They told of the meeting in the woods. Evin sat and listened, uncharacteristically quiet, but unable to hide his growing anger.

Johannes listened intently, nodding in awe. "Well, it seems the time I have been waiting for has come, indeed. I was unborn when the raids ravaged these lands. My mother and her family were devout followers of El Olam. I remember her telling me that many of the believers were targeted in the raids, but the sense was that the south was petty and not too dangerous. They seemed to be more jealous of god and intent on wiping the worship of him off the face of the earth. My grandfather was a chaplain in one of the small chapels along the western coast, and when my mother was a teenager, a small girl brought news that her island village had been attacked by the raiders. Already, the raiders from the south had broken the seal on the Holy Mountain and left us without hope of translating the book we had been entrusted with. It was a time of great hopelessness. Miraculously, the girl had two of the pieces of the seal with her. No one knew who had taken them from the mountain, but it would appear that it was the girl's father. She didn't know what she had but had been instructed to give them to my grandfather. Apparently, her dad and he were good friends. He split them up and found safe places for them, and finally the raids settled, and we reached a diplomatic solution with the south. For a couple of years, the girl stayed at the chapel and studied alongside my mother. Then, my grandfather heard news that your mom," he nodded toward Evin, "I'm assuming based on their story, had family on the other side of the mountain. My mom had married, and he decided to take yours to her family across the mountain, accepting an invitation to live among the people of the east. He was told that there was a lot of tension arising about El Olam and that the people there desperately needed chaplains who could hold the line of truth among the darkness that was trying to arise. I never met him, but my mom had only good things to say about him. I was born shortly after he left, and my mom and dad travelled to Fjall to study El Olam. My mom wanted me to follow in my grandfather's footsteps and become a chaplain, so they took me where we could focus only on the things of god without distraction. She intended to raise me to know everything about god and to learn to trust him without question, and she poured that into me for my first eight years. We saw the lords from the whole land come a couple of times while I was young that I remember. The second, my mom was very unsettled by the news they brought with their arrival, and she doubled down in her efforts to make sure that I understood everything she'd ever heard about El Olam. We spent every evening in prayer. I was only one of two boys being raised at the chapel, and we were a similar age and size. The other was the son of servants that did all the work around the chapel. When we were eight summers, soldiers secured Fjall." His eyes clouded with hurt at the memory. "They cleared everyone out of the chapel. All our possessions and especially anything related to the worship of god. My mother sent me to stand with the servants and told me to answer questions as they answered them. She put her hand on my head and prayed for me, and then sent me to stand with my friend. The soldiers moved through, separating us along invisible lines I could not then understand. However, when all was said and done, I was on one side of the line with the servants and my family was on the other side. Based on our answers, some servants were sent inside to clean and prepare the space for new inhabitants, and the others were sent to stand with my family. I answered in the same way as my friend, and we were among those inside. All of the people still outside were murdered." He stopped and relived the memory for a minute. "My friend's mother took pity on me and raised me alongside him. No one ever told. I've spent the last seventeen summers pretending to be the twin brother of one of the original servants."

Evin stood and removed the pouch he'd kept close around his neck. He cast it unceremoniously in Johannes's lap. "It's clear to me that your grandfather would have kept these for you if he had known you." He swallowed, fighting to keep his composure. "What they didn't tell you is that Lord Diederick wants me dead. He's apparently dreamed I'm going to kill him and he means to do the deed first. For that reason, Roald and my mom concocted this scheme to have me drag my unwitting bride to her apparent death so that I could be safe from him, and so I could fulfill a prophecy that I only just heard for the first time. They also didn't mention my inconvenient visions that indicate this god wants me to give my whole life to him, but I have flat out refused to do that twice. He has apparently chosen to move on."

With that Evin turned and stormed into the tent. The others looked dumbfounded.

Johannes dumped the contents of the pouch into his hands and held the pieces of the seal up to the light of the fire, examining them with awe. "That is something I never thought I would see!" He stuffed them back into the pouch and handed the whole thing to Roald. "I think we both know that these are going to have to find their way back to him when he's ready."

Roald gratefully took the pouch. "Thank you for not making that difficult. I knew I needed to get them back, but I wasn't sure how that was going to happen."

"Thank you for letting me look them over before I gave them back. Fascinating. Wasn't he born with the third one in his hand? I only saw two."

"He doesn't have the third one yet."

"Oh, I see," said Johannes as though he really didn't see.

"That's a long story that has yet to be written. I'm starting to lose faith in this whole process myself." Roald clasped his hands in front of him and the three of them sat quietly for the rest of the evening.

The next day, the four of them came in sight of the city of Cymbe. The outskirts were blanketed with vendors pulling brightly colored carts, and loud parties of citizens rejoicing. It was so far removed from anything any of them had ever seen that despite their exhaustion and grief, they stopped short and watched.

"What in the world is going on here?" Evin angrily glared at the festival atmosphere.

"Let's find some locals and ask." Roald was glad to hear him speak even if he was angry. "We need to find a place to stay and decide what we're doing next."

After a couple hours of searching, they had discovered two things. One, they had reached the town at the beginning of a month-long celebration leading up to the marriage of Lord Mikkel's son Micah. He was to be married to the daughter of the chieftain from the south to usher in a more diplomatic relationship with them. Two, there would not be a place to stay besides in their tents, but there were many places where they might be able to put those up.

None of them relished another night on the ground, but they were glad of the opportunity to be able to replenish their supplies. There was also a steady supply of water from a pump in the center of the city, so they were finally able to clean all the evidence of the fighting from themselves and their things. Johannes turned out to be a marvelous asset to the group. He seemed to know everything about taking care of everything. Evin finally assented to allowing someone to look at his wrist, and Johannes was able to find herbs and make a healing concoction. That ministration only served to make Evin angrier as it brought back memories of having his hand swabbed with the drugs at Fjall by this same man. Each day the young man's attitude grew darker and the space the others were giving him to make it through his grief did not seem to be working. He talked little, ate little, and never smiled. They spent many of the hours of their first day there asking the locals about bandits. The consensus was that bandits in the wilderness had become rarer than ever, and many seemed surprised they'd had a run in with them. The upcoming marriage had meant much more peace for the northerners. Since the news had been declared that the south had agreed to the peace treaty, they had felt a weight lift. They spent almost a week trying to get any information they could, but it was as if there was none available. It became clear that they needed to decide what to do next.

The afternoon of the following day, Roald stood and stretched. "Evin, let's take a walk."

"Not really interested, Roald."

"It wasn't a question, Evin." Roald's face didn't leave room for discussion. "We need to talk."

Evin jumped to his feet. "Fine, let's walk." He started off down the main thoroughfare of Cymbe.

Roald caught up with him quickly and they walked for a few minutes in silence, moving away from the streets crowded with encampments into the heart of the city where there were open spaces where camping wasn't allowed. A few people milled about, but there were far fewer than nearer the tent. Finally, Roald started talking, "Evin, I don't know what you're feeling, exactly. I can tell you're growing angrier by the day, and I understand, but have you thought about what your decision to abandon your quest means for everyone else that has a stake in everything that's happening?" Evin didn't answer, so Roald pushed. "I know you remember their stories and..."

Evin spun to face him. "I really don't want to think about other people's pain and my impotency to be able to solve any of the issues they're facing. I'm not trying to abandon those people, Roald. I have just become painfully aware of the fact that I have nothing to offer any of them. This has been an impossible task from the beginning. I had two pieces of an old rock that are part of a key to open an old lock on an old vault that houses an old book that no one can read. I needed three of them, and my dad has the other one, unless my visions aren't real, and then who knows where it is? If the visions are real, then it would take a miracle for me to get it now."

"What makes you think your dad has the other piece?" Roald looked at Evin like he was deranged.

"The Healer told me. I asked, and just like that," Evin smirked. "'Your father has it. He'll give it to you in time.'" He mocked and turned to walk on.

Roald grabbed his arm to keep him from strolling off again and fell into step beside him. "When did he say that?"

"Last time I saw him, when we were holed up waiting for Kai to heal."

"Evin, can't you see that El Olam is orchestrating things to bring us to this point in time with everything we need to find the key to free these people? He's chosen you to come here with the shards and he's going to work through you to take the next steps." Roald looked earnest.

Evin kept walking, looking straight ahead. "How far are we away from the Holy Mountain?"

"They call it Viberg. Less than half a day's ride." Roald said. "If we had horses."

"Get us some, and I will ride with you and we'll see what happens." He stopped walking and turned, putting a hand on Roald's chest to stop him from walking in front of him. "I'm telling you right now that if we go to this mountain and nothing happens, you need to join me in accepting that I am not the man god plans to use for this. I am not living up to anyone's expectations for me, not even my own. I have failed at supporting and protecting the one person I was supposed to be most concerned for, and there is no way I am going to watch that happen with that little band of people we left to wait for word. I am going to do this last thing for them, and then, I am going to settle over here where Diederick will never find me and spend my days finding out what happened to my wife."

"I will get horses today, and we'll go first thing in the morning." Roald said nothing indicating he would accept Evin's apparent resignation.

Evin turned and started walking back toward camp. "If that's all, I think I will turn in early. Have to be ready to get back on the trail tomorrow." Sarcasm dripped from everything he said.

Roald watched him out of sight and then set off to find horses.

~~~~~

Evin returned to the tents and with barely a word to the others, walked into the tent and closed and tied the flap behind him. He'd been going to bed earlier and earlier as the days went by, and now all he wanted to do was find solace in sleep. When he was asleep, he could be tormented by his dreams, but at least he couldn't torment himself. He thought of Inkeri, and the anger and resentment rose in him again. He pushed all of that down and just let his mind linger on their last good day together. He still loved the feeling he was starting to have of being part of something bigger with her by his side. He loved the idea that they could support and lift each other up. He loved the feeling that she might actually want to be with him, and that she loved all of these things too. He had come to understand that god had her here for a reason. He thought god was a good guy, because he would see these desires that Evin had and bring them so gloriously to life in Inkeri. At the beginning, he was willing to honor her and wait for her for an eternity. All of that had changed at the chapel. He felt like had treated her shamefully, and even though he knew they were
~~~~~

both under the influence of powerfully intoxicating herbal infusions, he had not been able to let go of any of his guilt over it. On top of breaking her trust, he had not been able to talk to her about it, barely summoning the courage it was going to take and just on the cusp of doing it when she was stolen from him so cruelly. He tried to block out the screams that were the last time he'd heard her voice. He screamed angrily and threw whatever he could find against the side of the tent, yelling indiscernible curses into the air.

Concerned voices from outside interrupted his fit of rage. "Evin?"

"Leave me alone!" He shouted menacingly. "I'm fine. I'm going to go to sleep now."

Mercifully, after a minute's whispering and shuffling, there was no more noise from out there, so he decided they planned to let him rest. He removed the shirt that had been hiding the wounds to stop the sleeve from rubbing against the sores. He picked angrily at the scabs on his wrist, which had started to look worse instead of better. He grabbed angrily at the things he'd thrown, and piling them up haphazardly around him, collapsed into them. He sobbed until his head ached and his heart felt as if it might rip in two pieces, and then he sobbed some more. When he could no longer breathe for all the congestion in his head, he inclined himself on the pile and gulped great breaths of air, trying to calm any part of his tortured soul. The breath would not come, and he started to panic, thinking that his sorrow was so deep it was going to deprive him of air completely. He hyperventilated, grabbing the pile of blankets and pillows he'd made and pushing them aside, forcing his hands to rest open against the firmness of the ground below. Finally, he was able to slow his breathing, pushing against the ground and focusing on nothing at all. The episode left him exhausted, so as his breath returned, he once more collapsed where he sat, welcome blackness overtaking his consciousness.

Seconds passed and he was awake. He groaned at his displeasure with the situation, longing for the blackness that he'd grown to love. As he came to awareness, he realized that there was grass under his face. It was soft and lush, and it reached to tickle the sides of his cheek and his nose. The anger that swallowed him every waking moment overtook him, and he grabbed the offending plants and ripped them from the ground, flinging them wildly in every direction. He sat looking with disgust at the chaos he'd created. He became aware that someone was sitting with him. He looked to his right, and there was the Healer. His face was sad, but there was no judgment in it even though Evin had just given in to a tantrum right in front of him. He took Evin's hand and turned it over, examining his wrist. Blood flowed from the parts where Evin had picked off the scabs. In places, the blood mixed with puss, and the wound had begun to smell and look like death. Red streaked down Evin's hand and up his arm, and it throbbed with constant pain. He'd ceased to care, and Johannes's earlier ministrations didn't seem to have worked. He had waited way too long to let him look at it, and for the last several days, he had just told him it was fine. He hoped it would kill him. The Healer looked into Evin's eyes, and the feelings that went through Evin were overwhelming and unnamable. Evin looked back to his wrist, impassively considering the consequences of this obviously grievous wound. He let go of Evin's hand and sat with him quietly for a moment. Evin kept his head down, struggling to remember the power he was sitting in the presence of. He looked again at the Healer, suddenly curious. "What is your name?" His voice croaked out, still filled with loss.

"Yeshua." The Healer looked at him again, and he felt too small to be here with him. Yeshua continued, "Evin, you need healing."

Evin looked at his wrist again, noting the heat and pain that radiated from it. "I'm sure it's going to be fine." He lied.

"There is a healing you need much deeper than that." He brought out the cup and offered it once more to Evin. "I've already paid for you to have this healing. Can you trust that and accept it?"

Evin jumped to his feet and grabbed the cup. His eyes flashed with anger and the Healer stood to his feet beside him, looking completely unfazed by his sudden movements. "I don't want your stupid cup!" he shouted. "I cannot possibly pile more pain on top of the pain I'm already carrying around. If you are El Olam, you should have been there for our desperate struggle in the wilderness. You cannot be seriously sitting here offering me a drink when you've allowed the best thing I ever had to be taken away. When you've allowed me to cause her pain and then allowed her to go through whatever she's had to endure since she was taken." Fresh sobs clawed their way out of Evin, and his aching ribs and raw throat burned afresh. "I am completely at the end of myself."

Yeshua watched as Evin stood broken in front of him. "Not completely."

Evin looked at him and his rage abated. This man was a conundrum. Then he remembered Inkeri's screams, and he screamed too, flinging the cup past the healer's head as far away from him as he could muster. "You can move things between wherever this is and reality. You can heal people when they're about to die. You can do all these miraculous things, and you let her die. You let her die!" He fell to his knees and grabbed the ground again, looking for purchase against the rocking hateful waves of emotion. Hands grabbed him and pulled at him, and he blinked, looking into the eyes of his friends and several curious onlookers. Roald stood at the edge of the camp with two horses on ropes. Evin rocked back to a seated position, shrugging off Kai's concerned hands. "I'm sorry, bad dream." He stood and blood dripped steadily from his wrist into the dirt at his feet.

Johannes turned to wave people away, and Kai muttered. "One of your bad dreams is going to end up killing someone, Evin. You almost threw yourself into the fire." He motioned to Evin's wrist. "The Healer run out of his miracle salve?"

Evin looked at his wrist, dismayed to see it looking the worst it had yet.

Johannes finished convincing the gathered people that all was well and returned to their side while Roald secured the new horses. He pulled Evin's wrist toward him and clicked his tongue. "You said it was better! By all that is good, Evin. You could die!"

"I certainly hope so." Evin grumbled.

"I am going to do all I can, but at this point, your hand is in grave danger."

"You can clean it up and bandage it or whatever you want, but tomorrow Roald and I are going to settle all of this nonsense and then I am done dealing with it."

Johannes looked at Roald, who looked more than a little concerned, but concluded, "I believe we are supposed to go tomorrow, Johannes. I know it may be ill-advised, but I get the sense we need to."

"Fine." He gave Kai a list and sent him for some supplies while he busied himself with various plants and pots near the fire. He fished several tinctures and small bottles from his bag. He told Evin to sit in front of him, and when Kai returned, he unfolded the new supplies and directed Evin to stretch out his hand. "Hold his arm still." He instructed Roald. "You don't let him jump up or move erratically." He said to Kai.

"What the hell are you going to do?" Evin pulled his arm back and looked suspiciously at Johannes.

"First Evin, we are going to cry out to the Healer on your behalf." With that, he knelt in the middle of the huddle of men and bowing his head, began to speak. "Healer, we cannot heal this kind of wound without your intervention. We pray that you will grant me wisdom to know exactly what to do and lead this process."

Evin scoffed. "I think the Healer already had his shot."

Johannes looked back up at Evin, disgust clear on his face. Then he dipped his hands in the water he had brought over and boiled, scrubbing at them furiously. "Evin. I have access to a tincture that will make this less painful for you. What I am about to do will hurt you, and I can lessen that, but this tincture is the same one that was part of the compound you and Inkeri had in the chapel, and I will not use it unless you ask for it. It would not feel the same way as that, but I thought you should know. He poured a very small amount of something into a cup and set it aside where it would not be knocked over. "I'm going to clean this wound aggressively and remove the dead skin. This is going to be the most painful thing you've possibly ever felt, but it is necessary."

Evin stretched his arm back out slowly, deciding he really didn't have a choice but to allow Johannes to continue. "I don't want the drugs." Roald grabbed his hand and his arm above the injury, immobilizing it. Kai stood at one shoulder, ready to hold him down should he try to stand. He closed his eyes and turned his head away, steeling himself for what he knew was coming. Using scraps of rags boiled with the water, Johannes mopped the same tincture he'd previously used all over the surface of the wound, cleaning up his arm and down into his hand, glaring at the stains of grass and dirt in Evin's hand, then giving Roald a questioning look.

"He has a way of bringing stuff back with him from his dreams." Roald stated flatly. "Looks like he had a fight with the ground this time."

Johannes shrugged and continued cleaning. "Let me know when it stops stinging." He told Evin. He sat back and waited while Evin winced.

"Ok." Evin indicated. Johannes began cleaning in earnest, not trying to be gentle, but instead scrubbing around the edges of the jagged cuts that had been left by the tent pole. Evin cursed under his breath, blowing air out through clenched teeth between mutterings.

Johannes gave him a short break. "You should have let me look at this every day. Do you have a death wish?" Evin opened his eyes and stared at Johannes, his eyes giving him the answer he didn't want to hear. "The healing you need is a lot deeper than this wound, Evin."

Johannes couldn't know the gut punch his words delivered. Evin just squeezed his eyes shut and tried to push his arm closer, forgetting he was restrained. The man bowed back to his work, focusing on the freshly cleaned flesh. "I have to remove some of this," he stated.

"Remove it?" Kai questioned.

"Some of the flesh is dead, and it is killing the flesh around it. I will attempt to stop that, but I will be honest. This is going to take a miracle." He looked at it critically. "I will do everything in my power." He took the scraper he'd asked Kai to purchase and began scraping the edges of the cut, pushing whatever dead material fell away to the side and wiping it off with the cloth. Evin grunted but held still, still breathing heavily. He finished that and looked at the other two. "Are you ready? Kai, grab his shoulders." Evin turned to look.

Johannes fished a tiny knife from a case in front of him, carefully wiping the surface with the tincture.

Evin struggled. "That's the same knife they cut our hands with." Panic filled his voice.

Johannes leaned forward and looked into his eyes. "Evin, I am not going to give you any drugs unless you want them. You do not have to fear me. This is not the same knife that was used on you. This one is mine and you have never seen it. You can trust me. I am not your enemy."

Evin stopped struggling but looked sick. He looked away again and gulped air. Johannes waited while he got control of his breath and then nodded at the others, who held Evin as tightly as they dared. He positioned the tiny knife carefully along the outside of the wound and began cutting, stripping away bits of diseased flesh, trying to leave as little extra damage as possible. Evin screamed out with each cut, and it was all Roald and Kai could do to hold him in position. After the first few cuts, Evin begged for the drugs that Johannes had offered. Kai took the small cup Johannes had set aside and held it to Evin's lips. He chugged the proffered drink, grimacing at the bitterness.

"Look at me." Johannes commanded. He didn't move for several minutes as he looked deeply into Evin's eyes, watching for a sign the drugs were having their intended effect. "It will take longer since he drank it. Give it a few minutes. Evin, don't touch your arm. We're going to let you go for a minute and let you rest. Keep your arm out here and don't let it touch anything. Roald released his arm, but let it continue to rest on his hand. Every few minutes Johannes looked into Evin's eyes, appraising the situation. After a time, he nodded, and the two men took their positions again. "It will be easier this time, I assure you." He commenced the careful cutting. "He is lucky that these stayed as close to the surface as they did. This would be a dangerous place to have to work deeper." Evin almost completely ceased struggling and allowed the work to continue while he sat in a stupor.

"Is he ok?" Roald watched Evin's head loll to the side.

"He drank all of it. I was only going to give him half at a time, but it will not hurt him. I didn't pour enough to kill him, but it is a big dose. He watched Evin's chest rise and fall. "He'll be in and out of it for the rest of the night, but he's fine." He finished up quickly and bandaged the wound carefully, tying clean bandages on as tightly as he dared. He sat up and looked at the others. "I don't have very much confidence in that to heal him completely, but it will slow it down and give you time for your mission tomorrow."

"Will he even be able to go?" Roald looked at the semi-conscious man as he helped Kai move him back into the tent.

"He will not feel well, but he will be able to ride by morning. He won't remember most of this."

"I have never seen the like of that." Roald clapped Johannes on the back. "You're a regular healer!"

"You learn a lot when you pay close attention. I'm usually just the one mixing the drugs and watching the patient while the work is done." He washed his hands again and began to tidy his space. "Now you two are going to tell me all about these visions."

Chapter 22

Morning dawned gray and sleepy. Evin struggled to wake, finally coming out of the tent well after dawn. He wasn't struggling as much this time with coming off the drugs, since they were different. Within the hour, Johannes had checked his bandages and cleared him to take the journey, even though it was against Johannes's better judgement. Roald left instructions for some tasks Kai and Johannes could take care of, including finding horses for themselves to replace their stolen ones.

Evin did everything as if he were in a fog. He moved mechanically from one task to the next, ignoring Roald as they cantered off toward the mountain. Viberg was more like a giant rock rising from the floor of the wilderness than a mountain. Stairs had been carved into one side of it, and the other side hung dazzlingly over the foaming sea. Evin had never seen anything like it. The beauty was extravagant, and the care that men had put into the site spoke volumes about the care they had taken of its contents. He hoped for their sake that he would be able to help them find what they wanted. He had precisely zero hope that was going to happen today, though. He knew he'd turned his back on the Healer, and he could feel the consequences of that in his mind and body. His self-hatred was fueled as well by the sluggish feelings that reminded him he had willingly taken drugs that he had promised himself never to have again. He couldn't remember any of what had led up to that, but his friends had promised him that his pain had been too great without it. Still, today none of that mattered. He just felt like the weakest man in the world.

He stood staring at the outside of the structure for a long time. What now? Here he was. His final destination. Here is where he was supposed to be able to free a useless book from its years of interment for some reason he couldn't understand that would apparently be made clear when the time came. Here he stood, mind muddier than ever and with a heart completely destroyed. He had nothing left to give this project. There was a time he would have prayed, or at the very least sought Roald's council. Instead, he climbed the many stairs slowly, watching as the view got better from each one. Before too long, they reached what appeared to be a solid stone wall with a wide porch carved in front of it. In the very center, a straight line cut down the whole surface was the only evidence of a door. Evin couldn't help but be impressed with the structure. For the first time in days, he felt a flutter of excitement at the sheer magnitude of engineering that went into this. He let his fingers play over the smooth stone surface, his amazement growing. Directly in the center of the door, a small circle was the only reminder that a seal had once resided there. The door didn't give to any kind of pressure. Evin pushed a few times in a few different directions, but the effort only hurt his arm, and he was sure it would do no good. Without turning, he held his hand out behind him to Roald. "I know you have the shards. Want to hand them to me?" He listened as Roald shuffled for the pouch and within seconds, he was holding the first. The one his mom had been given. He studied it carefully, again bewildered that such a little key would have the power to open such a gigantic structure. He puzzled over the piece for a minute, wondering at the symbol on it. He remembered in his first vision, the three separate pieces and the whole one. He tried to remember what the whole one looked like. He pushed the shard into the circular spot and rotated it until it seemed to find its perfect place. He reached his other hand back for the next one. When he had it, he stood for a minute, staring at the symbol on it. This was the one he was born holding. The one he'd handed to himself in a vision. The second part of the symbol fitted beside the first and he held them in place together with his fingers, looking at them and imagining them as three. "I think maybe it's a representation of the parts of El Olam. The Father, who we've been calling god, and this one, that looks like a river. That means we're missing the son, the healer, Yeshua." He felt the weight of his selfishness at just the mention of his name, but he breathed past it and marveled once again at the scope of the engineering that would make this work. "Roald, this is unbelievable." He let the pieces fall into his hand and turned to face the guide. "I can only imagine..." He was stopped in his tracks by what he saw when he turned around. Roald stood with the pouch in one hand and the third shard in the other. He held it out toward Evin, but Evin couldn't move to take it. He just stared at Roald. He looked him over thoroughly, taking in his height, his build, his eyes and eyebrows, remembering his goofy grin and his sense of humor. Evin blinked but still couldn't understand what he was seeing in front of him. Stunned, he took the third piece and fitted them all together. They stayed in three parts, but he turned and placed them in the space together, marveling in the beauty of the whole. The last piece was the Son.

Yeshua was the key. Evin's heart beat as though it might leave his chest, and his mouth dried out completely. Nausea overtook him like waves, and he struggled to focus on what he was doing. He held the seal in the space and tried to focus on willing it to seal together. Nothing happened, and he let it fall once more into his palm. He whirled around and looked the other man over again, taking the pouch from Roald's hand and returning the three pieces to it and handing it back to him. "Did you get this from my dad before we left?" He asked hopefully.

Roald stood in exactly the same spot, He took a minute and slid the pouch back over his head, watching Evin carefully. "No."

The simple pronouncement dashed Evin's hope of an easy explanation. Evin shook his head, then said in a mocking voice. "Your father has the third shard. He'll give it to you in time." He studied the ground at their feet. "How did I not see? I don't know what I thought. The shard was just going to fly across the whole country from my dad's possession." He almost choked on the words. His dad. So many of the things Roald had said and the ways he had acted made so much more sense now. His mom's embarrassment at the mention of the third shard, the differences in him and his brothers, his own grin that Inkeri had loved.

"Does he know. My dad? Does he know he's not even my dad!" Evin's voice raised, and he looked like he wanted to hit something.

Roald gave the same one-word answer. "No."

In that word were housed so many emotions that Evin couldn't even begin to process them. In his already weakened state, this felt like a final death blow. "Why in the hell, Roald. Why in the very real hell would you wait until right now to tell me this? Damn you, I absolutely cannot even imagine what is going through your head." He looked like a wild man for a minute, considering their vast height above the water as he looked for an escape. He made to move toward the edge and Roald grabbed him.

"Don't even touch me." Evin almost spat the words.

Roald kept holding on to him. "Then sit. Sit and I will let you go." He looked desperate. "I will not allow you near that edge."

Evin twisted from his grasp and sank against the wall, looking desperately toward the turbulent water. Roald squatted in front of him, on his guard for any sudden moves. He studied the young man; a longing look on his face.

Evin turned his head to look back at him. "I'm not going to do anything stupid, Roald. Don't worry. I'll do my part to make sure your bloodline continues."

"Evin... don't. You don't know the whole story."

His jaw was set, and his lips pressed together. He couldn't decide if that was a story he wanted to hear. "Did my mom..." he paused, gathering the strength to continue. "she wanted to be with you like that?"

Roald drew little circles in the dirt at his feet. "Wait, do you mean to imply..." he looked deflated. "By the gods, Evin. What kind of monster do you take me for?"

"I don't know," Evin shrugged. "Maybe the kind that lets another man raise his child. You're like one of those birds that leaves an egg in a different bird's nest."

Roald looked shaken. He stood back up and paced the length of the porch, looking out over the water. "Evin, I don't have a perfect explanation for you. You can think whatever you want about me, but I am very proud of you, and I will continue to be, no matter what you say to me. I never claimed any right to you. Damn it all, Evin, I didn't even claim any rights to your mom. I understand that she is the wife of another man. I am not making any excuses, and I will not be able to offer any explanations. When Erik came back from the war, he was greeted with a third son, and he was ecstatic. I didn't have the freedom to raise you. I got to just fade into the background and stay as close as I could and watch from a distance while Evin son of Erik grew up. I don't think I could have made a better choice. Imagine if the truth had come out. The law Erik loves so much would have been given free reign. You probably would have been left somewhere to starve after your mom and I were beaten to death in front of your brothers. Does that sound better to you than the choices we made, Evin?"

Evin let his head bang lightly against the stone behind him. "Why in the world would you do that? Why would you pick another man's wife?"

"I picked her long before she belonged to another man." Roald's explanation just made it worse.

"My brothers?" Evin started to wonder.

"Both Erik's." Roald walked back to where Evin sat. "Your mom and I lost touch for a couple of years after they married. I traveled around getting really extraordinary at my job. Then, I was given a job in your village, and your mom and I ran into each other." Roald paused. "Our relationship ended several years ago, Evin. We realized some really important things about honoring El Olam, and how our relationship wasn't doing that, so we stopped it." He looked very sad. "That wasn't what either one of us wanted, but it's the way it is."

Roald reached his hand down to Evin to offer to help him up. Instead, Evin pushed himself to his feet and continued to glare at Roald. "Are we going to keep up with this ruse or am I supposed to start calling you dad?" Evin smirked wickedly. "I can tell you right now what I am doing, Roald. This," he pointed to the door, "didn't work, obviously, so we've tested your precious prophecy, and now I am going to go back to that city that is the closest place I know on earth to the last place I saw Inkeri, and I am going to exhaust the days I have left searching this earth for her, just like I told you. You keep your shards, and the other three of you can come back sometime and see if you have better luck. I don't want you to do or say anything else to try to dissuade me from this course of action. I already do not care for anything you have to say to me. You, and my mom apparently, have been making bad choices for a long time, and you made some really awful ones for me without asking my opinion on the matter. I will no longer be considering your opinion." He turned and began his descent down the stairs, leaving a bewildered Roald standing at the top.

"Well, god, that's a mess." Roald started after him. "I might have made it, but it is going to take you to unravel it."

Chapter 23

Evin stayed ahead of Roald the whole ride back, his mind whirling through all the scenarios repeatedly. He had a lot of questions, but he didn't want to give Roald the satisfaction of answering them, so he just kept spurring the horse on. They made it back while the sun still had several hours in the sky. Johannes immediately took the horse from Evin and wouldn't allow him to do anything. He checked on Evin's wound and didn't look very pleased. He and Kai were fairly buzzing with news from the city. They had found horses that pleased them. Everyone in the city was gathering in the center near the palace that belonged to Lord Mikkel. Tonight, the people would get to meet the princess from the south that would make it possible for the two cultures to become one thriving whole. Micah was going to appear on the south balcony of the palace and introduce her to the crowd in an hour.

"I think we should go." Kai looked excited.

"Why in the world should we go to that?" Evin looked completely uninterested in the possibility.

Kai dismissed his gruffness as just more of the same. "Because, we have an opportunity to see how differently things work over here. Maybe we will discover if they still travel to chapels for the wedding, or what is different here. It is obvious," he waved a hand to indicate the charged atmosphere, "that something is very different about this place. I think it would help us to see what that is. Aren't we looking for help from here? We'll be able to infer some things from the way they talk."

"I hate to tell you," Evin countered, "but I am no longer a part of this resistance. I'm going to gather my things and find a place to live here and spend my days finding out what happened to Inkeri."

Kai just looked at him. "I take it the seal thing didn't work?"

"Worse than that, I'm afraid." Evin didn't elaborate. "Anyway, I believe sincerely that you are all better off without me."

Johannes stepped up. "That is fine, Evin, if that is what you have decided with the help of god, but you must stay with me until the arm is better. I will tell you when you can be on your own, but I insist you stay with us for now. We can stay right here." He indicated the tents.

Evin considered the situation. He hadn't cared if he died, but he had a renewed desire to find out what had happened to Inkeri. "I will admit I need you to help this to heal. I will be sleeping in my own tent, and as I'm sure my father's money," he looked at Roald with a menacing stare, "paid for all of these supplies, I will be taking at least one tent and some of the other things." He raised his hands up. "Why don't we go see a princess. I want to size up my new lord." He pantomimed a stiff bow. "Going to have to work on that." He started down the road, heading toward the palace.

Kai looked at Roald. "What happened?"

Roald finished moving the horses behind the tents with the others and held up his hands the same way Evin had. "That is a long story. Perhaps another time." He motioned after Evin. "After you."

The walk itself took almost an hour with all the foot traffic heading in the same direction. The announcement had been made that same afternoon, so as soon as people heard they moved in to try to get a place where they could see. Evin had never seen so many people gathered in one spot in his life, and he was comforted by the energy that emanated from them. It was like something had broken in his brain and he had become a different person. He liked the new confident Evin that could imagine his life alone. The thought crept in before he could stop it. Maybe he'd be just like Roald and wander the earth doing whatever he wanted without worrying about the impact it would have on other people. He'd never considered himself overly impulsive, but he thought it might be a good way for him to go about doing things from here on out.

They crowded onto a bridge with a fantastic view of the balcony. The bridge stretched across a street below that was also crowded with people. The palace loomed over the whole scene, the biggest building any of them had ever seen. Its light colored stone walls were the same shade as Viberg, doubtless quarried near the holy site. The distance from them to the balcony was far, but they would be able to see fine from here. The people in front of them were all shorter than they, so they were lucky. Hearing might be more difficult, but they would see. They were pleasantly surprised when a servant stepped out on the balcony and begin announcing Micah. Because of the buildings around the bridge, his voice bounced nicely back to them. The crowd cheered as the promised man stepped onto the balcony. He was impressive, but the crowds apparent love for him was unheard of in the east. Rulers were something to be tolerated and feared, and it was assumed the same would be true over here. Evin looked at Kai. "We need your glass eye thing."

Kai smiled. "Too bad I left that behind. We have a good enough view, though. You can tell he's a handsome guy."

That was true. He looked like a picture someone might make of a god if they were trying to describe one. Evin felt sorry for him that he had to marry this southern princess, because he could surely have his pick from all the women in the crowd if their reaction to him was any indication. He waved for a few minutes while the cheering continued. His head was covered with shiny black curly locks and his strong cheekbones, chin, and nose looked as if they'd all been commanded to be perfect and had obeyed. He was even more handsome because he knew he was handsome. In a minute, he raised a hand to indicate stillness and the people immediately ceased the noise they were creating. Everyone leaned forward in anticipation of the words he would speak. His bearing was perfect. He stood straight. He wore a long white and gold robe tied at the waist with a braided gold cord unlike anything they'd ever seen.

"It is with great pleasure that I stand before you today. As you know, I am to be married at the end of the month to the princess of the people of the southern lands." The people once again cheered their approval. When the noise died, he continued. "Until today, none of you have seen the princess. I myself only met her two days ago when she traveled here with a retinue of her people. I was the first to behold her beauty, but today, I wish to share her with my people. Years of tireless work by my father have paved the way for us to join with our friends in the south. We can now become one. One people joined in worship. Joined in peace. Joined in blood!" The frenzied crowd shouted their approval. "Please join me in welcoming my bride to our city." He stepped to the side and inclined his hand toward the curtain he'd come through only minutes ago. "Princess Siria!" The crowd cheered wildly as the curtain parted. Everyone strained to the front to catch a glimpse of the much-acclaimed beauty. The four men joined the crowd in their eager anticipation. A woman strode through the curtain hesitantly with her head down, looking at the floor of the balcony. From their viewpoint, only the top of her head was visible. She continued to study the ground as she stepped to the front beside her husband-to-be. Micah leaned toward her, seeming to coax and encourage her to look at the crowd, lifting her chin gently. Evin was confused by her hesitancy. He had been expecting a proud march out of the curtain and the same sort of display Micah had given. Her hair shone in the sun in a way that seemed familiar to him somehow, and he remembered Inkeri's hair shining that same way in the light of the morning sun when Roald and Johannes had awakened them at the chapel. He sharply took in a breath and held it as she raised her face to the crowd. She didn't smile or make any friendly gestures, but at the sight of her face, the crowd went berserk. It wasn't the beauty of her face that made Evin began to scream with the crowd, it was the face itself. As he stared off the bridge to the balcony yards away, he stared into the face of the woman he knew as his wife. He began screaming her name, but the crowd drowned his voice, and he sounded like any of the others welcoming her to the city. He suddenly felt sick to his stomach. The impact of seeing her alive would have been strong enough under any circumstances, but under these, it was crippling. Somehow in the month since she'd disappeared, she had managed to become the princess of the southern people. Adrenalin filled him and he pushed people out of the way and surged to the railing. Hands grabbed him from behind to keep him from leaping to his death and started to drag him off the bridge. He wrestled free and stood where he could watch her. Time froze as he stared, memorizing all the little things he'd forgotten. Could it be someone who looked like Inkeri? He observed her movements and beautiful expressionless face while the crowd cheered. It was her. His palms were sweaty and his heart threatened to beat through his chest. Micah began to speak again, but Evin focused on Inkeri instead of listening. It was as if he was watching all of this happen to someone else. He felt like a piece of his heart was being ripped out and he couldn't stop it. Taking a breath became a chore as he struggled to control his emotions. She looked more beautiful than he'd ever seen anyone look. Her hair was swept up and gathered in curls all over her head. Precious stones glinted from various places in her hair, around her neck, and around her waist. She wore a gown that shimmered like fire in the setting sun. Evin stared as Micah reached up and swept the hair off her forehead. He clenched his hands into tight fists, remembering wanting to do that himself several times and never having the confidence. Micah was clearly pleased with her. He treated her with kindness and respect, moving around her like a good man should treat a princess. Then, he took her hand and held it as he addressed the crowd. Evin stared at their clasped hands and the weight of the day seemed to find its fulfillment in that one act. Everything he'd thought was his was no longer his. He no longer had a safe homeland. His father was no longer his, despite all the memories and all the care that Evin had taken for granted over all the years he'd been raised in his home. His wife was no longer his, and even though their history was short, he knew she had a part of him he could never have back or replace. He could never love someone the way he loved her. Micah finished talking and released Inkeri's hand as he waved at the crowd again. The cheering recommenced around them, but Evin could only scream her real name again, undoubtedly seeming insane to the people close by. As he watched, horrified, Micah slid his arm around Inkeri and they walked out of sight through the curtain. Evin moved toward the edge of the bridge again as if to follow the only way he knew how, not caring anything for the open spaces that prevented him from reaching her. Hands grasped him again, more firmly this time, and dragged him off the bridge. He didn't struggle against them this time, and soon they were joining the crowd as people made their way back to where they were sleeping. The crowd buzzed with news of her beauty and girls giggled nearby and talked about wedding details, wondering how she could be even more beautiful on that day. Evin allowed himself to be led along like he had no will of his own. He snapped out of it when a man on the other side of them made a rough comment about wishing he was Micah on the wedding night. The men around him laughed raucously with him and Evin started to push through the crowd at them.

Roald grabbed his arm. "This is not the time, Evin. These people will think you've lost it, and you're going to get yourself in worse shape."

Evin glared at him, but instead of saying anything, allowed himself to be led away. So much for the impetuous version of himself he had started to like for a minute. He was gone, again replaced by this uncertain boy who was still trying to figure things out.

The rest of the walk back to camp was silent. Evin concentrated on blocking out the conversations around him. He wasn't sure if he would ever recover from this one day. He'd been very sure of the path he was ready to take when they had set out to see the princess, and then he had discovered that she was his missing wife, and now he was conflicted. He wanted to hate Roald. He vehemently wanted to blame him over and over for all the trouble in his life now, but he kept coming up short of the power to do that. He had seen too much of the man's good character and his care for others, including himself. He had been planning to walk away from the situation. That way, he would never really have to think about it again. Roald could go away, and he wouldn't have to work out how to treat him or what things to trust him with. Now, it looked like he still needed him. He needed the counsel the man could offer. He needed the ideas that came from his years of experience. Needing his help stung more by far than the thought of walking away from everything had stung. Evin thought of Erik. The man he had always known as his father had always treated him fairly. He had shared his wisdom, his love, and his home with his youngest responsibility. He hadn't wanted to think about him as the enemy. Even when he had heard the words "war hero" used to describe Erik and later heard the details of what the soldiers were involved in during the last war, he didn't let his mind go there. Now he pondered the reserved, smart man he had always called "dad" and he felt sorry for him. Evin never wanted to be that man who poured his life into making a happy home with a woman he grew to love while she was actually with another man behind his back. He thought of Inkeri standing on that balcony, apparently already betrothed to the most eligible bachelor in the country, and he felt the pain of being that very man. What did he have to offer her next to Micah? What had Erik had compared to Roald? Evin looked at Roald, who was walking just in front of him talking animatedly to Johannes. He had always looked tough, probably just because he was, but underneath was that grinning boyishness that was always winning people over. Evin had been won over by it too, and now he saw that it was the same as his. Rather his was the same as Roald's. Something wonderful that had been unintentionally given him by a man who had never intended to help create him, much less raise him. He felt the resentment swell again, but he heard Roald's words from Viberg. What choice did the two of them have? Could they have run away? Would he have thought better of his mother if she had left two young boys at home to fend for themselves? Roald looked back and caught Evin staring at him. That boyish grin fought its way to Roald's face, and Evin recognized the unsureness of that expression. Roald wanted to win his affection. He hadn't given up on the surly boy he had been trapped with for the better part of this journey. Roald went back to his conversation. They reached the tents and exchanged a few words. Darkness had completely covered them as they walked, so Evin made his way into the tent to rest. He wasn't feeling well, and today had been too much. He was asleep before the others were even thinking about bed.

Chapter 24

Johannes was sitting patiently by the fire, poking at the newly relit embers when Evin stepped from the tent. He waved him over for the now ritual check of the wound. Evin had become familiar with the pain and heat that radiated from his arm. He had forced his bound arms over the tent peg in his desperation to be free, and as he pushed against the peg with the ropes, he had also dug several grooves into the flesh of his arm. Debris and dirt and dried blood had stayed there while they had fruitlessly searched the wilderness, and now his sewn stubbornness was reaping its reward.

Johannes removed old bandages and frowned at the carnage on Evin's arm. The work he had done on it had slowed the progression of the disease, but it was looking bad again. "Leave the bandage off for now, just try not to touch it." He put his hands in his face, and Evin thought he must be praying. He had a habit of that.

Evin sat quietly beside him. "I don't feel well today, Johannes."

"I would imagine not." The man said quietly.

"There is something you're not saying." Evin looked at him.

"I would say the same is true of you." Johannes returned his gaze.

They both looked back to the fire, confirming to one another that there were indeed a lot of unsaid things between them. The others eventually came to sit with the pair of them.

Johannes looked at Evin again and addressed the others. "We have to find some other help for Evin." He looked back down at the fire. "We need someone who can help decide whether to remove the arm before the arm ends up removing Evin."

Evin straightened up and looked angrily at Johannes. "Who are you to decide we might have to just lop my arm off?"

Roald and Kai looked at the two. "Are you sure?" Roald asked Johannes.

Johannes nodded. "I have rarely seen such a stubborn infection. It seems no matter what I do, nothing helps. I think it doesn't help that he refuses to allow his mind to fight it."

Evin just looked at him.

Roald stood. "Today, we're going to throw ourselves on the mercy of Lord Mikkel. Yesterday we wouldn't have had a chance to even see him, but today we have information he definitely needs, and maybe he will take pity on Evin and help us with the care he needs."

Evin looked appalled to have no control once again over his own circumstances. "Wait a minute! We're going to march up to the palace and ask them to help figure out if we need to cut my arm off right after we inform them that we're pretty sure their celebrated princess is my wife? Who could even think that Inkeri would want to see us now that she's found herself the perfect man? This does not sound like a good plan. I would really like to keep the arm and go on."

"Think about it, Evin." Kai said. "Inkeri isn't in that palace of her own free will. She's still a captive. There is this big wedding planned that's supposed to unite two kingdoms that have been warring with one another forever, and the south gives them a fake princess? I do think that is something they would like to know."

"Even though they seem to have developed far differently than we have to the east, these are our people, Evin, and I feel like they're the victims of treachery." Roald implored him to see. "Also, your best chance lies in the hands of the physicians they are bound to have in that palace."

Evin shrugged.

Johannes stood. "Oh, we're back to that, are we? You just want to let death claim you? What of Inkeri? What of your commitment to her? I stood and watched you make that commitment. I saw the love on your faces, and even though I have spoken very little to her, I have no doubt that she will be as delighted to lay eyes on you as you should have been to see her." He walked to Evin and pulled the necklace roughly out of his shirt, holding the silver pendant. "She didn't give you this lightly, Evin. Instead of thinking the worst of her, maybe you should be examining your own heart. You've been spending so much time beating yourself up that you can only think of yourself. Well, do you know what that drug cocktail that was mixed for you did, Evin? It was designed to awaken all the senses and encourage the feelings that you already have to flourish. That one was given to you because you both indicated that you were pleased to be with the other to your separate attendants. Neither one of you did anything you didn't want to do. It's the whole thing I mentioned before about positive experiences being tied to the things they want you to remember. We call the mixture Solace, because it forces people to a place of peace in a mind that may have been disquieted before. I'll bet you can still quote all those sections of the law you repeated that night, even though you only said them once. It's important to the process that they find out what both people want and make that happen in order to be able to manipulate their memory." He paused, letting the pendant go. "You're assuming how she feels without even talking to her about it, which I understand at this point is not your fault, but you need to fight to get that opportunity, Evin. You had better wake up and be willing to fight for your life, or your body is going to take the cues you're giving it and give up the fight itself."

The outburst from Johannes was so out of place that the others just stared at him. Evin finally stood and looked at the group. "Let's go try to lose an arm and get the girl, then." He looked at the others after a second. "Maybe sooner is better than later?"

They wasted no time once they were on the same page, and as the sun grew strong in the sky they stood next to their horses in front of the palace. It was situated in the center of the city on a square surrounded by an ornamental stream spanned with a footbridge. The man-made stream provided no protection but was a beautiful accent to the unusual tan colored stone that reminded Evin of the Holy Mountain. They tied the horses to posts meant for the purpose and continued on foot across the bridge. There was no resistance to their entry of this part of the palace. The gardens were open to the people during the day. A few people walked the ground working in the plantings. Evin assumed they were gardeners preparing the place for the wedding that was set to happen here too soon. They took in the sights of the garden, wondering where to go from here. Evin thought of Inkeri, hidden from him somewhere in this giant building. What did she think had happened to them? As they moved to the interior of the gardens, they came upon a large staircase that wound into the upper levels. In a large landing where the staircase became two smaller ones, a pair of guards stood. Above them the stairs continued, showing little of what they might expect to see at the top.

"This looks like the right place." Roald indicated the guards. "Take a deep breath and look friendly, guys." With that, he started up the stairs.

The guards watched them approach. "There is no audience with Lord Mikkel today." One of them impassively intoned.

Roald bowed lightly. "I completely understand, and I would generally agree that is the best policy, but we have a critical piece of information regarding the princess that we need to see he gets in person."

The guard appraised the group. "You understand that if you claim to have important news, and then if you do not actually have news, even if you think it is important, you will be imprisoned." He said it with no emotion, as if it were common information.

"Of course. Please, sir, the news we have could be of the utmost importance." Roald let the man know they meant to make the commitment.

"I will go and ensure that Lord Mikkel wishes to hear news today. While I am away, these other guards," he nodded to a group of four that had appeared from nowhere, "will search for and remove any weapons you might have. If you are allowed to enter, you will be surrounded by guards, and you can be cut down at a second's notice. Do you understand?"

Roald understood perfectly. "I do. We will do whatever is needed to gain an audience."

"Very good." The guard turned and walked off while the four were each poked and prodded in the search for anything that could be used as a weapon. When the guards had removed their swords and were satisfied they had nothing else, they stood coolly appraising the rag tag group.

Finally, footsteps echoed in the hall above and the first guard appeared at the top and beckoned them to follow him. "You have found Lord Mikkel to be in good spirits. I trust that you will be careful to see that he stays that way."

"I'm sorry," said Roald, "but we cannot assure that we will leave him in as good a mood as we find him."

The guard merely pressed his lips together at Roald's declaration and led the group through a maze of hallways and staircases until they reached a room with an open door. The room was massive, and the door was the same design as the one on the holy mountain. Two solid slabs of heavy stone stood inexplicably apart from one another. The room was one of the ones that boasted the balconies that were the building's most outstanding features. Mostly empty, it was nonetheless very inviting. The stone floor led to a pile of cushions on the left and an ornately carved desk on the right. The rest of the floor lay barren. Designs carved into its surface told a tale that would have taken quite some time to decipher. Filmy sheets of silk hung on horizontal poles suspended from the ceiling, giving the room an ethereal quality. Seated at the desk was a man who most of the travelers had never seen. Despite that, they were all equally sure he was the man they sought. His bearing and his kind face radiated wisdom that seemed to be even too great for a man of his advanced years. There was, however, a hard edge to his eyes, something that commanded respect. Each one of the men, upon making eye contact with him, let their eyes drift to the carvings on the floor. The guards positioned themselves in strategic places in the room, and the one by the door slid it shut almost noiselessly.

"Well, I didn't expect to have guests of such an interesting caliber today, but change can always be good, I think." He carefully considered each man's face and clothing, and he must have seen something in Evin's face that drew his attention. He motioned for him to step forward. "You look honest, so I would like for you to explain this important business of yours."

"Evin looked up, this time making and maintaining eye contact with the seasoned ruler. He thought carefully and decided that since honesty was apparently important to Lord Mikkel, he would not try to make their sudden appearance look more official than it was. "You have my wife."

His blunt declaration had quite the impact on Mikkel's face. He raised his eyebrows and stared at Evin, receiving the same look in return. "Well, I thought you were honest, but as you are too young to have a wife, and I lost my wife long before you were born, I can't make sense of your point."

"I'm sorry, my lord." Evin quickly corrected, bowing his head. "I didn't mean any impertinence. I will explain myself if I may." Mikkel kindly inclined his head, so Evin continued. He told his abbreviated story, cutting out everything that didn't have a bearing on Inkeri's disappearance and carefully led up to seeing her on the balcony the day before. "When I saw her, and I knew she was alive, I was astounded. Seeing her downcast and understanding that she might somehow be being forced to agree to this marriage, I had to come."

Mikkel stood and walked back and forth behind the desk before sitting on the end of it, looking out at the balcony, absorbing the information he'd been given. "I know you cannot come close to understanding what is at stake here. Enemies beset me from every side trying to stop the union between our country and the south. For decades, I have strived to no other end, and my son's marriage to Princess Siria is to be the bond that I have long struggled to see solidified. It troubles me greatly to be faced with this quandary. If I believe that you tell me the truth, then I believe that the people I have befriended in every way possible for almost half of my life are trying to deceive me. The fact that they might steal some traveler's wife to do so troubles me. If I believe them, then it means that at least four men," he pointed at them, "in my own kingdom will go to any lengths to try to stop the union. Tell me traveler, who should I believe?"

Evin held his gaze steadily under the scrutiny. "I think you would do best to ask the woman you call the princess. Have you spoken to her?"

"For her own safety she is kept under tight security by her own people until the wedding. There are many in the south that would see our efforts toward peace thwarted. I have not spoken to her and have only seen her briefly. Until now I had no reason to doubt her identity. She fits the description of the princess that we have heard. I think it should be as you say, though." He briefly considered for a moment. "Micah has begun seeing her every day leading up to the wedding. They are using the time to get to know one another. I believe he is the man that can get close enough without suspicion to ask about this. It may be difficult. They keep her closely guarded, but the balconies are large, and I think he can get out of earshot. We will make that a priority."

Johannes stepped forward, "If I may, my lord." He waited patiently for permission to speak.

"Something is very familiar about you." Mikkel said to him. "Where could I have seen you?"

"I was until very recently a servant at Fjall. I have served you many times on your trips to council."

"Ah! Yes! I have seen you there."

"If it pleases my lord," he looked at Evin, "our friend has a grievous injury he sustained while trying to free himself when we were bound, and his wife was taken. I have given it all the care I know how to give it, but it has reached a critical time, and I think he will die if I continue his treatment course." He looked at Mikkel. "I know you might prefer him dead at this point, but we throw ourselves on your mercy. Do you have someone who could look at the wound?"

Mikkel nodded one more time at the guard, "West quarters." and Evin imagined how glorious it must be to have people know exactly what you needed all the time. "I would love for you to stay close for the moment anyway. I'm sure you understand. I do not mean to make you prisoners, but it would be very helpful if while we work on this, you were to stay on. I would like to say you are a contingent of our brothers from the east come to wish Micah well on the occasion of his marriage, and that you will be given quarters in the palace until after the wedding." He said it like they had a choice, but it certainly felt like a very strong suggestion. "I will have my physicians look at this young man's injury."

Roald looked at the others. "I think it's a good choice to stay here. Evin can get the help he needs, and we can learn more about how things are done on this side of the mountain."

The others nodded assent.

Mikkel seemed pleased with the decision. "Please feel free to come and go, but you will be escorted wherever you go in the palace by guards, and of course, much of it will be off limits for now." He seemed satisfied with his plan. "I will send fresh clothing to your quarters, and as soon as we have been able to speak with the girl, we will talk again."

He motioned, and the guards came over and indicated they should follow.

Within the hour, they were clean and dressed in simple clothing, their old clothes whisked away for mending and cleaning. Evin had seen the physician, and his arm had been treated to some more painful prodding and covered with fresh linen bandages.

They had been assigned to a suite of rooms that were situated in the corner of one floor of the palace two floors above where they had been with Mikkel. There were bed chambers for each of them surrounding a central room designed for gathering. Although all of the footprint could have fit inside the room where they'd met Mikkel, it was still by far the most spacious accommodations they had managed up to this point. They trickled into the central room as they each finished cleaning up and changing to discuss retrieving their things and horses. Roald spoke with the guard, and it was decided that Evin would stay behind and rest while the others went. As they rose to go, a knock sounded at the door and without a pause, the door slid open.

Framed within it, Micah looked even more imposing than he had on the balcony. He was strikingly handsome, but now they could see that much of that attractiveness oozed from his bearing and mannerisms. He was tall and strong, and although he looked every inch royalty, his face had a kindness that couldn't be manufactured. He looked at each of the men in the room in turn, no doubt summing up in seconds what each of them were capable of before stepping in. As seemed to always be the case, guards were nearby if needed. "Friends, welcome to our homeland."

"Thank you, Lord Micah." Roald dipped his head in a sign of respect.

"Oh, not quite yet!" The man laughed and everyone in the room felt at ease immediately. "We'll let my father keep that title for a while longer." He looked introspective. "I was going to spend a little time falling in love, but it seems one of you is claiming my betrothed as his wife?"

Evin stepped forward. "That would be me."

Micah looked over the youngest member of the group and whistled. "I would have thought you a servant because of your age! How are you the husband?"

"Marriage has become a condition of the young in the east." Johannes interjected. He looked at the others and lowered his eyebrows. "It makes for more..." he struggled for a word, "pliable citizens."

"Well, I must admit now that I see it, that Siria looks a little younger than the age ascribed to her, but perhaps she just looks youthful." He looked steadily at Evin, as though he could see into his soul, gauging his reaction to the mention of the princess.

Evin's face, as always, showed everything he was thinking, clouding over with a bevy of emotions, not the least of which was anger. Still, he did manage to keep the anger from his voice. "Her name is Inkeri."

"Very well." Micah wandered to one of the many seats in the room and sat, indicating the others should join him. "I wanted to see you and speak to you, Evin. As you can imagine, I am disappointed by this news for many reasons, but I am not going to lie to you, one of them is because the woman you call your wife is indeed quite breathtaking. Are you married to her, or only promised to be married?"

"Married." Evin clipped the word, not liking the insinuations behind the question.

Micah graciously ignored his tone but looked disappointed by the answer. "If it is as you say, then I too am promised to another, although it is looking as if the plan might not include me meeting her. I am going to meet with Siria in a little while, and I will be attempting to get her alone enough to ask her about you. If she is indeed the princess from the south, I run the risk of her thinking I'm insane. I would much prefer to ask her by seeing her reaction first to information she knows that I shouldn't, so I know whether to proceed."

"Ask her if Alia is well?" Evin said. "Inkeri has a good friend who should have a baby anytime.

If it's Siria, it will be easy to make her think you got a name wrong or something."

"My wife." Interjected Kai.

Micah looked over at him. "By El Olam, they do marry young on your side of the mountains. Congratulations." A shadow crossed over his face. "While I can't imagine the circumstances that would have pulled you away from her, I am sure you want to get back quickly. I can't promise being able to speak to Siria alone for some days. I'm just getting the guards to leave our side now. It may take longer to get away from them enough to speak freely."

"What did you say?" Roald stood and looked at Micah's face earnestly.

Micah looked confused. "I said I can't be sure to..."

"No, did you say, 'El Olam?'" Roald looked excited.

"Oh, yes." He pondered for a second, then realization broke over his face. "You really are from over the mountain, aren't you? I won't apologize for mentioning God's name to you, but I had forgotten that we have to be careful when we're with our brothers from the east, because they have forgotten his name and frown on its use."

"Do you worship him?" Johannes took a turn getting excited.

Micah's face lit up and he smiled broadly. "Of course, man! Who would we worship other than the true God?"

"Do you have a library here where we can read more of his worship?" Johannes was beside himself.

"Do you also worship him? I was under the impression that was not allowed on your side of the country?" Micah looked thrilled.

"Indeed, my lord," said Johannes, "but we must hide among our own. We would die for openly worshipping him."

It was Micah's turn to look angry. "I am aware of this treachery. It is one of the reasons we so desperately seek unity on this side of the mountain. We need to be united should that mindset try to spill over the mountains. As for a library, we do have one, and you are welcome to its use, but there is little there to help in our limited understanding of God. Unfortunately, we are locked out of a vault where we kept a book about him, but that was not in our language. I would have the finest scholars working on deciphering it were I able to access it." He stood. "I will have the guards show you the library anytime you'd like to use it," he said to Johannes. To everyone, he said, "I would like to speak more with you, but I have another engagement. Soon, I will return." He walked over to Evin, who had stood with the others, and placed his hand on Evin's shoulder. "Do you worship him?"

Evin looked startled. "I want to, but I may have squandered the opportunity." He opted again for honesty.

"May it be he will pull your heart to his. Such a fine girl as I am starting to imagine you probably have, deserves a man who can lead her in his worship." He stared into Evin's eyes, again looking for something there. "I promise you that I will treat her honorably. Until I know for certain whether you are telling the truth, I will treat her accordingly. However, I still have the ruse of smitten husband-to-be to play. You will understand, I hope, that I must keep the same tone and appearance in my interactions with her for her safety." He moved his hand, keeping his eyes locked on Evin. "I see the war you are fighting inside, Evin. I want to be your ally and not your enemy." With that declaration, he turned and left the room, his confidence still remarkable to each person left watching him go.

Chapter 25

Things were retrieved and horses were settled in stables, and life took on a different rhythm than they had previously known. Each day involved healthful and plentiful food and clean surroundings. Johannes spent much time in the library, soaking in all the information he could and sharing much of it with them. Micah came at least one time a day to talk to them and learn all he could about their home in the east. He also shared the way things had gone since the last war that had destroyed the chapels. They had, in essence, pretended to make the same changes, and had met at council to maintain appearances. Evin still struggled with the meetings, seeing only a much more capable, much more deserving man than himself. His arm was still a matter of concern to the palace physicians, and they were in the habit now of checking it twice a day. On the third day, he was completely despondent. Mid-afternoon came and Micah left, and Evin could only imagine the man leaving to go spend time with his wife. It wasn't that he didn't think he could trust him, for he seemed exceedingly trustworthy, but he had come to the point where he didn't know if even he wanted anything else for Inkeri than Micah. He was everything Evin could never be. Already a seasoned warrior, already a lover of El Olam, and already old enough to have perspective. Aside from that, a woman would have to be dead to not be attracted to him.

Evin wandered down, followed as usual by a guard as far as the door of the palace, and then alone into the gardens. He meandered around, trying to find something to occupy his tortured mind. In addition to the mess with Inkeri, he still did not want to talk to Roald, and their interactions were short and strained. He had a lot to work through, and for the last day, he'd felt exhausted and fuzzy. Finally slowing down had kicked his body into rest mode, and even just thinking too much made him feel sleepy. He wandered to the shaded part of the garden, where the morning sun had shone, now pleasantly covered in long shadows. He plopped himself down on a square of grass, thinking perhaps sleep would still his mind. As he lay back, he was rewarded with a magnificent view of the back of the palace, its many balconies jutting out here and there into a beautiful picture. It wasn't the balconies that caught his attention, though. Instead, it was what he saw on one of them. On a higher one, bathed in glorious light, was his wife. She was smiling and her face was transformed from the worried girl he'd seen on a different balcony some days before. Her grin turned into a laugh, and she turned and leaned against the railing, staring out over the city. She must have an incredible view of everything from up there. She looked to the side and motioned for someone to join her, and out of the shadows of the building stepped Micah. He strode easily to her side, and she pointed to something in the distance. He nodded and talked to her, apparently explaining whatever it was. They seemed to be joyfully enjoying each other's company. It was a side of her he had only seen once.

A side unrestrained and relaxed that he had only witnessed when she was under the influence of drugs. He felt sick but couldn't look away. He raised to his elbows in the grass to see better. She looked unmistakably happy. She reached out her hand and touched Micah's arm and looked up at him with a smile. She could have just said his name if she needed his attention. They chatted animatedly for what seemed to Evin like an eternity, laughing as if they had been friends for their whole life. Evin struggled to pull air into his lungs.

The sight seemed to confirm his worst fears that the woman he loved was much more pleased with this other man than she'd ever allowed herself to be with him. After a long time, Micah said something and grasped her elbow, pulling her toward the palace. She turned and walked beside him out of sight with no resistance. Evin watched the spot where they had disappeared for a long time, then convinced they would not reappear, he imagined all the places they could have gone. He collapsed on to the grass and put his fist to his mouth, stifling the angry yell he wanted to make. Instead, he shook with the emotions. Rage filled him and pushed the sadness aside. Life was surely not fair. He felt betrayed, destroyed, and alone. He had come to uncomfortable terms with his traveling companions before Roald's pronouncement that he was Evin's dad, but since, he had not felt a part of the group. Now he felt his resolve to abandon them return with a vengeance. Still, this pesky arm would not heal, and he felt the need for rest. He would bide his time for another day or two, but the need for escape in this moment was real. He returned to his rooms, where he submitted to his evening bandaging of his wound that was meant to protect it at night while he slept. Instead of sleep, though, he rose and dressed again, glad to have the long sleeves covering the annoying bandages. He stalked through the main room and headed out the door.

"Evin?" Roald's voice broke into his disjointed thoughts. "Where are you going?"

"None of your business, Roald. I just need to get out. Don't worry. I will come back."

He spun and left, not giving the man any time to ask for an explanation. He breathed a sigh of relief when the guard stopped following him at the edge of the gardens, and at the footbridge leading away from the palace, he turned and looked at the breathtaking place. He wished that he were able to enjoy the unreal opportunity to stay here. His mind landed on the thought of how fantastic it would be to live here with his wife, and the rage returned with a vengeance. She was probably very happy to entertain the idea of making this her forever home, but he was decidedly not the man that was able to make that happen. He stepped out into the streets alone, determined to just wander aimlessly while he tried to quell his rage enough to make it through the next couple of days. He walked with purpose toward the part of town where he knew the celebrations went on into the night. Shops and inns lined the narrow streets and wine and ale flowed freely from the casks inside. Evin stopped at a couple of different ones, listening as he drank to the men talk about all the seedier activities available in this place. He was disgusted at these people who claimed to be worshippers of the god he was trying to understand on the one hand, and on the other hand, glorified their own passions so openly. He left another of the inns, finally feeling his emotions eased some by the strong wine he found on hand there.

A bonfire in the middle of a nearby square caught his attention, and he remembered the bonfires to the gods in his hometown. He wandered over to stand amongst a group of men intently watching something in the middle. They cheered and laughed. The fire burned bright, and his eyes took a moment to adjust, but when they did, he was rewarded with the sight of scantily clad women dancing around the fire seductively. Each of them wore very little that could actually be called clothing. In all his days he had never seen anything like it. They seemed to melt into the fire and reemerge before eventually making their way closer to the now excited group of men. As Evin watched them closely, his initial disgust turned quickly to desire, and he joined the men in cheering the girls closer. The circled men pressed in as the women moved out, and soon they were mingled together. A pretty girl caught his eye, and when she saw him looking at her, he was rewarded with a smile. She moved close beside him and did a dance that seemed like it was only for him. The glass beading on her filmy dress made her sparkle like a fire sprite. Then, as if from nowhere, she produced a small bottle and offered him a drink from it. The second it hit his lips he felt the familiar astringency of the drug he'd become unfortunately familiar with. He refused the drink, pushing the bottle back to her, not roughly, just forcefully enough. He was going to walk into this with his eyes wide open and he was truly going to have control of how he remembered it. He grinned as he refused the bottle, and she pondered his refusal for a minute. It became clear to him he was supposed to take the tincture without complaint, but he hadn't, and she had to decide if he was still safe. She looked him up and down, smiled back at him and intertwined her hand in his. He pushed down the feelings that threatened to destroy his focus. He ignored the memory of Inkeri's hand in his and followed this girl toward a building off the square. She led him to a small, sparsely furnished room behind a curtain, one of several in a row together. He let himself be drawn in close to her, overwhelmed by the sickening sweetness of something she'd applied to make her smell appealing. She pulled at his shirt, helping him take it off. She threw it on a small chair in the corner. She leaned up and kissed his ear, moving her hands all over his chest, bending to trace where her fingers had been with her lips, sprinkling kisses all over his chest. Every one of them seemed to burn into his skin. He pulled her in close and tugged at her skimpy dress, pulling it over her arms as she lifted them, continuing to push back the rising shouting in his mind that he should not be here.

She pushed back against him, now almost completely naked, still smiling approvingly. "What will you use to pay me?"

He was a little put off by the question. "Don't you think I should get what I'm after first?" His conscience pricked. What was he after? He decided he wanted to relive the night he could never forget. The one he'd shared with his wife. It wasn't like he'd ever get another one from her.

"That's not the way it works. You have to pay first." He let his arms drop to his sides, and she circled his neck with her arms, letting her body brush against his, masterfully distracting him. With uncanny skill, she slipped the necklace from around his neck. "How about this?" She dangled Inkeri's pendant in front of him and then slipped it around her own neck.

He stood stock still for a second. All the disgust and anger he had been leveling at the revelers around him came back on his own head and crushed him. His mind flashed to Inkeri's face at the camp the night before they had made it to the chapel. She had meant for him to keep that pendant. Forever. It was to be a symbol of their promises to one another. She gave it in good faith. He was faced with a flood of memories, and he was able to see there were other perspectives aside from this destructive pity party he was having. He owed it to Inkeri to see her and ask her the questions he was letting torture him. Realizing what he'd been about to do, he snatched at the necklace. "No! Give that back!" He lunged toward her, grabbing her arm.

The girl screamed, and within seconds an extremely burly man was bear hugging Evin from behind, pulling him toward the exit without his necklace or his shirt. Evin fought back furiously, knowing if he left here, he would not ever see his pendant again. "I want my necklace back!" He screamed furiously, all the rage he had felt in the last weeks rushing to the surface. He managed to wiggle free from the man's grasp and start running back toward where the girl was.

He realized his error too late. Suddenly his feet were swept out from under him and the wind was solidly knocked out of him when he hit the ground. Struggling to get a breath, he was dragged feet first over the sill of the door and thrown into the street. "Show him why he should never do that again." A rough voice said as its owner disappeared back inside.

Still struggling to breathe, he rocked from his side to his back. Just as he rolled onto his back, he caught sight of something swinging fast through the air toward him. He raised his bandaged arm just in time to intercept the swing. White light exploded in the edges of his vision as his already damaged arm absorbed the crash of the blow. He turned on his side and curled into a ball, taking the next hit on his hip. A boot struck out and kicked dirt at him. "Don't come back," a disembodied voice barked.

Hands grabbed at him, and he turned to fight, trying to lift his arm to defend himself. Sickening pain threatened his consciousness and he lay still. "Evin, it's me. Do you think you can stand?" Roald's voice made this situation worse if that were possible.

He moaned and rolled tighter into a ball, willing Roald to just go away and leave him here to die. A hand tugged at his good elbow. "Try to get up."

He realized he just needed to listen for now. He was in no position to argue. With help, he sat up slowly, then climbed shakily to his feet. "They have my pendant. I have to get it." He pointed at the building from which he'd been dragged.

Roald looked at the building for a minute, and at the dance continuing behind Evin. "I think you had better be happy you got out of there alive. That pendant is gone." He maintained his hold on Evin's good arm and steered him away from this part of the city. They went slowly, stopping whenever Evin wanted to, until they reached the footbridge.

Evin looked up at the palace, and the image of the tranquil stone structure wrecked him. He walked to the middle of the bridge and sat slowly down with his legs dangling over the edge. He held his injured arm close to his body and stared out into space. Roald sat down between him and the palace and looked out over the water, not sure whether to talk or just sit. Suddenly, Evin lurched forward and leaned over the edge of the bridge, giving in to the waves of nausea he had been feeling. Roald put a hand on his back and sat quietly with him, waiting out the bout of sickness. In a few minutes, Evin rested his head against the rough wood of the bridge, staying in the awkward half sitting, half lying position he had ended up in. He started sobbing quietly, his shoulders heaving under Roald's hand.

Roald waited for the sobs to slow, then quietly said. "What is going on, Evin?"

Evin stayed where he was and asked a question of his own, "How did you find me?"

"I followed you when you left, but I lost you for a few minutes. The next thing I know, you're on the street getting the life beaten out of you with a club. You weren't in there for very long, Evin. Surely nothing..."

"She stole my pendant, and when I tried to get it back, they dragged me out and..." he started sobbing again, sorrow tearing him apart. He groaned and pushed himself on to his good elbow, managing to find a seated position again. His head hung and his breath heaved in and out of him. "I can never face Inkeri again." He barely managed to say the words, put his good hand over his eyes and cried uncontrollably.

Roald once more stared into space, struggling to find anything redeeming to say. He was sad for Evin, but he was also angry with him in a way he had never experienced. The sheer selfishness that could drive someone to these lengths astounded him, and the pride he had always felt when he had looked at what he had considered a fine young man had taken a gut punch. Now he felt like he was looking at a younger version of himself. His mistakes of the past all wrapped into one fateful evening. There was no doubt Evin had drank too much, but there was never enough wine to be able to blame the drinks for his bad decisions. Roald knew Evin was angry with him. Hell, Evin was angry with the world. Roald did the only thing he knew how to do. He reached out and put his arm around Evin and pulled him over, hugging him close. He had always wanted to do that, and he wasn't prepared for the emotions that rose in him when the young man didn't resist.

The two sat for some time like that as Evin cried until there was nothing left to cry. Then he sat up and wrapped his good arm around his injured one, rocking himself slowly back and forth.

"Where's your shirt?" Roald noted that Evin smelled strong like the unmistakable scent of a woman who had been closer than close to him.

"With the pendant." He looked down at his feet. "It's a miracle it's only my shirt. A few more minutes and I wouldn't have had any clothes at all."

"What could you have been thinking, Evin? I am just trying to understand. You have Inkeri waiting here for you, and you find your way to a brothel, and try to get with one of the very questionable women there just days after you find out your wife is alive?" He emphasized the words for maximum impact and stared at the broken young man.

"I don't have anyone here, Roald. Micah does. I saw the way she was looking at him earlier today. They were on the balcony having a fabulous time."

Understanding dawned on Roald's face. "You think..."

"I know, Roald." Some of the fire came back into his eyes. "Do you know how I know? Because I've seen that look on her face before, but she could only give me that look when she was on some pretty powerful drugs." He looked disgusted. "Apparently she didn't need drugs for Micah."

"I think you are the most impetuous, hardheaded, stupid boy I have ever met. If you would pay attention, you would know that Inkeri wants to be with you. You can ask anyone who has been with the two of you. I have led some betrothed couples to the chapel and the whole thing felt like a funeral march. She has been put through hell because she believes in you enough to hang around when she experiences scary things, and this is how you repay her? You run away from an inscrutable circumstance into the arms of a prostitute?" He turned away from Evin, his anger finally finding purchase. "By the gods, boy, you know those two have to pretend to be a happy couple."

"That wasn't pretending."

"Maybe they're friends, Evin. She's probably delighted to have someone to talk to that isn't threatening her life if she doesn't toe the line. That's probably the only part of her day when she's not afraid. You should be thrilled that she looked happy, and instead you're trying to destroy yourself, and your relationship with her."

The words hit Evin like a punch in the face. He let himself fall backward on the bridge, not even trying to slow his descent. He hit his back hard and jarred his arm, then moaned and grabbed it again. He lay disturbingly still, looking ashen in the low light of the torches that burned on the ends of the bridge.

Roald took in the sight. His son. Abject, beaten, and so completely broken. He didn't know what to expect at the beginning of this journey, but this was a scenario he'd certainly never considered. He let his gaze fall to Evin's chest, its movement the only evidence he was still in the land of the living. No shirt, no pouch with the shards and map, no pendant. Every reason people had put on him to come on this journey was removed. All that remained to keep him here was the threat on his life that was very real at home. He was struck again by Evin's boyishness. He was enraged at the people who had stolen the pendant. They used his obvious youth and inexperience to take advantage of him, and Roald was incensed. This anger at someone wronging your child was something Roald had never felt, and it was otherworldly in its power. Yes, Evin was wrong to put himself in that place and in that position, but only evil would see him there and exploit him. He sat, waiting for Evin to move for a moment, then looked a little more carefully at the arm he had been cradling. It had slipped out of his other arm and now lay awkwardly beside him. The bandage hung half off it, and the edges of the ragged wound blazed red. The angle of the whole thing was somehow wrong, and he knew the arm must be badly broken. He had seen the force the man used on Evin. He reached out and touched the arm, alarmed to find that Evin didn't react at all. He realized that the heat he had taken for raw adrenaline and emotion was radiating from Evin even though he had been still for several minutes. He shook Evin's good shoulder. "Evin." Nothing. "Evin!" Still, there was no response. Roald shot to his feet, all his anger evaporating, replaced by sheer panic and terror. He scooped Evin up, careful with his arm, and ran as quickly as he could with such a burden toward the palace. "Help, help!" A guard appeared at his side, recognition dawning on him.

He investigated Evin's face. "What happened?"

"He was beaten and robbed. Can you help me get him to his room?"

The guard motioned to a couple of others, sending one to fetch the physicians and enlisting the other to help carry the unconscious man to his room.

Chapter 26

Despite the careful care Evin received, he only opened his eyes once briefly. He took in the room and Roald and then closed them again. Fever raged in him, seeming to grow exponentially since taking hold. Micah showed up, having been alerted to the situation because he oversaw security for the palace. Kai and Johannes were roused by all the noise, and the electric air was punctuated with their very appropriate questions. The physicians came quickly, examined the arm and the comatose Evin, and looked grave.

Micah gestured to one of the guards. "Get Garrick."

The man left and returned before the end of the examination with another guard in tow, this one obviously higher ranking. The two men greeted each other warmly and Micah brought him up to speed quietly.

Roald stood to the side watching the flurry of activity in a daze. Johannes walked over and put his hand on his shoulder. "What happened, Roald?"

"I'm going to let him tell you." Roald nodded his head toward Evin.

Johannes looked at the unmoving body of the boy. "He doesn't look like he's going to be in a position to do that anytime soon."

Roald buried his face in his hands, swallowing his emotions, then raised his head and said, "He had a run in with some nasty people, and they took his pendant. He fought them for it, and he lost."

"Well, they sure smelled nice. Did they hit his head?" Johannes tried to make sense of Evin's condition.

"No. His arm. His bad one is shattered, and he's burning up with fever."

Johannes' mouth drew into a hard line, clearly indicating his hopelessness. "God, heal him." His prayer was simple and straightforward, but Roald was convicted by it. He should have been praying that for days over Evin's emotional state.

The physicians finally turned away from Evin. His arm lay useless looking at his side, twisted and swollen. "We aren't hopeful, but we have to remove this arm in the hopes that the poison from it hasn't overtaken his whole body. We think there is a minute possibility this may save his life."

Everyone looked grim, thinking about what they had said. Roald watched as the physicians gathered their things and left to go prepare a different chamber for the removal of Evin's arm. They would come back for him when they were ready. He was less restless than he had been, and Roald wasn't sure that was a good thing.

As the physicians moved out of the way, Micah moved up beside him and motioned for Garrick to do the same. "This is Garrick," he said to the others by way of introduction. "He's a warrior in many ways, but if I were to fall ill, it is his prayer I would covet." Kai watched the situation unfold from the far side of the room. Johannes paced; his fingers pressed to his lips. Micah continued. "We're going to cast our anxieties about Evin onto God and leave them. He knows the healing Evin needs," he gazed at the sick, half-undressed, sweet-smelling man for a minute, then said, "inside and out." He looked up at Roald. "This afternoon, I finally got an opportunity to tell Inkeri you are here. She was a different person, transformed by the news that he had come for her." He gazed at the boy in front of him, obviously wondering about the missing shirt and the broken arm. "She looked genuinely happy. We should also pray he survives for her sake. She loves him, I think." Micah managed to look only slightly disappointed by that pronouncement, no doubt wondering if Evin was worthy of that. Roald looked devastated, sat roughly in a nearby chair and dropped his head into his hands. Johannes strode over to join the men getting ready to pray, and each of them laid their hands on Evin. Micah began to pray earnestly.

Evin stirred slightly, then settled again. Roald stood and walked over to where the others stood praying, hands still on Evin. He touched the feverish brow of the young man. "You have a lot to live for, Evin. I know you don't think so, and I know you just want to end all this suffering you perceive. I want you to fight. I want to know you the way I have always longed to. I want you to be proud to call me your father."

Kai stood straight and looked surprised, but realizing it was not the time to jump on that, he just ran his hands through his hair and took the seat Roald had left, bending over in thought.

Roald left his hand resting on Evin's head, joining the others in prayer. The physicians moved back into the room quietly, allowing the praying men the space they needed to continue. When they became aware that the physicians had come, they backed up, except Micah. He looked into Evin's face, then prayed out loud. "God, I do not know this man as well as I'd like, and I can see that he needs you to heal him in a much deeper way than to remove these physical infirmities. I pray that you would help him to know you the way I have come to. May he live to fulfill the plan you have for him." He moved back and the physicians lifted Evin's bedding, using it as a makeshift carrier to take him to the other room.

Evin sat by a stream, his arm hanging useless at his side. He looked at it as if it weren't a part of his body, wondering where he was. He kept moving between here and the room with all the people and the pain. Here, the pain was blessedly less, although still present, so he chose to stay here, shutting out the agony and low serious conversations in the other place. He stared into the stream, watching as crystal clear water flowed past him with a happy popple.

Yeshua's voice broke his reverie. "You seem to have come to the end of yourself." He smiled a little in Evin's direction.

"Is this what that looks like?" Evin swept his good arm around, indicating the glade in which they sat. Inexplicably, all the horror of his last day flooded into his memory and he groaned and dropped his head, the shame and disgust replaying in his mind over and over. He reached for his neck, willing the pendant to be there, and cursed when it wasn't.

"More like that," said Yeshua.

"I am not worthy to be here right now. I'm the absolute worst of the low lives in the entire world. I cannot even begin to tell you what I've done. I am an unredeemable mess." Evin let tears fall unimpeded from his eyelashes.

"Some of that is true, and some of that is very untrue. The enemy likes to use the partially true to convince us of the untruth." Yeshua said. "I can redeem anyone."

Yeshua watched Evin work himself back into a desperate state of mind. "They're praying for you." He looked carefully into Evin's face. "For the healing you definitely need."

Evin looked carefully into Yeshua's face. "I think I am beyond healing. I am certainly not worthy of being healed. I have chosen willfully to hurt people I love."

"Truth and lies mixed together again. You have chosen to do what is wrong. You have hurt people you love. You are never beyond healing." He touched Evin's arm, looking at it. "As for your worthiness, that is not a question, I've already paid to return your standing to where I created it to be. I'm worthy so you don't need to be. Now you have to choose whether to step into that standing. You have heard of El Olam, and you know part of my story from your own history. I and the Father are one. I paid for you through my sacrifice on a Roman cross."

"The sacrifice of the Son." Evin looked down at his good arm. The hand of the Healer rested lightly against it. He had heard of the brutality of crucifixion. He reached and took the fingers, turning the hand over and looking in wonder at the scar where hand turned to wrist. He looked again into Yeshua's face. "Why do you pursue me? Why not let me die and end this?"

"I pursue you for the same reason I pursue everyone, Evin. I love you. If you choose to die in this state, you can certainly do that, but I want to see you accept the work I've done. You have a part I've prepared for you to play in helping other people know about me and do the same." He moved his hand off Evin. "Don't walk away from healing every time it's offered."

Evin felt like the breath had been knocked out of him. Nothing seemed worse right this second than failing to fulfill the purpose Yeshua had designed for him. He dreaded facing any of the people that awaited him should he wake again. All of them had every right to be angry with him. He would gladly close his eyes forever to that reality. Here, though, he couldn't imagine living without. Here, there was unmistakable and overwhelming peace. Here, there was incomprehensible love. Here there was unfailing mercy. He needed what this man had been offering him, and suddenly he was desperate for that healing, even as he loathed the idea of being bodily healed and having to face the consequences of his choices. He knew in his mind that the two would come hand in hand. The pain would walk alongside the healing. He remembered the first time he'd tried to drink from the cup, and the searing pain, but he recognized that if Yeshua stayed with him, he could manage to walk through it.

As if reading his mind, Yeshua continued. "I have drunk the hardest cup, Evin. The cup I swallowed contained all that same shame and sin and failure you feel. Full to the brim of the ugliest of the ugly things that humans are capable of. Full of the wrath of the Father. I accepted it willingly, but it was not an easy decision to accept it. I'm offering you a cup that contains some pain, sure, but none of the wrath. I already took all of that, and I bore it alone. The Father couldn't even bear to look at me. I did that so that I can always be your advocate. I'm never going to leave you alone, and though we might not always keep meeting this way in your perception, my Spirit, the Comforter, will inhabit you, because I always keep my promises. In time, you will come back to see me, when the Father, El Olam, decides it is time."

Evin looked stricken. "I've rejected you three times. I've said no to following you. I have been enraged at you."

Yeshua smiled. "Well, you're not the first to do that, Evin. I have a knack for changing the most stubborn of you into the most miraculously transformed. It's what I do. You'll just have to trust me." The look on his face was one of the sincerest love.

"I've worshipped other gods, and I've hated Roald and I've judged Kai. I'm not sure how you feel like you can use me now." His head dropped again. "Those are the small things. I have become the worst offender I can imagine. I have taken the love of a beautiful gift, straight from your hand, and I have tarnished it with my own desires. I have tried to buy a counterfeit of it to soothe my own angst about it. I am deeply wounded. I have deeply wounded."

"I am faithful to forgive all of that, Evin. Even what you think of as the worst of it was in that cup I drank, remember. Those things may follow you and shape how you must live in this life until you're back with me, but I have taken all the punishment that you should have had to face for all of that. You can keep putting that back on your own shoulders, or you can let me have it." The Healer once again reached towards Evin with a cup.

Evin looked at Yeshua again. "I'm missing the key. I know you're the key, but the seal didn't go together because I'm missing something. He took the cup and looked at it. "Is this it?" He wondered.

"I took all that punishment and I died."

Evin looked quizzically at him. "If it killed you, how are you here?"

"Evin, if I had stayed dead, then I wouldn't be here. If I had stayed dead, then all there would be is this forever death. People would be without hope. There would be no forgiveness. There would be no place with me. My resurrection from the dead is the key, because through that one act, I defeated death and forever removed its power. People who choose me will face the death of their bodies, but they will never actually die."

Evin looked hopeful. "You won't always heal my body?"

Yeshua laughed. "You won't always need it."

Evin knew he had to trust Yeshua with whether to heal his physical body, but he felt an awareness that his time to make this decision about drinking this cup was near an end. This was the last time. These were the last seconds. He stared into the depths of the decision and without hesitation or fear, tipped the cup up and drank the whole thing down.

~~~~~

The physicians transported Evin to the room where he was to lose his arm. They had laid out various instruments, most notable a saw that looked as if it would be used to cut down a tree. They had decided it would be best to sedate him further even though he was already out, so that was to be the first order of business. They settled him on the table, and as soon as the motion of the blanket stopped, he sat up sleepily, blinking at them. They looked at one another, then the head physician moved to his side and touched the skin on Evin's head. He looked at the others and beckoned they come do the same. Evin watched them for a minute, then raised his right arm and looked at it. There was no evidence of injury to the arm at all. They were all staring at him with mouths agape. He moved to get off the table, and they tried to restrain him.

"You should rest." The physician looked unsure of his pronouncement.

"Why?" Evin countered. "No fever. No broken arm. I just had a nap."

They all looked at each other and shrugged. Evin looked for the guard he knew would be nearby. "Will you take me back to the others?"

~~~~~

The others stood quietly in the room, waiting for news of Evin's surgery. He had only been gone ten minutes, but nobody had dared to speak. Micah stood. "Have the guards come and get me as soon as you hear anything at all."

He started out of the room, but as he reached the door, he almost collided with Evin coming in. He just walked in and stood in the middle of them as if it were typical for a man so near death to suddenly rise and come back to his bedroom. "Hey, guys. Can't a guy get some peace to sleep?" He smiled at them. They were much too astounded to speak. Each of them just stood there with disbelief written all over them.

Kai was the first to move. He picked up Evin's arm and looked at it, then he turned a paler shade and walked out of the room without a word.

Micah stood in front of him with a gigantic grin. "Evin! I am so glad to not have to give Inkeri bad news tomorrow."

Evin looked at Roald and all the emotions he was hoping to avoid threatened to overcome him. He tried to force a smile to his lips but did an atrocious job. "That is good."

"I was telling Roald that I finally told her this afternoon. Well, I suppose yesterday afternoon now. She was delighted to hear you had come for her. She finally let herself relax some. She's quite definitely your wife." Micah looked a little puzzled at Evin's lack of exuberance. "You're a lucky man."

Evin took a deep breath and held it to just keep his head above water. What in the world was he supposed to do now? He had really not been hoping to get well for this very reason, but he could see that the Healer must have a purpose for him to fulfill. He thought of the prophecy and grabbed the chance to change the subject. "Roald, I think we need to try to fix the seal again."

Micah looked back and forth between them; his interest piqued. "What seal?"

Roald just stared, speechless.

Evin looked at Micah. "How about we tell you the whole story after we get some rest?"

Chapter 27

It was late the next morning before the flurry of activity had slowed. Evin sat alone in the central room of their lodgings. Johannes had left early for the library as had become his custom. Roald came out and sat with him, and the two of them quietly watched each other for a time. They shared a secret that everything in Evin just wanted to bury. Roald had told everyone that Evin had been beaten and had the pendant stolen, and that was the story he wanted to continue to tell everyone, but even he knew that because of the state he'd arrived in, there would always be conjecture that something else had happened that he wasn't saying. Would failing to address those questions erode the trust others needed to have in him? They sat like mirrors across from each other, each leaning forward with his elbows resting on his knees and his hands clasped.

Evin finally sat back and sighed. He wished all his anger at Roald had disappeared the moment he had been healed. Instead, it was as if the power of it had been replaced. All the hard work was still there, but instead of blinding rage when he would let his thoughts wander to his mom and Roald, he thought he might want to hear more of the story. Still, there was a level of anger that seemed appropriate. Last night had made him realize that he was excusing himself of every kind of misdeed while he expected everyone around him to be perfect. Understanding that didn't make this situation any less complicated. Evin had always hoped that when they found the help they needed and marched across the mountains to free people, that the love Erik had for him would help him to see that what Evin was bringing would be better, and that they could live once more as family. He had this idea that he and Inkeri would settle near his parents and raise their own family and that everything would go on much the same way it had seemed to after the last war. After he found out Roald was his dad, he gave up completely on the idea of being some kind of chosen leader, but now he knew unequivocally that he had work he had been called to do from which he couldn't continue to run. Now these two ideas had to meet in the middle somewhere.

Roald contemplated Evin. "Something is different about you this morning."

Evin grinned. "Yeah, you could say that. Had an interesting conversation with Yeshua while you guys plotted to take my perfectly good arm off." His smile made it clear he was joking.

"It's good to see a little of your sense of humor." Roald considered Evin closely. "Does this mean you're over some of the anger you've been leveling at me? I'm really sorry that I've wrecked your perception of your life, Evin."

Evin's smile turned sad. "You're right about that. Every single thing in the world seems to be up in the air. I am still angry with you, Roald. That's going to take time, but I'm interested in hearing your side of the story. I've seen Johannes and Micah pray, and I'm convinced they're talking to Yeshua in the same way I have in my visions. I know Yeshua's the wisest person I've ever encountered. He's god, after all. I'm going to ask them to show me how to talk to him without needing to pass out or sleep." His smile returned. "Then I'm going to try to learn to listen and let him walk me out of this angry place. Until then, be patient with me. I can't promise I won't lash out when I'm under pressure, and there is a lot of that right now."

"That's more than I could have hoped for, Evin. Thank you. I do want to tell you what happened sometime." Roald considered Evin's last statement. "I'm not going to say anything to Inkeri, Evin."

"I know, Roald," he looked back into the other man's eyes, "I think I should be the one to do that."

Roald just stared back at him. "Why would you do that? No one knows any of what happened except for you and me, and since nothing actually did happen, I think you should just consider it a tough lesson learned and move on."

"Everything did happen, Roald. In my mind, I had already completely decided to do what I wanted. If the girl hadn't slipped that pendant over my head and shaken me back into reality, we would have had a very different situation." Evin ducked his head again, swallowing to steady his raw nerves. He looked up at Roald. "Whether or not I actually succeeded in touching her doesn't mean I didn't intend to."

Roald sat back against the cushions, still watching him. "What would be the benefit of crushing Inkeri like that, Evin? You need to think through that decision carefully."

Evin gazed at Roald for a minute and dropped his head into his hands. Kai walked in quietly and stood to the side listening. Oblivious to Kai's presence, Evin continued, "I just get the feeling she deserves to know even if it means the end of my marriage. She could still go back to her family if that's where she wants to be." He sat back up and made eye contact with Kai, then let his eyes drop.

"Just be careful, Evin. Consider the consequences before you make a choice." Roald glanced at Kai and changed the subject. "Last time I had any idea of what you were doing, you were planning to settle here and abandon this journey we're on for a life on this side of the mountains looking for Inkeri. Do you want to bring me up to speed now?"

Evin looked relieved. "We talked about the seal last night, and like I said, I'm fairly sure I have the key to that now. I'd like to try that again. At some point, I have to get an audience with my wife and decide what to say to her. " He glanced at Kai and continued. "I still don't see where I could fit into leading an army. I don't see that happening, but a lot has happened that I didn't see coming." He looked up at the ceiling. "What I want to happen is a quiet life with Inkeri in a nice home with no danger."

Kai leaned against the wall. "I want that last part too, Evin. With Alia." He gave Evin a stony look. "I don't know what's going on here. I will admit I am completely over any ability to understand what is up in your private life, Evin. I do know, though, that I have cast my lot with you, and that you have spent the last couple of weeks making sure I regret that decision. Every day at least once I have thought that my most rational course of action would have been to sneak back in and steal Alia all over again and make another go of it in a different town, and that's an unbelievably impossible mission. Right now I can't even get her to wake up to the idea that I'm alive. That just goes to show you how unhinged whatever this is feels to me." He looked down at the floor for a minute, trying to frame his words. He looked back at Evin. "I'm not typically a selfish person, Evin. I do want to have a part in freeing the people over the mountain. I have really examined all of the choices I've made, and I would make them again, but I am about to ride away from here and go back home and risk my life to at least lay eyes on my child one time."

The weight of how all his selfish decisions had impacted the people around him once more rested heavily on Evin. He and Kai had come to terms with one another, and he thought Kai had forgiven him, but he could clearly see the other man's point. "I promise that all of the things we have to do here will be done as quickly as possible to get us back over the mountain. I know that Mikkel's allegiance is to his people and the work he has to finish here, especially in light of the news that Inkeri is with us. I feel like the fastest way for us to get from here to there is to go through that with him as we talk to him about whether he's interested in helping us. He must be the help we've been looking for. Something has to be resolved by the day of the wedding, obviously, which is coming quickly."

Kai narrowed his eyes at Evin. "Sounds like, from what you were saying when I came out, that you might not have a marriage to pick up the pieces of when we get to that point." His voice wasn't accusatory, just questioning.

Evin looked at him, thinking about what he should say. What was he going to tell the people that were going to ask questions? Roald sat quietly, just watching. Fresh shame washed over him. He considered sticking to the basic story, but he knew he had already piqued Kai's interest in the overheard conversation with Roald. He had no choice but to trust him. "I lost the pendant Inkeri gave me as a promise for our wedding to a prostitute, and it was when I tried to get it back that I ended up with the shattered arm."

Kai's face transformed into complete disbelief. His mouth dropped open and he stood up.

Then, still looking at Evin, bent double and put his hand over his mouth. "By the gods, Evin." He breathed. "What in the world?" He stood back up and just stared, hand still over his mouth, obviously trying to think through what he had just heard.

Evin felt relief at having said it out loud, but fear flashed to the surface. He hadn't wanted this ugly thing he had done floating around where it might be heard by others. He wished there was some way to reverse course and bury it, but now it lay out there in the open, feeling like a threat.

The other man recovered some from his horror and began to pace back and forth in the small space afforded by the room. He muttered a curse under his breath, fresh disbelief filling his mind. "Have you even looked at your wife, Evin? I cannot even imagine where you were in your head." He stopped and looked at Evin again, growing angry. "You weren't even thinking, just following your lust wherever it wanted to take you."

Despite the inaccuracy of part of the statement, Evin just let it go, hoping this was the last time this was going to come up in conversation. He understood his character was obviously lacking in that moment. He let his eyes drop.

Kai looked at Roald and back at Evin. "I'm going to guess something here. I'm going to assume the best about you, Evin, because I thought I knew you better than that. I'm going to guess that you might have gotten some disquieting news in the last few days that might have thrown you off. Namely, you heard that Roald is your dad."

Evin looked up, astonished, then looked at Roald with a question in his eyes.

"I didn't say anything." Roald spread out his hands in front of him.

Kai looked at them. "Honestly, when I first saw the two of you, I assumed you must be related. You're a lot alike. But when I found out you weren't, I didn't think any more about it. Then last night, I overheard Roald say to you when you were clearly about to die, that he hoped you could be proud to call him your father. The wildest thing to me this morning is that we're not talking about the fact that you were probably within a day of dying late last night. Instead, we're sitting here talking like the most glaring thing that's happened to you in the last day is a run in with a prostitute, which I will admit is up there."

"Nothing ended up happening, Kai. I told you the truth about it, so I need you to believe that I couldn't go through with it. The girl tried to take the pendant as payment, and everything went downhill from there."

"Wow, Evin. I would not want to be you if you intend to tell Inkeri about this." Kai looked devastated by the situation.

Evin stood, wiping his palms on his pants. "I haven't decided what to tell her. Right now, I cannot see my wife, so let's work to get to that point so that you can get to the same point. I think it's time we find out where Mikkel stands."

Chapter 28

Only days remained before the wedding, and those days would have already been full of activity without the extra layer of obvious malice that was floating just below the surface. Now the furious pace of activity was insane. Someone intended harm of some kind, and after much discussion out of earshot of even the palace guards, it was decided that it was likely the enemy intended to use the wedding ceremony to incite some sort of violence. The easiest choice was to just cancel the wedding and go on, but it made sense to everyone to instead prepare to face the threat and allow the uprising to root out the traitors that must be inside the palace. The four travelers, Micah, and Mikkel were the only ones to initially gather, followed soon by Garrick. They discussed all the other guards in the palace and decided they could also trust Tavas, who had served the family as a guard alongside Garrick since they were both children. He was called to join them. Mikkel laid out his concerns. He had been working on this treaty for many long years, and he and the leader of the people to the south had ironed this out ten years ago, promising their children to marry as a token of the joining of the two peoples. They had worked out the transfer of power, and the lordship of the region of the south, which was to fall to the only son of the current chieftain. He was unambiguously convinced that the chieftain of the south was a man of his word who was also eager to see this union end the hostilities between the two peoples. When Evin and the group had shown up and made him aware there could be an issue, he had sent a messenger to him to gauge if everything was going as planned. That man, and another he sent had yet to return and he feared the worst. Now he had to face the idea that something had happened to his ally, and the plan was to destroy any hope of the treaty. Because of his former resistance to becoming a lord instead of the chieftain, the son that was to take over the lordship was assumed to be behind the nefarious change of plans. Mikkel feared for Micah's life, so they plotted for the wedding ceremony itself to take place at the foot of the giant staircase in the gardens. This still permitted access for many spectators but would allow an escape route for the couple and ensure they could be surrounded by the faithful guards on the list. Micah would carry his own best weapon instead of the ceremonial one that had initially been planned for him to wear.

The opportunity came for Evin to talk to Mikkel a couple of days before the wedding. The lord summoned him alone to meet with him. He sat behind the desk looking older than he had when they had first arrived. His eyes crinkled into a welcome smile as Evin entered. "Welcome, Evin. How is the arm?" Evin just smiled and Mikkel continued. "I know we have talked about several of the reasons your group made its way to this side of the mountain, and I know you intend to try to fix the seal." He looked at Evin. "What I need to know is what you intend to do if you are able to free the book. Also, what are your plans after you get Inkeri back?"

"I know we have told you some of the suffering of our people on the other side of the mountains. It seems the second part of my mission is to find a way to free them. I have hoped that perhaps you are the help I have been seeking to accomplish that. I think the book should stay in this city where it can be safely held and studied. Kai has a wife and maybe a baby by now on the other side, so we are going to do everything in our power to make sure that they are able to have a home together, and that other people aren't forced to make decisions far worse than the one he made. We are going to have to go back across the mountains and work to somehow free our people."

"Are you convinced the freedom you're supposed to be offering them is physical?"

Evin looked stunned. "I haven't considered this before, Lord Mikkel. I don't think I can just leave the people over there suffering without an actual physical solution to their problems, but I will think about it."

"Pray about it too, Evin." Mikkel seemed to be staring through him. "Consider too, with the smaller numbers of people who are seeking to uprise, whether or not they should consider relocation." He watched Evin carefully. "All along, I have wanted to strengthen our position enough to cut all of our ties with our brothers to the east. I think this is a solution worth thinking about. If you have people over there who want to leave, now is the time they should do that, before things get more tense. Even though it's a small number of people from what you say, I would welcome the boost to our population."

Evin was astounded with the offering. He had expected the help, because this was the only place where it could possibly be, but this was a twist he wasn't prepared to meet with a response. "I will try to talk to Yeshua about it."

Mikkel watched the younger man carefully. "Evin, I see El Olam moving around you in a powerful way. Still, I can see that the path that has brought you here has been hard and fraught with danger. I want to offer to allow Inkeri to stay here in safety while you go back to finish your mission. I hope to take some of the burden off of your shoulders of having to divide your attention between your mission and her safety."

Evin felt sadness fill his chest at the thought of being separated from her. "Thank you, Lord Mikkel. I think she should at least be given the choice to stay here if she wants to. I am extraordinarily grateful that you have considered her needs in this situation."

Mikkel stood and thumped Evin on the back. "It may seem too hard to be away from her, but I know you desire to protect her. I'm glad to be able to offer some assistance in that regard."

Evin felt a sting from the words, but managed a warm smile for Mikkel. "I will talk to her about it when I am able."

For a time, they discussed some of the particulars of the various scenarios that might arise, and then Evin headed back to his quarters. As he walked, he let himself wander through the halls of the palace, the footsteps of the guard following him aimlessly. He stopped at a window and looked out over this city that was so different from anything he had ever known in his life. Could he ask a group of families to leave behind the lives they had always known to come here? How would that even be accomplished? He watched as people moved in and out of shops on the straight road that cut through the city. Colorful awnings marked spots where various goods were being sold. Would these people welcome a group of aliens into their midst without tension? Truth be told, he could see himself leading this group of people far more easily than he could see himself commanding an army, which would just be ridiculous. He wished he could sit by that stream in his mind and talk to Yeshua about what he was supposed to do

Chapter 29

The wedding day dawned with a brief rain. Since there was very little of that in this area, it was considered a divine portent. Weddings on this side of the mountains were a one-time affair that happened in front of a priest, not requiring the trip to the chapels that Evin and Inkeri had discovered were used in the east as an attempt at control. The energy that pervaded the entire city was palpable, but in the groom's room, it was all the tension without the excitement. The group that had been assigned to guard Micah sat with him. He paced a lot and spent time on the balcony, watching the day unfold around him.

He walked in and sat near Evin. "I just wanted to tell you something, Evin. Today, I'm not going to try to keep the admiration out of my eyes when I watch Inkeri walk down the stairs. Every man there is going to be filled with awe, and I'm sure I will be as well." He watched Evin to see how he received this news, "What I've learned from spending so much time with her is that the beauty she has inside makes her worthy of every admiring look she gets. Today, you're going to have to not think too much about the words we're saying and the looks we're exchanging. We have discussed how to make this realistic while trying to make it less painful for you. I wanted to let you know she's thinking about that while she's standing with me today. One thing I'm sure of; I don't know if there's still a princess for me, but I do know this one's for you."

Evin hoped Micah was right. "What if I can't protect her today, Micah? I'm sickened by the thought of losing her." He let his head fall.

You mentioned wanting to learn to talk to Yeshua without falling asleep, Evin. Let me show you how I would do that if I were in your situation. He reached out and put his hand on Evin's shoulder, and as if Yeshua was in the room with them, he told him about the situations facing them today, and asked that they would be able to be cross through with his blessing. As they finished praying, the guards informed them that they were all wanted in Mikkel's office. They made their way there quietly through the halls, nerves feeling raw.

They entered the room and Mikkel smiled at the forlorn looking group. He strode up to Micah and wrapped him in a giant bear hug. "You guys look terrible, cheer up. God is in control." You could see in Mikkel the representation of what Micah would look like in his old age. The two smiled at one another with unfeigned genuineness. "I had hoped this day would come and be the most joyful day of your life, Micah. You know, I have worked for this moment for much of my life and all of yours. I promise you that whatever happens, I will do everything in my power to see that the next time you prepare for your own wedding, it will be more than just a big show to draw out some scheme."

"I have to admit, it will be hard not to mean the words I'll have to say today, but it will help me to have this group nearby as a reminder that this bride belongs to someone else." He looked at Evin. "Don't find yourself in a position where you take her for granted. Always remember that you thought she was gone, and God gave her back to you. She must be precious to you. Don't forget to consider her in the decisions you make. She is more than just a beautiful girl." It seemed to Evin as if god must be speaking directly to him through Micah.

Mikkel patted his son heavily on the back. "Your day will come, Micah. Perhaps the girl she was meant to replace will still be open to the possibility of marriage once her brother is removed. Now you must have some idea how beautiful she is since they must have tried to steal someone who looked similar to her. Remember, that beauty will fade, but if she learns to love God, she will only grow more in true beauty." Mikkel walked into the big open space in front of his desk. "Let's acknowledge God's infinite wisdom in bringing about these circumstances we'd all rather not have a part in." Mikkel indicated they should each take the other's hands until they were formed into a circle in the middle of the room. Eight men, each considered trustworthy and upstanding, prayed together in a way that Evin, Kai, and Roald had never experienced. Mikkel lifted their purpose to God, concentrating on God's goodness and abilities, and putting little weight on their own. Evin was humbled by being in the presence of these two rulers who possessed every good thing materially yet did not feign to see themselves as more than men dependent on a powerful God. He felt the presence of El Olam in much the same way he'd been used to feeling it in his visions. He found himself wanting to stay here and surround himself with the knowledge and presence of God, but he realized that was impossible. By the time the last words lifted to the heavens, it was time for the group to make their way downstairs.

The guards filtered down the stairs and into their appointed positions. Tavas and Garrick would flank Micah, and Evin and Johannes would be near Inkeri. If anything happened, Johannes would lead Inkeri to safety, and Evin would help the others fight. Roald and Kai would be in the very front of the crowd to have a little bit of a different perspective on everything that was happening. Fifteen minutes before the decided time for the ceremony, Micah appeared on the stairs and walked to take his position with Tavas and Garrick. He smiled and waved at the gathered people, and they cheered raucously. The crowd was huge, and included many families, children perched atop their father's shoulders to get a better view. Evin was uneasy about the inclusion of children in the crowd, but Mikkel had planted soldiers among the crowd to try to provide them some protection, and an orderly escape should anything happen. Apparently anytime there was a big crowd, this was a common way to manage them. Mikkel watched the wedding from the second floor, a viewing gallery having been created with the perfect view of the festivities. An empty seat beside him reminded the group that the chieftain of the south had never shown to take his place for his daughter's wedding. A messenger had come just that morning saying that he had been forced to leave the party because they had experienced an unexpected delay, but that they would be there later in the day in time to take part in the post-wedding festivities. Hearing this had set everyone on edge. Micah seemed perfectly at ease, and Evin was once again impressed at his poise. Music began to play from above, and the crowd strained forward to catch sight of the bride whose arrival it heralded. Evin took turns joining them to watch for her and keeping an eye open for anything out of the ordinary. It struck him how out of the ordinary the whole thing was. How many men would watch their wife walk down the stairs and pretend to marry another man? Probably not many. Micah stared at the spot where Inkeri would emerge in exactly the way one would expect him to.

He looked enraptured, and Evin had to look away. He remembered Micah's words, and he decided to believe him, in spite of the evidence on his face. A gasp from the crowd made him turn his attention back to the stairs where his wife stood, looking like a vision. She wore another stunning gown completely covered with shimmering stones that somehow enhanced her own natural beauty instead of taking away from it. Curls of her hair hung beside her face, and the rest cascaded over her shoulders and down her back. It reminded Evin of the way it had looked when he'd pulled the pins out of it after their own wedding. He was suddenly having a hard time focusing. Johannes stood close at his shoulder. "Wow, Evin. You're an incredibly lucky man."

Evin looked sideways at him and grinned, then watched as the priest moved down the steps carefully with Inkeri. This whole journey had been punctuated with wedding ceremonies, and he was frankly ready to just run away with her and settle down somewhere and forget all of this. He looked away as Micah reached out and took her hand, a smile passing between them. The priest wasted no time starting the ceremony, and Evin became painfully aware that one thing that hadn't changed much from one side of this country to the other was the vows that passed between the bride and groom. The words echoed the ones they had said at their hand-fasting.

"Till death divide us,
In good faith,
Two bodies, one heart."

The words cut deep into his heart. He had only thought of them once since he'd promised them to this same girl. Now he stood off to the side while she held another man's hands and said them to him. He felt himself sinking into his former despondency, but he was reminded in his spirit of the selfishness of the thoughts he was tempted to entertain, and of the actions he was tempted to take when he allowed himself to go there. He allowed the truth to wash over him as he remembered their relationship. That relationship was in peril, and he knew it wasn't the man standing across from her that was to blame, or her. Instead, he was the only one to blame. He was the one who hadn't considered these vows.

It happened more quickly than Evin could have imagined possible. One minute, the wedding ceremony was in full swing, and the next minute he saw one of the guards at the edge of the crowd starting to look apprehensive and uncomfortable. The change in the man's mood seemed very out of place and put Evin on guard. Evin flashed a warning look at the others, then watched as the man reached under his cloak for his short sword. A shout arose from somewhere and the guard Evin had been watching drew his sword and plunged perilously toward Micah. Before he could connect, he was grabbed from behind by Roald and knocked off balance. Kai cut the man down as he fell and the two of them turned to repel any other attacks. Evin spun and grabbed Inkeri's arm, pushing her toward Johannes. "Get her out of here, now!" he screamed. Then he whirled back to where Micah was drawing his sword and stood his ground beside him. Where had Tavas gone? It was his job to guard Micah from this side. He had never experienced anything at all like the fury with which the enemy surged forward. In case one assassin was not enough, there were plenty more. The intent was clear as every one of them pushed toward Micah to try to make a quick end of him. He was an expert with his sword, and as soon as he mowed one over, he stood ready for the next one. Even though it had been expected, it was nonetheless disconcerting to be in the middle of a wedding one minute and in the middle of a skirmish the next. Since they'd had a forewarning, they were able to put up a good fight. People clashed everywhere he looked. Townspeople were fleeing noisily, adding to the congested confusion. Some members of the army shepherded as many as they could out of harm's way, but Evin saw a few commoners fall as they fled. Adrenaline and fury fueled him. He had never experienced anything so detached from reality in his whole life. His movements didn't seem to be his own as his mind thankfully brought back the training he had been doing. He fought beside Micah, who seemed to cut down everyone who tried to get near him. It was evident that the enemy wanted to destroy the morale of the people by destroying their leaders. Evin glanced where Mikkel had been and found he too had been removed to safety. He felt the responsibility of keeping these dangerous men out of the palace where Mikkel and Inkeri were. He redoubled his efforts next to the others, stomping out the enemy. It was clear they hadn't expected such opposition, but also that they had infiltrated a large group of Mikkel's own soldiers. The attack served to weed out those traitors, and short work was made of them by the ones remaining loyal. The opposition started to falter and fall away one by one, each one pulling back to save himself from the unexpectedly effective resistance. The carnage made Evin feel sick.

Micah stood next to him oblivious of it, surveying the scene for further danger. "It seems we've squashed them." He stowed his sword back in the decorative sheath.

"At least for now." Evin's voice was flat because of his sadness at the sudden realization that everything Mikkel had worked for diplomatically would have to be taken militarily. A few guards at the edge of the courtyard were still engaged in skirmishes, but the clanging of weapons was giving way to the groaning of the wounded, dying, and frightened.

Micah surveyed the scene and turned to Tavas, who'd reappeared. "We need to get these people some help. You take a couple of the guards that fought with us and get a place set up where the physicians can look at the wounded. As he spoke, he put his hand on the man's shoulder.

"I can't do that." Tavas's face transformed as the others watched. He looked at the hand on his shoulder and a storm broke out in his features, as if he were fighting a great and necessary war with himself. "Goodbye." The word was full of both grief and resentment, and its meaning dawned too late on the others. Kai flew forward first, bringing his sword up to strike. Within less than a second, Tavas swung his sword from his side and drove it straight up into the soft flesh under Micah's ribs as far as he could. It was a blow meant to kill immediately, but his aim was thrown off as he also tried to avoid Kai. Kai brought his sword down in the same moment, cleaving straight into the man's skull, and the two men fell together. Evin was aware that everyone was yelling, himself included, but it all felt like it must be happening to someone else. Everyone who had seen it happen rushed to the side of the fallen man. The now clearly dead Tavas was pulled away from Micah. Kai jumped to his feet, uninjured.

"Get a doctor here, now!" Roald's booming voice sent several servants scattering to find the nearest physician. Suddenly Mikkel appeared in the circle of them, and Evin realized he had been somewhere where he could see the events unfolding. He knelt carefully beside his son, examining the wound himself with a supernatural calm. Micah's eyes were full of pain, but he managed to look at his father. Mikkel gave him a little smile; one that contained no reassurance. Micah slid his hand into his father's hand, pulling it slowly away from the wound.

"Leave it, dad. Let the doctors..."

Mikkel squeezed his son's hand and quickly moved back to trying to staunch the flow of blood. "The way you're bleeding, Micah... I need to try to stop it."

Micah closed his eyes and lay still. Everyone was galvanized by the failure of even the most careful planning. Guards rushed to secure the scene. With the help of the physicians, Garrick moved Micah quickly upstairs where they could work on him in the safety of the enclosed space. His father stayed with him. Garrick also refused to leave his side, standing guard outside the room, his whole demeanor one of defeat and sadness, his clothes covered with blood. He had thought Tavas a trustworthy friend, as Micah had, and to find out differently in such a horrific way was devastating.

The remaining team that had surrounded Micah moved themselves back to their rooms to wait for news. Johannes joined them shortly, bringing news that Inkeri had been safely returned to her quarters. Evin wondered if she might be able to come and join them, but he didn't even know who to ask for that right now. They prayed for the fallen man earnestly, pouring out their requests that he be healed and be able to stay with them. Kai paced and watched them. The night passed, and news came before first light.

Chapter 30

Death is a hard thing to imagine, even after you've seen it happen. To Evin, it was all surreal. He had seen many people killed yesterday, but he couldn't get the image of Micah falling so tragically out of his mind. The quiet that had settled over the palace was quite different from the former sounds of celebration and then battle. The clashing of swords had ceased, and what had once looked like victory had taken on the hue of horrifying defeat. Evin stood at the window in the room that had served as his own since his arrival here. Mikkel had retreated to his chambers in dismay a couple of hours before. The festival atmosphere had quickly been abandoned, and now the streets, still littered with former signs of glee, had been deserted in favor of the tents that served as a safe harbor outside the mourning city. It had been too late when they'd realized that the intent of the enemy was to kill no matter what. Their infiltration had been complete and well-planned, and Tavas had been the last resort. Evin was sure it was the intention that he stay undetected close to the two rulers, but when all else had failed, the horrible job had fallen to him. Today others would be isolated and questioned to determine if there was anyone else among them who couldn't be trusted. Some people really did not want to see this place unified. With Micah gone, the reality of a union between the two groups of people who had been so close to a resolution seemed at best an unlikely prospect. Micah was to have been sent to oversee the leadership of the south, and to bring their people together with his own. It was his purpose in life, and it had been the reason for his untimely death. Evin watched the sun color the sky as it rose. The bright colors seemed mocking and false when his heart was filled with grief. He had seen an upright man killed. To have been present for such a horrid thing would be a weight he would carry in his heart forever. He had not been able to sleep, thoughts continuously buzzing in his mind. How would they leave this place and continue with their mission? What would be the best thing to do now? How could any of this happen without Micah's strong leadership? He decided to try to lie down again, but as soon as he stretched out on the bed and closed his eyes, images of the day came flooding back. The smiling face of the triumphant bridegroom, and the gruesome picture of the same fine man laying too still on the cold stone floor of the palace in a pool of blood that was only mostly his. He vowed to himself that he would be available to do whatever he could to avenge the unjust death of this man. He had to admit that he had resented Micah's obvious admiration of Inkeri, but now the resentment was completely washed away, replaced by guilt. He wanted to be rested when he went to see Inkeri, but he was not able to muster any sleep. When morning was fully ripe, he asked the guard to be taken to his waiting wife, and as they walked through the hallways, he prayed. What was he going to say to her? He had spent much time contemplating Roald's words. Should he allow his indiscretions to stay buried? Would Kai say anything to her if he didn't? He felt panic build as he drew closer to her quarters. Would he be able to make a good decision about this?

They wended their way to one of the upper floors of the palace and emerged from a staircase into a courtyard alive with the sound of running water and a plentiful assortment of beautiful plants. Benches were strewn here and there, providing a glorious place for relaxation away from the cares of the rest of the palace. Arched doors led in several directions away from the courtyard, and as they walked through, it became clear to Evin that this was a floor where royalty lived. One of the arched doorways they passed was covered with black silk, and Evin's heart was struck again with the immeasurable sadness of untimely death. The guard stopped beside a different set of arches and indicated that Evin should proceed through. Inside, the archway became a foyer. A large stone door stood partially open.

"She's expecting you." The guard said when Evin paused.

He walked through the door and into the most luxurious apartment he could have ever imagined. Obviously decorated with a princess in mind, bright cushioned spaces and beautiful flowing fabrics adorned every part of it. The feelings of inadequacy tried to creep back in. There was no way Evin could ever offer her any of these beautiful things, and what if she had become accustomed to them? Why couldn't he shake these thoughts? As he stood contemplating, swift footsteps refocused his attention and he was suddenly swept into a fierce embrace. The woman he had been doubting and mistrusting buried her face in his shoulder and grabbed him as if she might never let him go. He wrapped his arms around her, reveling in the warmth of her embrace. He bent his head and drew in the sweet smell of her hair, gently kissing the top of her head. He closed his eyes as he was powerfully reminded of how unworthy he had acted of her unbridled affection. What a fool he had been! He squeezed her tighter, only letting her go when she finally pushed away. She looked up at his face, and her red-rimmed eyes were a testament to the fact that she had spent the night the same way he had.

"Evin." The way she said his name cut through him like a knife. "Isn't it devastating, what has happened to Micah? He told me he was enjoying getting to know you. I think you may have been good friends someday." Her eyes dropped and tears welled up in them.

Evin lifted her chin with one hand and wiped her tears with the other. "We were fast becoming friends, Inkeri. He was a hard man to dislike."

She looked at him quizzically, hearing something in his tone. "Did you try to dislike him?"

Evin sighed. "I didn't try." At least that was honest. Hatred had been something that had come easily to the Evin of the past few weeks.

She leaned up and kissed his cheek, intertwining her hand in his and leading him further into the apartment she'd been occupying.

"This place," Evin was dumbfounded. "It's incredible." He fought hard against the memories of the girl in town leading him away in much the same way Inkeri was leading him now.

She stopped in front of a wide, low bench upholstered beautifully and covered with cushions. She let go of his hand and collapsed on the pile, crossing her legs and indicating he should sit next to her. She wiped at the tears that wouldn't stop coming. "I want to tell you about my life since I saw you last." Evin desperately wanted to hear that. Now that he was here next to her, he couldn't imagine telling her how he had acted while she was away. He was glad she intended to talk first. He sank into the cushions and listened carefully as Inkeri spun the unbelievable tale of her capture. She had been sure that the men who had taken her meant to violate and kill her, so she had been overwhelmed with gratitude when she had discovered they intended to use her as a stand-in for someone who apparently looked a lot like her. It was blessedly important she be unharmed. They kept her in squalor for a few days, then they took great pleasure in watching her bathe and dress in more royal garments, which was the most humiliating thing that she had ever been forced to endure, but still, she knew it could have been much worse. Evin leaned forward, anger rising in him. He suddenly wanted to brutally murder each of the jeering men she described. "Evin, I just talked and talked to the healer you had described to me. I kept asking him to spare me safe and whole for you." Her words knocked the breath out of him. "When we reached here and I began to be allowed to spend part of every day with Micah, sometimes without those awful men nearby, I had hope that I might be able to share the truth with him and find you. Before I got the opportunity to do that, he asked me about Alia out of the blue. It was unbelievable! Then I knew you were here. I've waited all this time to see you. It was so hard not to run to you when you were standing at the bottom of those stairs yesterday."

"What about what happened at Fjall, Inkeri? Weren't you disappointed in me? I promised you one thing and then the next day acted in complete opposition to that promise."

She smiled in a way that made his knees weak. "Apparently, I wasn't any more eager to wait than you were. If I had been, the drugs would have heightened that desire to run away. I don't remember running." She reached up and laid her hand on his cheek. "I love that we won't ever forget that. I would say that's a good side effect of everything that happened at the chapel."

He had felt perspective shifts before. Learning lessons was something that happened a lot as you grew up, so he was as familiar with the sinking feeling that accompanied the realization that you were wrong about something big, but the absolute grief at his error, compounded with the grief he felt over his treatment of Micah when he'd had the chance to trust him was like being crushed under one of the huge slabs of stone in these buildings. His head fell and he stared at the ground, blowing air through his lips, trying to maintain a semblance of control. His absolute anger at his stupidity grew and he felt as if he needed to escape. It didn't matter what had happened with Roald, and it didn't matter if he thought another man was taken with his wife, he had never had the right to take matters into his own hands and turn his back on her. Here she was, apparently ready to pick up where they'd left off, and he was just barely surviving under the weight of unimaginable guilt. He knew despite his fight against it she'd be able to see the emotions racing to show on his face.

Sure enough, her hand left his cheek. "Evin, what's wrong?"

"I have quite a story to tell you, too." Maybe he could play off all his negative emotions on the impossible things that had happened while they were apart. "While you were away being forced to act like the beautiful princess you are, I managed to give myself a severe injury escaping from the ropes they tied us with when they took you." He indicated the place on his arm where his injury had been. "Then I thought you were dead, and I lost all interest in living myself. On top of that, I found out that I'm the bastard son of Roald, so I haven't had the best time." He paused and took a breath.

"Roald is your dad?" Inkeri looked astounded. "How is that even possible?" She looked his arm over carefully. "I assume the injury healed?"

"He is. I still haven't really heard his story, but I know he and my mom apparently had a very loving and long-lasting relationship." He looked at his arm, once again startled at its wholeness. "The injury was going to kill me. I was probably a day from dying. They were getting ready to cut my arm off."

She looked flabbergasted. "What happened?"

"The Healer. Remember the cut on your forehead. He healed me. Inside and out." Evin looked at her.

She took his arm in her hands, looking it over carefully. "It's just like my head, not a sign it was ever injured." She appraised him carefully. "It sounds like it's been a hard time. I'm sorry you had to go through thinking I was dead. You could come stay here with me until we leave?"

He pulled her into his arms again, desperate to remember what it felt like to be so close to her. She fit perfectly, her head resting on his shoulder. He was sorely tempted to glaze over the truth somehow or try to hide it. The comfort of her closeness was something he hadn't realized he needed until this moment. She was inviting him to be here with her every day until they left. She was ready to leave with him. He realized what a valuable comfort they could be to each other in this extraordinarily sad time. They had both lost a friend. Surely the healer wouldn't want him to bring more pain into her life right now. It sounded so good, but immediately when he had the thought, he felt that prick of conscience to which he was going to have to learn to pay closer attention. Immediately he knew what it would mean to not be honest with her. He might be able to squish these emotions and pretend everything was okay. He might even be able to go on for a time convincing himself that he was doing the right thing. After all, he hadn't actually slept with that other woman. He knew, however, that if he dragged out the time and then the truth somehow came to her, that the consequences could be far greater and possibly even involve the family they would hopefully have. Right now, he would be able to give her back some of the choices he inaccurately felt like he'd taken from her. She would be able to decide if she wanted to stay here with him, or if she wanted to dissolve their union and go back to her family. He kissed the top of her head and closed his eyes, steeling himself to do the worst thing. He took her by the shoulders and pushed her back where he could see into her face. "I have one more thing to tell you." He let his finger trace her cheekbone, wishing he had let this love he could feel for her lead him through the last several weeks instead of letting all his anger rule his actions. She sat beside him, looking curious and concerned. He folded his hands in his lap and twiddled his thumbs, trying to consider how to start. "I was in a much worse place than I have ever experienced, Inkeri. Remember I said Yeshua healed me inside and out?" At her look of confusion he said, "That's the healer's name. Before that, I let my anger at Roald and El Olam grow until it poisoned me. We failed when we tried to open the vault, even though Roald had the third piece we needed. My pesky arm wouldn't heal, and I gave into needing those stupid drugs again for pain. I felt useless and bitter. I failed to accept the healing Yeshua offered to me. I was so angry I threw the cup he offered back at him. I thought he had allowed you to die, and I was prepared to settle here and try to find out exactly what happened to you without regard for anyone else. Then we saw you that day on the balcony with Micah, and my mind told me all sorts of lies. Even though I knew the truth in my head, I was really struggling with thinking you might prefer him to me. I also wanted you to have someone as worthy of you as he was." He looked down, grief washing over him again at the mention of Micah in the past tense. "I watched you on the afternoon he told you I was here. I didn't know that's what you were talking about, but I was down on the lawn watching you have a wonderful conversation, and you gave him a look. I thought..." He let out a shaky breath, tears fighting to rise in him. "I thought you were in love with him, and I was going to be the last person you would tell. I had only seen that look from you once when we were in the chapel at Fjall, so I let my mind run wild."

Inkeri looked dismayed and alarmed all at once, losing her usually calm composure. "Why would you think I would so easily turn on my commitment to you, Evin? Do I seem like that kind of person to you?"

"Not at all, Inkeri. I said I wasn't thinking. To be fair, we haven't exactly spent a lot of time getting to know each other. How was I supposed to know what you're thinking?" His question didn't sound harsh, but it came off as though he was trying to deflect some of the blame to her. "It's just, I mean, he seemed to be the perfect man. What could I offer you compared to that?"

"Maybe you feel that way, Evin. That doesn't give you the right to assume every woman on the planet is going to swoon at the first sight of him. I was already very much taken with someone else." A little fire sparkled at the back of her crystal eyes and Evin knew this was bound to not go well.

"I wish I had gotten that idea from here," he said, pointing to his head, "to here." He laid his hand on his chest, feeling the conspicuous absence of the pendant under his hand. Instead, I let all of those negative emotions drive me to do something stupid."

The color drained out of Inkeri's face, her mind running wild with possibilities. "What did you do, Evin?"

"I went into the city. I had a lot to drink. I only managed to numb a little of the pain I was feeling. When I was down there, I came upon a dance outside..." he looked up at her, hoping to find the strength to go on, but just seeing her calm face,

"...a brothel." Tears brimmed in her eyes as she imagined where he was going with this, forcing him to look away to keep from losing it himself. "They offered me drugs and I didn't take them. I decided I wanted to relive the night we had together, because I imagined that's what you were doing. So, I went with one of the girls and I was fully prepared to just lose myself in there, but she took your pendant from around my neck and asked for it for her payment. That jarred me back into reality. I remembered your promise to me too late. I remembered my vow of good faith. I'm not making excuses, but it is like I had been asleep, and someone slapped me awake to what I was about to do. I fought to get the pendant back, which they took as aggression to the girl, so they threw me out on the street and broke my already injured arm with a club."

She dropped her head, looking into her lap, thinking quietly for a long minute. Then she looked up and pushed his shirt aside, her fingers sliding where the pendant's cord had once lay. "It sounds to me like you were willing to ignore the meaning of it anyway. It seems apt you lost it." Her words chilled him to the bone and as her hand dropped away from his collar bone, he felt a desperate panic rise that he might never feel that touch again. He looked back at her, and this time tears rolled down her face and fell off her chin onto her lap. He reached out to wipe them and she turned her head away from his touch, wiping at them furiously herself. "I think maybe you're not the man I imagined you to be, Evin. I want to trust you and I have loved you despite how difficult that has been, but I'm going to have to spend some time with this information before I decide what I need to do with it. You admitted you planned to have sex with this other girl. What's my guarantee that won't actually happen if things get tough for you again?"

He looked hurt. "I would never make that mistake again, Inkeri." He looked her in the eyes. "I think tough is a little light a word."

"Even when life completely crumbles down around you, Evin, I would think that you would have remembered more easily what you vowed to me. I would have thought you would have clung to the reality of our relationship, young and tender though it was. I would have hoped you would be able to draw strength from it instead of turning your back on it for one night with a prostitute. Damn it, Evin. You knew I was alive!" The tears had stopped, and the fire was back. She stood and walked to the big window that framed the beautiful city. Her back to Evin, she said, "Lord Mikkel says I can stay here to be safe while you're finishing your mission, Evin. I was prepared to go with you wherever you were going, but for now, I think it would be best if I stay here and consider what you've told me. You go finish what it is you need to do, and I will be here. When you've got all of that figured out, come back, and I will let you know what I've decided." She turned and walked back to where she could see his face, now tear stained, and locked eyes with him. "You can be sure of one thing, Evin. I am still going to uphold all the vows I made to you, regardless of what you choose to do, until we see each other again. Don't let your mind imagine that anything else is happening. If I decide to follow you into the future, I want that to be a decision that I made when I was able to think clearly. I think I'm too sad and angry right now." She crumpled back on to the cushions across from him. "Just go, Evin."

Evin looked at her for a long minute, taking her in, hoping she would say something else. He could see the absolute hurt he had caused, and he wished he could go back in time. She was folded up on the cushions with her face buried in her hands. She was finished looking at him. Desperation and hopelessness filled the center of his being, and the pain of great sorrow seemed too strong for any man to bear. “I’m so sorry, Inkeri.” His voice was broken and quiet. “May the Healer help you forgive me.” With that he stood and walked out of her room.

Chapter 31

Inkeri's reaction wasn't a complete surprise to Evin, but that didn't mean it wasn't devastating. Fortunately, she hadn't completely written him off, and the few minutes he'd spent holding her had reignited his desire to fight for her. She wasn't insisting that he take her back over the mountains to her family, and there was a lot to be said for that. He knew he had always wanted to be with her, but he had convinced himself she wanted something different, and that was up to now his life's greatest regret. Now he was living with the consequences, and for the first time, he was ready to take responsibility. Still, he'd been unable to smile at all in the day following his meeting with her. The atmosphere was so heavy with the weight of Micah's death that he was able to just keep to himself the fact he'd seen Inkeri. He didn't really want to rehash it. It was decided that in two days Micah would be laid to rest near Viberg with the ancestors who had gone before him. Also on the same day, they would make another attempt at the seal. Much discussion had ensued surrounding the idea that maybe the people who wished to live in freedom should be relocated to this side of the mountains. There had been good arguments on both sides, but since Mikkel's army wouldn't be able to fight two wars, and since it appeared that one might be brewing in the south, any attempt to overthrow the lords in the east would amount to a suicide mission for the tiny band of travelers that would be left to try it. It was decided that prayer and consideration should go into the decision, so it was left until later.

The day of the funeral dawned fair. A knot of people followed the body, carefully laid in a closed box which rested on a cart, all of this built to make the transport easier. The whole group moved without any extra noise, the sounds of wheels grinding against the ground and horse tack rattling the loudest things. A gathering was due to be held for the people in the city, but this was the one where his father and his best friend would say goodbye to him. They rode, one in front and one behind the cart, and the picture created was one of hopelessness. They left as the sun rose and arrived midway through the day. Evin rode behind Garrick, his thoughts a tangle of confusion. He was aware he could trust Yeshua, but some things didn't make sense, and this was one of them. The pouch was back around Evin's neck where it belonged, and he was feeling the weight of getting it right this time.

Garrick may as well have been burying his brother. The pair of them had grown up together, one the servant and the other the lord, but to ask Garrick, you would never hear that the difference had mattered to Micah. He had treated every man with respect and loved people without reservation.

They placed the box with the body in a freshly dug pit, which was covered with mounds of dirt as they watched. He had been left with the sword that had served him well in his life. Unlike the people of the south, the northern people didn't sacrifice animals and precious objects to bury them in the soil with the people to whom they belonged, but it seemed as if the sword belonged with him.

They stood silently, mourning the great loss. Inkeri had come as well, wishing to say goodbye to the man who had treated her with utmost tenderness and honor. She stood near Mikkel, which was not lost on anyone there. Evin was glad there were no expectations about how he and Inkeri would interact. He stood a short distance away and struggled valiantly to contain the emotions that kept threatening to swallow him every time his eyes wandered to her or the grave.

As the last of the dirt was piled on the mound, a great wail arose. Hands raised toward the sky, and the sound of abject sorrow went with them. Faces turned up and tears flowed freely without embarrassment. The sound was an unearthly expression of untamable grief, the sound of a people who long for hope. Evin listened and watched along with the others from the east. At home, funerals were accomplished in much the same way everything else was, with fire. A great pyre was raised, and the body burned as the favor of the gods was sought. Here, hands lifted to heaven, the people were crying to El Olam for comfort. Evin bowed his head and listened to their cry. In the midst of it, a spark lit in him. He felt the clear and awesome presence of the comforter moving among his people, reminding them that they were his. Reminding them that they were loved. Working his truth into their hearts. Evin could tell that the connection was unmade. The comfort was unfelt by most. The wails continued unabated as the great injustice of Micah's death weighed on the hearts of those who loved him. Suddenly like a great bonfire lit, the connection flared in Evin's mind like a flash of lightning. The key that was absent from every worship of El Olam he had ever been a part of was this: the people moaned and wrestled under the oppressive weight of a spirit without hope! He knew firsthand the hope they were missing!

His hands raised with theirs, and as their wailing receded, he was compelled by the raging fire in his chest to speak. "From time immemorial, El Olam has been. Seated high on his throne he has existed forever, separate from us. We cry out in our pain, longing to be with him, but we are the lowest beings, unworthy of his affection. He is uncreated, we are created. He is perfect, we are flawed. He is everlasting, we pass away. Our hands are raised, El Olam, hear our cry. He has heard us in our sorrow. He has known and cared about the depths of our grief, yet we cannot feel the hand of the Comforter as he moves among us. The sting of our frailty bears down on us and in death we are undone. We are a people with a flawed picture, incomplete because we have no teachers. In your faithfulness, you remind us of Yeshua, the Healer. The rift between us is too great, but Yeshua binds our wounds and heals the space between us so that now you hear us. Teach us of his sacrifice. Great is the story of his coming, God made into human flesh to reach down to us, and we thank El Olam for his perfection that walked among us. He told me that he sacrificed himself, perfect and lovely, for us, broken and entangled in our own filth, drinking the cup of El Olam's wrath for us. Thank you, El Olam, for the execution in our place of your perfect Son, Yeshua. Once enrobed in glory sent to us enrobed in flesh like ours. More has not been fully understood until very recently. That is that Yeshua did not stay dead. His sacrifice was not an empty display or an incomplete victory. Indeed, the Spirit of God in great power raised him from the dead, destroying the bonds of his grave, this grave, and the grave of any other man who follows him. Our mortal bodies are merely a place we live temporarily, like a tent in the wilderness. When they are gone, we live on. El Olam, Yeshua, and the Comforter are three parts of one." Evin felt warmth begin to emanate from the pouch around his neck. He reached his hand up and felt the overwhelmingly comforting warmth. "I believe you died while you lived with us, sacrificed for the iniquities we have performed, bearing the punishment we deserved, and I have now come to understand that you were raised again and returned to the Father so that the bonds of death would be forever without power in our lives. For our comfort, your Spirit moves among us and dwells in us, reminding us of you. We send our beloved friend, brother, and son, Micah, to you too early for our liking. But who are we to wail as people without hope when we now know that where he is, with you, we will also find ourselves in your time? Our day will come when you choose not to heal our mortal bodies. You will bring us into your presence with the same rejoicing that no doubt welcomed Micah. Thank you."

He stopped talking and raised his hands in worship to the sky, overwhelmed by the beauty of the finally made connections spoken to him by Yeshua and confirmed by the Comforter. Tears streamed down his face, and the weight of glory forced him to his knees, head down, eyes closed. It was as if the pouch around his neck had become a weight that dragged him down, and he took it off and lay it on the ground in front of him. Then his arms raised back to the sky, he rocked back and forth on the ground on his knees, unaware of any of the people he'd been with all along. Instead, the true beauty of Yeshua poured into him and he could not contain the vision. He could not forget his own interactions with him. His own anger at him. The unworthiness next to the holiness was an unbearable picture, and without the healing he'd tasted, he felt in his spirit that the weight of it would kill him. The absolute truth of his own failure pressed him completely to the ground, face in the dirt, tears flowing freely. As he lowered himself, his hands once more closed around the pouch and he grabbed it, marveling at its immense warmth. Moving back to his knees, he opened his eyes in wonder to gaze at it. He poured the fragments into his hand. The others watched without a sound, but Evin wouldn't have heard them anyway.

He looked at the shards in his hand and held them up to the sky, again finding his voice. "El Olam, you sent Yeshua to heal, and the Spirit to comfort. We seek you. Heal the shards and give us access to the truth we have walked too long without. Give us a path to understand the things written about you. Make us strong in our faith so our knowledge of you no longer feels inadequate." It was as if his hand was filled with hot coals, and his instinct was to drop the shards, but he surrendered himself to be the vessel by which they would find their way back to one and held on through the searing. A ring of white light shot out from his upraised hand, bathing the whole scene in an unearthly light for what must have only been seconds but felt like ages. When the light left, Evin carefully lowered his hand, afraid of what damage he might find when he opened it. He held it in front of him and uncurled his fingers, palm up.

Johannes, who was standing next to him, knelt and gazed into his palm with him. "El Olam!" He exclaimed and looked at Evin with amazement on his face. Evin took the now single piece from his palm and held it up, looking at it with wonder. It glowed with an emerald light, and the formerly clear etchings across the surface shone like finely spun gold carefully woven into the stone. Johannes grabbed his hand and touched the palm. "Evin, you have the seal seared into your hand!" The unmistakable image of the complete seal was burned exactly into the flesh of his palm. He looked at the two side by side, taken aback at the perfect representation. The skin on his hand was already completely healed, leaving him forever marked with the indelible imprint of the three parts of the Everlasting. The culmination of months of his life into this one astounding moment felt like a beginning and an ending to Evin. This fulfillment was proof to him that he didn't have to rely on himself. El Olam stood ready to do the work. He held the seal aloft, a jubilant smile transforming his features. He marveled as it caught the sunlight and scattered it into a million points of dazzling emerald light, bathing the formerly despondent company in the light of a future full of hope.

Enjoy this preview of the first chapter of the next book in the series.

Chapter 1

Evin, Mikkel, and Johannes stood in front of the massive stone door. Evin looked once more at the seal, seated perfectly on top of the art it had created in his palm. He flipped it, wondering what was next. Panic gripped him as he considered what he might do if the seal didn't open the vault. Others watched him quietly, assuming that the hardest part was over. He didn't even understand the everyday operation of these gargantuan stone slabs that the people over here used for doors, so he was sure he was going to flub the opening of this special one. He looked at Mikkel, reaching toward him with the seal. "I don't even know how to make these doors work," he admitted, "will you show me?"

Mikkel smiled warmly at him. "Place the seal where it belongs, and I will show you." He nodded toward the door.

Evin reached the up with the seal and held it in front of the door, rotating it to the orientation he remembered from when he and Roald had first come here. He looked over his shoulder to find Roald watching intently along with the others. He closed his eyes and drew a long breath, blowing out steadily to calm his nerves. Then, he focused his vision back on the seal, breathing a silent prayer as he pushed it forward toward the door. This time, when the seal made contact with the door, it clicked into place and stayed as if held there by magic. He smiled, relieved, and looked back to Mikkel, who stood beaming beside him.

A shade of sadness played across Mikkel's face. "Micah would have given anything to see this." Then he looked at Johannes. "Opening these doors initially takes two if they are the same as the ones in the palace. Beside you, toward the bottom of the door, there should be an indent in the stone. I have one here." He bent and found the space he was talking about. "If at the same time, you and I push in and up, while pushing in up here," he indicated a spot about halfway up the door to the inside, "it should swing in."

The two men bent to the task while the others watched, pushing the doors forward for the first time in decades. Disbelieving laughter flitted through the spectators, each craning to see what could be seen as light filtered into the stone chamber for the first time in years. Evin still stood centered in the doorway where he'd affixed the seal. He watched as it swung away from him into the room, then focused his attention on the room. It seemed to be a bare chamber, except for a column of stone that rose from the floor, carefully carved to hold a much smaller volume than Evin had imagined. The book lay closed, several signatures bound together into one unimpressive whole. He knew that it wasn't the outside that was important, but he couldn't help feeling like the moment would have been more awe inspiring if a thickly bound volume awaited them. Instead, what looked like several smaller volumes bound together simply into a plain, thin leather cover greeted them. He stood still, staring along with the others as the doors finished their course and ground to a halt. As with the other stone doors Evin had seen opened and closed, it seemed to take little effort for the men to move the doors. The corners of the room were still shrouded in darkness as the group stood looking in. Different faces reflected different emotions. Johannes was absolutely glowing as his eyes locked on the long sought-after tome. Mikkel's face still held the echo of sadness that had crossed it when he thought of doing this without his son by his side. Others showed interest and disbelief. What had been out of the realm of possibility for a lifetime stood open once more.

Evin looked into the corners of the room, his eyes attracted to some perceived movement in the corner. What started as a simple shifting in the light that he attributed to the movements of the people behind him grew into something more. As he watched, it became clear to him that something was moving toward him out of the darkness. His eyes grew large and flashed to the others, and then back to the shapeless moving darkness. The others seemed oblivious. He was so astounded, he made no sound as it formed into a robed figure and stood before him, positioned inside the stone doors in front of the book. It was then that others noticed, and he heard gasps behind him. He couldn't move his eyes from it, even though terror seemed too light a way to describe the fear that filled him. The figure lightened to gray and stood shifting before him. It was as though the image was not solid enough to hold position for long. Now a clear representation of a man, he reached up and pushed the hood back that had shrouded his features. Evin glanced at Mikkel to make sure he wasn't the only one seeing this vision and satisfied with the expression on the other man's face, he looked back at the robed man. Still gray, but in a way that seemed to allow for the possibility if life, the man stood before them, looking like he'd reached a significant age while he waited in the stone room. Flowing gray hair stuck out at odd angles, moving and shifting with the rest of him. His skin was darker than Evin had ever seen, as if he'd seen the sun far more than they. He had dark, sharp eyes, and he stared toward the group, his disconcerting gaze the only unwavering thing about him. He raised his hands, the robe falling back to reveal more of his arms. Hair covered his arms, wafting in much the same way as that on his head.

His voice boomed out. "An oracle concerning those who have deserted. Those who have forgotten El Olam, who saved them for his purpose. Stubbornly, they refuse turn from ancient error, even when given absolute truth. Listen to the words of El Olam. Woe on them to a thousand generations! Though I have shown mercy, I will now show none. They will be abandoned for a thousand generations. Teaching will come, but they will be unable to hear. They will erect buildings to my name, but their hearts will remain empty. Their land will be a land of war, torn again and again by rulers who seek to control but never will. Their people will become unwanted, their land unfruitful, and their leadership like children. The land will produce fruit for others. Though they stretch toward power, they will never find it. The darkness they have chosen will walk with them into the future, and though they wail, their gods will never answer. Turn and return, oh faithless people. Return and flourish and spread. Abandon the gods that never answer and return the way you came." The eyes that had been staring toward the whole group locked on Evin's face, boring into his eyes. The apparition stood still for a minute, as if considering Evin, then said, "Lead the advance." He was gone much more quickly than he'd appeared. He just ceased to be there as if he never was. Evin thought his heart might stop because there is no way it could keep the furious pace it had reached for any length of time. He was in company with all the others as they drew in the first breath they'd allowed themselves since the man had appeared. They eventually began to look at one another, unsure if there was anything to say that would be the right way to follow up what they'd just witnessed.

Johannes finally broke the stillness by moving forward through the space where the strange man had been, up to the almost forgotten book. He reached out reverently toward it, his face the picture of excitement as he gently touched its leather face. Mikkel stepped beside him, looking at the volume with curiosity. He nodded to Johannes. "Bring it home with us."

Johannes lifted it carefully from the place where it had languished unstudied for far too long and turned to face the group. What could he say in this moment that would matter at all? Instead of speaking, he moved forward.

Kai voiced what everyone else was thinking. "What in the hell was that?"

They looked again at the spot where Johannes now stood that had recently contained the unexplained. Mikkel did his best to lessen the man's fear. "Our minds are too feeble to be able to offer an explanation for everything we have seen. Over the coming days, we will no doubt benefit from telling the tale over and over to one another to strengthen what was seen in our memories so that we never forget any of it. Today, it is too big for the telling." With that, he moved past Kai and the others and began down the steps, followed closely by Johannes and the book.

The others padded silently after them, almost afraid to make noise and frightened enough to feel as if the leaving was also a kind of escaping. Evin watched as Inkeri turned to follow the others.

He stood still, watching her go. She had handled the unexpected intrusion in much the same way she handled everything life threw at her. His heart swelled with unabashed admiration as he watched her move away from him. He wanted to rush forward and begin the retelling with her. He wanted to see the excitement he knew would reach into the corners of those incredible eyes and watch her as she told what had happened from her perspective. He became aware he was not alone and looked to the side to see Roald watching him with that familiar grin. "What?" He tried to deaden the expression he could imagine had found its way to his face.

"You're gone, Evin. She's got you right where she wants you."

"I hope she wants me where I am." He let his eyes wander back to her as she walked down the stone steps.

Roald moved closer and put his hand on Evin's shoulder, drawing the young man's gaze back to him. "Sounds like you've been given another opportunity to lead, Evin. I'm sure she's going to be among the people following you. Breathe out thankfulness every time El Olam lets your eyes see her. Believe me, you should cherish that every time it happens."

Evin looked down at the sea below, rushing as it did everyday toward the bottom of the structure. He remembered the helplessness that had almost caused him to throw himself into that foam. Now it seemed to be pushing him away toward an unknown future to lead an enigmatic advance. "God help me." He turned to follow the group that now gathered at the foot of the stairs to wait for the stragglers. Something was different as the group wended back toward the palace. Unlike the crushed company that had come this morning, this procession had hope stirred into their misery.

Acknowledgments

If I tried to write a thank you to all the people who have impacted me enough to write things down on a blank page that feel real and can have a positive impact, then if I were honest, I would have to thank the people who have most deeply hurt me. Because of you, I know what it feels like to have a panic attack. I know what it feels like to have to find the ground and feel it with my hands to feel like part of any semblance of reality. I'd have to think this world for its constant assault on anything innocent and beautiful. I'd have to acknowledge that no doubt there is a spiritual assault that never lets up that has managed in whatever ways to give me ideas that were so terrible that following through with them has caused me to wreck myself. At the very least, life has given me a well full of interesting material from which to draw.

Instead, first, thank you God for being angrier than I could ever be at all this misuse of your intended creation. Thank you for giving some of us the gift to see many sides of a story and redeem the worst of them into something that looks beautiful through a glass darkly. We can't wait to see it clearly like you do.

Second, thank you for people who hear your voice and reach into our mess and show us part of what you look like. Thank you for my community. Thank you that I never fit in with any group of "normal" people. I like these oddballs much better.

Third, I have to say thank you to Jackson Tobin, and Jason Queen for showing interest in the words I put on a page. You guys have helped me find something I didn't know I'd lost. Then my mom, McKenzie,

Karma, and En for coming alongside me and helping read, edit, and design. To Steve Kite for helping me re-write the lackluster back cover. To my other children for giving me the space to work at the kitchen table, and for believing me when I said I had to work. I have a unique and inspiring family.

Thank you, Jeff, for putting up with my mind that works differently than anyone else's you have the pleasure of interacting with. I know I drive you crazy. Just take my hand and let me be crazy with you beside me.

A Dirt Road Crime Story

SURGEON GENERAL WARNING:
GUN FIGHTS MAY BE HAZARDOUS TO YOUR HEALTH

Time for a road trip. On a dirt road. Beautiful. Scenic. Nothing but you, a soft breeze in the trees, and sweet, musical birds.

And hard drugs. Rednecks that have them. Dixie Mafia that wants them. Newark leg-breakers that want them back. A farmer with everything to lose and a couple of nitwits with guns.

What could possibly go wrong?

CHECK OUT THESE OTHER TITLES FROM INDIE LIT!

My Life Was Mercy Creek is a coming of age story told from the point of view of a boy growing up in Virginia during the Great Depression. Will the Morrissey family rise together from the depths or scarcity or will the brutal realities of the rural world they live in separate them and destroy their hopes and dreams?

The World Comes To Mercy Creek is a continuation of the series of Morrissey Family Novels. The year is 1941, and threats of War from across the ocean combined with bulldozers, bank robbers, and a mystery on the moun-tain to jeopardize not only the families of this rural Virginia community, but a way of life that values the pursuit of life, liberty, and happiness above progress, power, and politics.

At Indie Lit we love summertime and we love short stories, so we decided to combine those ingredients and create our own *Summer Brew*. This collection of stories was written by six authors of varied backgrounds, styles, and experience. There's a little something for everyone in this collection, and we hope you enjoy each and every one of them!

Rachel Himelright is another among many who put the pen to page and watch as a story unfolds. It is her hope that something in the stories she crafts resonates with you, and that you'll want to pick up the next and the next. She is a wife and a mother who loves things that don't talk back, like coffee, plants, and books. Most days she loves people too, especially her people. Music keeps her sane. She is blessed to live in one of the most beautiful places in the USA, the iconic Shenandoah Valley.

Made in the USA
Middletown, DE
06 December 2021